DUNGEON SCHOOL

TOROTH-GOL BOOK II

KENNY GOULD

Dungeon School (Toroth-Gol Book II)

Copyright © 2024 Kenny Gould

BOOKS BY KENNY GOULD

<u>Toroth-Gol Series</u>

The Castle of 1,000 Doors

Dungeon School

Prey House

The War of Fangs

<u>The School Beneath the City Series</u>

The Potionmaster

<u>Other Work</u>

The Midnight Carnival

Monster Summer Camp

THE EMPIRE

The Wastes
Peakskill
Portside
Argoston
Helios
Spiderhead
Steel City
Ironwood
Mick
The Crescent
Atlantis
Tabura
Reo
Binti
Irbo Jamrain
Arid Dominion
Hub
Shining Dunes
Fain
Brigadoon
Cort
Oriel
Bourdaux
The Great Basin
Bellablanco
Velda
Sanmar
Barrier's Pavilion
Palmer's Pavilion
Crystal Keep
Red Hills
Aramel
The Sea of Paradise
Lobster Isles

RECAP

Confirming... Live on *Elvis Madden's Hunter Talk* in 3... 2... 1...

Ladies and gentlemen, welcome to my show! Elvis Madden here, host of *Elvis Madden's Hunter Talk*. I have to say, the action doesn't get much better than this.

If you're just joining us, we're currently following King Crow, the former gutter rat turned lightball player who, along with his father, Sal Valentine, was convicted of treason against the Empire.

What have you missed since Crow entered Toroth-Gol? Quite a bit, actually! Enough to give your kindly host palpitations. Oh my poor, weak heart!

As any civilized person knows, the Hunt begins with the prisoners choosing their starting weapons. This year, things happened a little differently for Crow, as he mouthed off to the guards and was held back for a bit of a lesson on respect. Because of that, Crow was the last to enter the dungeon, and so he got the last pick of weapons. Fortunately for him, the only weapon left was something he knew well: a pair of lightball gloves. Only, they didn't shoot a lightball, but a potato.

With his 'weapon' in hand, Crow headed deeper into the dungeon, appearing in a mysteriously convenient secret room where he had a chance to spin a wheel and earn a magical prize. After his spin, his potato evolved into Spud, a sapient entity and one of the most popular characters we've had in the Hunt in a long time. Once Crow exited the secret room, he used a Fountain of Wishes to upgrade Spud with a power called Hot Potato, which let everyone's favorite sidekick light himself on fire.

This would be a good time to mention that we have official Spud plushies available at our store in the Stadia. Realistic sounds! Simulated flames! Limited supplies! For only thirty Empire marks, you won't find a more coveted gift this holiday season.

Now that Crow had an upgraded weapon, he entered the Castle of 1,000 Doors. Better late than never, right? He fought white slimes, nearly blew up half the castle, and ran afoul of another group of fan favorites: the former pirate captain Cara Thorne, daughter of the late Nile 'Whitemane' Thorne, and her siblings, Skeev and Marland.

Not long after meeting the pirates, Crow accidentally earned the ire of Geeta, a reptilian from the Emerald Isles, and fought a battle with Cravag, the last of the giants. I won't say anything more about that engagement, because you've got to see it to believe it! We'll be replaying it after our highlight broadcast at nine o'clock this evening. Tune in!

Crow would've died as the castle collapsed around him, but he was saved by Geeta, the very reptilian who'd previously threatened him. After going through one of the castle's many doors and finding themselves in the Dark City, they made a plan to infiltrate a dwarven stronghold called the Electric Fortress. Once again, Crow delivered on the action! After a series of near-death experiences that included a run in with Metalhawk, a giant mechanical bird, Crow and Geeta arrived at the fortress, where they met with a Thuin soldier named Jocko, a mechanic named Brynn, and a strange cultist named Rayne.

That's *right* when yours truly got involved, dear viewer. It was my solemn duty to fulfill the will of the people by sending Crow a single magical item from the stockpile recovered by brave Empire soldiers between hunts. Suddenly, Crow didn't have only one piece of sapient ammunition, but *two*. You voted, and we sent him Peristopheles Magnesis IV—aka Perry—a brilliant young tomato with serious little-brother energy who spits corrosive acid.

What will happen next? Will Crow continue to deliver on the action? Will you get your hands on a licensed Spud plushie before supplies run out?

The suspense is absolutely gripping!

PROLOGUE

Sal Valentine surveyed the room he was about to enter. His hands rested on the head of his signature duck-head cane, and his eyes twinkled with the confidence of a man who knew his business.

We arrive at the Overgrown Hive. That rhymed! The level looks as expected.

Sal leaned forward, careful not to let any part of himself cross the threshold. The room beyond was a fifty-foot square, the walls made of light-brown wood and covered in black protuberances that dripped sticky liquid. In some areas, the knobby bumps oozed strands so thick that they gathered in ropy piles on the ground.

"Per your request, I have replaced the visual ramblings a normal hunter might receive with a salient, audible summary curated by your brilliant AI," said a voice in his ear. Nineteen was a supercomputer built by Sal himself, with a little help from Thuin mechanics. "The danger presented by this room is nominal compared to other rooms on this level. The main threat comes from golden bees, insects that live in those dark prominences."

"Do you have an entry for the creatures?" Sal asked.

"Yes. Golden bees are swarm insects. They don't sting like regular bees, but their abdomens are filled with molten gold."

Sal thoughtfully drummed his fingers on the head of his cane. "Sounds like my kind of bug," he said. "I've never minded bees. Industrious little critters."

"Should you get within two feet of the golden bees, they will explode, showering you with molten liquid," Nineteen said.

"Ah," Sal said. "Well, maybe we should avoid them, then. Anything worth taking from that wall?"

He lifted a hand and pointed across the room to the wall in question. On it, shelves held various potions in glass jars, each glowing a different color. He also saw three daggers, one with a handle wrapped in red leather, one with a grip of yellow leather, and one with a handle of neon green.

"All the items on the wall to your right are decoys except for the dagger with the green leather wrappings," Nineteen said. "However, if you get within four feet of those shelves, the rest of the items will transform into tonguelings. Remember tonguelings?"

Sal scratched his head. "Mouthy creatures? Paralytic venom?"

"Those are the ones," Nineteen said. "Good memory. Who said you can't teach an old dog new tricks? Ha. Ha. Ha."

Her laughter came out as monotone and robotic. *Not like a human would sound at all. Something to fix when I get out of here.*

"Are you *sure* we don't want the green dagger?" Sal asked. "It looks fun."

"As we have not created a build capable of wielding daggers to maximum efficiency, I'd advise you—with all the seriousness of which I'm capable—*not* to approach that wall," Nineteen said.

"That settles it, then," Sal replied. "No daggers."

"Thermal scans tell me the protuberance at your four o'clock has an eighty-seven-percent chance of releasing bees before the others," Nineteen said. "I will update this metric in real time as you enter the room. Your most effective strategy for dealing with the bees is to freeze the cysts before the insects can exit."

"Let me stretch," Sal said. He brought one arm across his chest and massaged some life into his stiff joints.

I'm not getting any younger.

"As the supercomputer responsible for your protection, I should note this is a *timed* level," Nineteen said. "Each second spent in the service of something other than finding your way to Dungeon School lowers your chances of survival by point-zero-zero-one-two percent. This is not insignificant."

She was right, of course. With a crack of his neck, Sal turned the head of his cane ninety degrees to the right. When it clicked into place, there was a soft whirring sound and gray mesh sprouted from his right wrist. It slithered toward his elbow like a fabric snake, folding over itself in a complex lattice to form an exoskeleton of gray mesh.

"Still tickles," Sal said as the mesh started up his bicep. The flexible armor was practically impenetrable, capable of withstanding a wetsnake's bite. Sal knew that for a fact, because he and the Thuin engineers had tested it.

"It's good the mesh tickles, as its purpose is to provide you with pleasure and not, say, protect you from the horrors of the dungeon," Nineteen said. "Ha. Ha. Ha."

Sal shook his head. *Brynn asked me to let her run the sarcasm module, and I listened! I should know better by now.*

He knew Brynn was still alive. He had an implant in one of his molars that buzzed every fifteen minutes as long as her heart was still beating. He had another implant for Jocko, one for Rayne, one for his son, and a final one for his man on the outside.

The mesh stopped at Sal's right shoulder, fully encasing his right arm. When he cleared the Overgrown Hive's final room, he'd find a chest filled with enough glassinine to make mesh that would cover his left arm as well as his chest. He could then build out the full suit of armor from there.

Eye on the prize. One foot after the other. Isn't that what you always taught Crow?

"Are you ready to engage?" Nineteen said. "Once again, I find myself stressing the need for haste."

In response, the rune on Sal's palm flared to life, glowing a soft blue.

"Locked and loaded," he said. "Shall we steal some honey?"

"Yes," Nineteen said. "Attack the bees at will."

1

———

*O*ne *foot after the other*, I thought as I stepped through the portal to the next level of Toroth-Gol. *That's what my father always taught me.*

That thought turned to, *I'm gonna be sick.*

I stumbled onto a circular platform that sat in the middle of an ocean. My stomach heaved from my recent teleportation, and Jocko caught my shoulder before I could fall.

"Not a bad view, *pacho*," he said. I grasped his arm to steady myself and let my stomach settle. "I could've done without the nausea, but I'm used to it. And we're here! Gotta count the wins."

Before me, at the end of the platform, was a long, curved dock that led to a tower of tan stone that jutted out of the water, rising some thirty or forty stories into the air. To my right and left, two other docks ran to similarly sized towers of green and black stone.

"Where are we?" I asked. In the distance, behind the black tower, the sun crested the horizon, painting the wide sky in brilliant purples and oranges. Water lapped gently below me, and little crabs chased each other along the sandy bottom of the sea.

The tranquility was shattered as Spud screamed into my ear.

"You don't read well, do you? This is Dungeon School! And it's *way* better than I expected. I mean, I thought we were goners."

I glanced at the timer in the upper-right-hand corner of my vision. Before I'd stepped through the door from the Dark City to Dungeon School, I'd had four days until it hit zero, which had meant four days until certain death if I hadn't been able to escape. I thought it might reset when I got to Dungeon School, though the timer still showed four days.

That's good news, at least. At a minimum, I've got another four days of life.

I turned around. Behind me was a fourth tower, this one made of gray stone. A small boat approached, moving lightly through the reeds that surrounded the tower's base. When the boat reached the tower, strange creatures appeared on the deck. They were each about three feet tall, their bodies obscured by dark-brown robes and their faces hidden deep within the folds of their cowls. The only parts of their bodies I could see were their glowing yellow eyes. They used ropes to secure the boat to metal pegs embedded in the stone, and then they started unloading wooden crates from the prow of the ship.

"It's good to meet an industrious people," Spud said as I watched them work. "And how *adorable!* I'd love a robe like that."

Text popped into my vision.

Welcome, hunters! You've survived the Castle of 1,000 Doors. Now, you face Dungeon School.

This level of Toroth-Gol is all about preparing for the War of Fangs, a challenge you'll face deeper in the dungeon. Soon, you'll find yourself against some *very* angry enemies, and we need to make sure you're prepared!

Now, you get a choice. Surrounding this platform, you'll see four towers, each of which contains a school that offers different abilities, gear, and specialization. Pick the tower that best speaks to your skillset.

Good luck, and happy hunting!

"Well, this isn't great," I said.

"Why, because we have to fight more?" Spud asked. "Side by side, together, good guys taking down the bad? Second to none, there can only be one, Spud Squad, Spud Squad, rah rah rah? Come on, Crow. The Spud Squad *loves* that stuff. Don't be such a downer."

"I don't really like fighting," Perry said from his spot at the bottom of my bandolier. When no one responded, I patted his bristly green stem.

I turned to Jocko. "Are these descriptions being written by the dungeon or the Empire?"

The Grass King's eyes twinkled in the bright light. "The dungeon, *pacho*. That piece of machinery in your face broadcasts footage back to the Empire, but the text and the timer are both generated by Toroth-Gol. You'd see them even without your mechanical eye."

I ran a hand over the stubble on my scalp. In better times, I'd shaved and oiled my head at least once per day, but finding myself consigned to a murderous dungeon hadn't really let me maintain my personal hygiene.

"I'd like to keep us all together, if possible," I said. "Though the text makes it sound like the dungeon is trying to pull us apart."

Jocko approached the dock that led to the tan tower. A wooden sign hung from a post and he pointed to it. "I think it makes sense to split, *pacho*. Here, read this."

I walked closer.

Dungeon School (Talon Lake)

Welcome to Talon Lake! If the words "poison blade" and "cloak and dagger" make your spine tingle with excitement, you've come to the right place. Our graduates are so sneaky, their enemies never see them coming. And then, *bam*! They're dead.

For all you stealthy scouts out there, Talon Lake offers two classes

per semester, plus a killer enrollment bonus: *Jade Cipher's Book of Poisons*. Get ready to become the ultimate ninja assassin!

Class Type: Scout

Classes Per Semester: 2

Enrollment Bonus: *Jade Cipher's Book of Poisons*. **Written by Talon Lake's mysterious founder, Jade Cipher, this is the definitive resource on poisons, toxins, and more.**

So that's what the dungeon meant when it told us to choose a tower that spoke to our skillset.

"See?" Jocko said. "Talon Lake is perfect for someone trying to augment stealth abilities. Someone like Geeta."

I scanned the platform for her before realizing she stood beside me. True to her nature, I hadn't heard her approach.

"Come look at this one," Brynn said from behind us. I turned and saw that she stood before the dock leading to the tower made of gray stone. "Crow and Jocko, I think this might be a good one for you."

Dungeon School (Gray Moor)

Welcome to Gray Moor! This is the tower for fearless warriors. Our graduates lead their fellow soldiers on the battlefield, and they always come out on top. If you're ready to command a team with sweat on your brow and blood on your blade, then Gray Moor is the school for you.

Gray Moor offers three classes per semester, plus an enrollment bonus that's worth fighting for: a personal advisor!

Class Type: Soldier

Classes Per Semester: 3

Enrollment Bonus: Personal Advisor. Upon entry into Gray Moor, each student meets with an advisor who helps tailor the course load to their individual skillsets. Meetings last one (1) hour.

I agreed with Brynn: this had my name written all over it. And she was right in that it was probably the tower for Jocko, too.

But if Geeta goes into Talon Lake, and we go in here, we'll be splitting up. I only survived the Castle of 1,000 Doors because of her. Without Rayne, we wouldn't have made it through the Electric Fortress. It seems like our group should try to stay together.

"The Personal Advisor seems interesting," I said to Brynn. "I wonder about this 'classes per semester' thing, too. Talon Lake only has two classes per semester, but Gray Moor has three."

Jocko joined me at the sign. "I'm not really the resident expert on the towers, *pacho*. From what I've experienced so far, the dungeon likes to balance the playing field. I imagine each tower has its own set of advantages and disadvantages. Look at the book you get with Talon Lake. Maybe that's better than the enrollment bonus at Gray Moor. But it could be that Gray Moor students gain an additional opportunity for specialization."

"Let's see what Rayne is looking at," I said.

We walked up behind the strange woman, who stood before the tower of green stone.

Dungeon School (Wicked Field)

Welcome to Wicked Field! If you prefer to stay behind the scenes and help others succeed, then this is the tower for you.

Wicked Field offers two classes per semester, plus an enrollment bonus: *Flame Child's Set of Schematics*. It's the ultimate collection of ten essential schematics that successful engineers need in order to survive the dungeon.

Class Type: Engineer

Classes Per Semester: 2

Enrollment Bonus: *Flame Child's Set of Schematics.* **Penned by the most successful engineer ever to run through Toroth-Gol, this collection of ten essential schematics prepares students of Wicked Field for crucial support roles.**

"Oh yeah," Brynn said from behind me. "This is the tower for me."

Another wedge in the group, I thought, just as Spud said, "I wonder what's in the final tower. Let's go look!"

Our group walked to the last tower, which was made of black stone.

Dungeon School (Winter Ridge)

Welcome to Winter Ridge! Here, only the toughest of the tough survive. If you're the type of person who loves a good challenge and doesn't mind getting your hands a little dirty, then consider Winter Ridge.

Who needs a warm blanket when you can have a heart full of fire?

Classes Per Semester: ?

Enrollment Bonus: ?

"We need to split up," Jocko said. "That much is clear. Geeta, I imagine you'll want Talon Lake, right? Brynn, Wicked Field is the obvious choice for you, and Crow and I will go to Gray Moor. Rayne, you could choose any of the towers."

"We only just got together," I said. "I don't think we should go our own ways yet."

Jocko's jaw tightened. "Can I speak to you for a minute, *pacho*?"

"Sure." I opened my arms and gestured to the group. "We're all listening."

Jocko raised a hand. He held the four pill-shaped devices that had generated the Aural Containment Field in the Castle of 1,000 Doors.

"Privately?"

He wants to talk to me where the Empire can't hear.

"Oh," I said. "Yeah. Got it."

I followed him toward one side of the platform.

What could he possibly have to say?

I was about to find out.

2

Jocko set the four cylinders on the ground in a square around us. Although I knew the Empire could see what we were doing through our mechanical eyes, they were powerless to stop us. When the cylinders were in place, the pink sound-blocking field sprang into existence.

The world around me fell silent.

"What's up, *majoré?*" I said. "What's going on? Why are you so insistent we split up?"

Jocko wrapped his fingers around the hilt of his sword, and it gave him strength. "I don't know how to say this, *pacho*. In truth, I thought I'd be doing this a little later, so now I'm trying to think of the best way to tell you some important things without hurting your feelings."

"You can hurt his feelings," Spud said. "Actually, I encourage it."

Jocko glanced down at him, then back to me. "First of all, *pacho*, your father is alive," he said. "I know because I've got a tooth that buzzes every fifteen minutes as long as his heart keeps beating. Last buzz was less than two minutes ago."

"Sal is alive?" I had a thousand more questions. "Is he okay? Where is he? Can I talk to him?"

Jocko held up a hand. "Slow down, *pacho*," he said. "Let me try this. Have you, uh, suspected Toroth-Gol of being a little too easy?"

I'd heard his question, but I was too distracted by what he'd already said to answer. *My father is alive!* That's all I wanted to hear about.

"What does this have to do with Sal? Tell me more about that."

Jocko threw up his hands. "I'm getting to it, *pacho!* Just answer the question: have you suspected Toroth-Gol of being too easy?"

I narrowed my eyes at him, though I could tell he wasn't going farther unless I played along. So I considered what he'd asked me. The giant I'd fought in the Castle of 1,000 Doors hadn't been the friendliest creature, but the death hyenas hadn't been too bad. The slimes had been a piece of cake. Every time I'd been in real danger, I'd been whisked away to those prize rooms. There, I'd faced the implication of death, though deep down, I'd known everything would work out.

"Uh, yeah," I said. "I never watched the Hunt, but given what I've heard, I guess so."

"Have you wondered why?" Jocko asked.

"He *knows* why," Spud said. "He's had help from the most impressive weapon of all time. That's me, in case you were wondering. Not Twinkletoes Magnesis the Fourth."

"That's not my name," Perry said.

"And yet you knew I was talking about you," Spud said. "Twinkletoes."

Again, Jocko glanced toward my chest.

"Ignore them," I said. "I want answers, Jocko. Now."

Jocko shifted uncomfortably. "I've already told you we prepared for this. Your father and I spent twenty years watching the tapes. Like you do in practice, right *pacho?* Sal got access to footage from past Hunts. The first two levels are always the same, so that let us prepare how we wanted to run them."

I raised an eyebrow at him. "What are you saying?"

Jocko rolled his eyes. "Come on, *pacho*. I've seen your aptitude scores. Do I have to spell it out?"

"For a smart guy, Crow is actually pretty dumb," Spud said. "You might have to spell it out."

Jocko stared down at his feet. He looked like a child who'd been asked to explain why his hand was halfway into a cookie jar. "You've never been in any *real* danger, *pacho*," he mumbled. "The castle was a practice round. A warmup lap. We wanted to get you acclimated to the dungeon, so we walked you through from start to finish. Got you in the right mindset while the stakes were low."

That doesn't make any sense.

"I don't understand," I said. "What about the death hyenas? The winged imago? Metalhawk? Those creatures seemed pretty dangerous for a warmup."

"I don't like where this is going," Spud said. "Someone's ego is about to get busted, and I think it's probably mine. Or maybe Crow's. Actually, yeah! Poor Crow."

"The death hyenas were puppies, *pacho*," Jocko said. "Evil puppies, but you've faced lightball enforcers more dangerous than them. Call the winged imago a calculated training risk. And Metalhawk was never going to kill you. Just rough you up a bit. Make the danger feel real."

"It felt pretty real when that evil bird came crashing through the windows and almost blew me to smithereens," I said, remembering the piercing sound of the creature's screech as it smashed into the abandoned party store where I'd been hiding.

"Right," Jocko said. "At which point you were promptly teleported out of danger and presented with an opportunity for an upgrade. Pretty strange coincidence, wasn't it?"

I stared at him. "That was *you*?"

Jocko nodded. "We got two special items that came with Brynn's loadout. Single-use, very rare. They bring a player to a secret room and give them a chance to win a prize. We triggered the first because you needed a boost after mouthing off to Lucca Bert, and the second because you ran inside what was literally the only house in the entire level that was booby-trapped."

My head spun. "You've been following me through the dungeon this whole time?"

I glanced over to where the rest of our group was hanging out near the center of the platform. Rayne was crouched on her haunches, but Brynn was staring at us. She made a "hurry-up" gesture with her hands, but Jocko looked at her and held up a finger. Geeta, who stood nearby, had her stiletto in one hand and was sharpening the blade against her whetstone.

"Geeta," I said. "She's been in league with you all along, hasn't she? She's my protector. I knew it was too much of a coincidence for her to have dragged me through the door to Dark City!"

"What? No. We've never met Geeta before the other day, *pacho*. We've had Rayne tailing you. She has this power where she can build shapes out of bone. Ladders, cages, that sort of thing. It lets her get to some unusual vantage points, so she used that to stay out of sight."

"Don't feel bad for thinking Geeta was on their side, Crow," Spud said. "My head went to the same place."

"I've had protection this whole time," I said. "And I *still* needed two lifelines? And now Brynn doesn't have any more?"

Jocko exhaled. "No," he said. "But don't worry about that, *pacho*. You were supposed to make mistakes. Better to do it now than later. The thing to realize is, we've got you. The only true danger you faced before this was the subterranean wyrm queen."

"I never fought the wyrm queen," I said.

"That's my point, *pacho*. We took care of it on our own because we were on level one, and you'd already burned through both contingencies."

"I feel like I should be offended," Spud said. "I'm not, because I'm awesome, but this is a shocking revelation."

Jocko held up his hands defensively. "I'm not trying to get anyone worked up. I'm saying that if I'm pushing for something, I'm doing it for a reason. I trained for this, *pacho*. So let me do my job. I'll guide you for one more level. After that, it's anyone's guess what the dungeon will throw at us, and the training wheels come off."

I wanted to hit him, but I knew that'd probably end with a blade at my throat. Besides, something else had caught my attention.

"What did you mean when you said we faced the subterranean wyrm queen on level one?" I asked. "That was level *two*. The castle, then Dark City, and now this."

Jocko looked down at his feet. "About that."

"Oh, for crying out loud!" I said. "Dark City wasn't the second level?"

Once again, the other man held up his hands. "Easy, *pacho*," he said. He looked back toward the group and waved at Brynn. When she saw him, she said something to Geeta and Rayne and jogged over to us.

"What's up, boys?" she said after she'd stepped through the pink wall. She stuck an index finger in her ear and wiggled it around. "Wow, it's *really* quiet in here. I forgot about that. That's disorienting. I should probably allow at least a little ambient sound. Something to fix later, I guess."

"Can you readjust Crow's eye?" Jocko said.

Brynn pulled her finger out of her ear and wiped it on her overalls. "Now? I thought we were getting him through this level first."

"We're changing plans," Jocko said. "Go ahead and make the adjustment."

Brynn shrugged. "Okay, boss. Whatever you say."

I couldn't believe what I was hearing. "My eye? What are you talking about?"

Brynn looked at Jocko. He sighed.

"I told you we'd planned for this, *pacho*," Jocko said. "We have someone on the outside. He arranged your seat on the rail car, as well as your eye. It wasn't cheap, but your father stacked a few things in our favor."

"Why do I have a special eye?" I asked. "I thought the eyes were just cameras. How is mine different from yours?"

"We have data from thousands of lightball games and practices," Jocko said. "We know how you react to different situations. If a problem looks insurmountable, you rise to the occasion. So we thought, for someone of your personality type, what would be more motivating than easing you into the dungeon, getting you prepared for the deeper dangers, and then taking off the training wheels and letting you know you weren't as deep as you'd previously thought? You'd be unstoppable. So your eye has an extra component that warps the dungeon's descriptions before you process them. For instance, it told you the Dark City was the second level, but it was really still part of the first. The eye also has a training mode that makes everything seem a little, uh, *sillier* than it really is. A little more fun."

Before I could say anything, Brynn grabbed my chin. Luckily, she did it with the hand that hadn't been in her ear.

"Don't move," she said. With a thumb and index finger, she held my eye open. Then she fished a circular glass lens out from a pocket of her overalls and raised it toward me. Her magnified eye peered at me through the glass, her brown iris flecked with gold and green.

"Hmm," she said. "That's not good."

"What's not good?" I asked while trying to keep my head as still as possible.

"You're stuck between modes. The switch is caught halfway between the training mode and the real thing. But I can fix it."

Brynn dropped the lens back into her pocket and then *flicked* my eye. Her fingernail clicked against something and I stumbled backward, hands flying to my face.

"Ow!" I said. It hadn't *actually* hurt, but no one likes anything touching their eyeball. "What the heck was that for?"

"Per the boss's request, I moved you to the big time," Brynn said. "Whoever installed that thing must've hit the switch by accident. Got you all jumbled. I can't imagine what your prompts looked like. What'd you get? A mix of fun and serious? Jubilant and less jubilant?"

I thought back to the prompts. Sure enough, some of them *had* seemed strangely manic, while others had been explanatory and matter-of-fact.

"By the Dregs." I didn't like that Jocko and his people had kept so much hidden from me, even if they'd done it in what they thought was my best interest. I stepped back and rubbed my eye. "No more secrets.

If we're going to work together, I want to know the truth. Is there anything else you haven't told me?"

Brynn and Jocko glanced at each other.

"One time, in Potato Hell, I tried a fire stick," Spud said quietly. "The other people down there told me it was the cool thing to do. But the smoke hurt my tummy, and it wasn't cool at all."

Jocko ran a hand over his head. "We're on the same page now. I promise I'll help keep you alive. Can you trust us?"

Trust you? After you lied to me for days?

Yet, he wasn't wrong about what motivated me. I understood myself well enough to know that. I got excited about big, complicated tasks. It was one of the reasons I performed so well under pressure. One of the reasons I made a great competitor.

He wants to help you. I'd never seen the Hunt, while Jocko and his team had not only seen every second, but had spent two decades planning how to beat it. For the next level, at least, they knew all of the ins and outs.

If you can forgive him, you're guaranteed to survive another level.

I swallowed my pride. "I need your help, so I'll take it," I said. "You say we split up, I won't argue with you. But moving forward, I want the truth. Agreed?"

"That's the spirit, *pacho*," Jocko said. He clapped me on the shoulder. "We're on the same side here. We're gonna get through this together."

He started to shut down the containment field.

"Jocko," I said. "Are we in agreement?"

"Hmm? Of course, *pacho*. You got it."

It wasn't the reassuring answer I'd wanted, but it was as good as I was going to get. When the containment field was down, we walked back to Rayne and Geeta. This time, when I looked at the towers, different text appeared.

Dungeon School (Talon Lake)

Talon Lake specializes in a stealthy approach to combat, where

victory is achieved through shadow and silence. Graduates are renowned for their ability to strike without being seen, making them formidable opponents.

As an enrollment bonus, students receive *Jade Cipher's Book of Poisons*, written by the tower's mysterious founder. The book contains comprehensive information on poisons, toxins, and more.

Class Type: Scout

Classes Per Semester: 2

Enrollment Bonus: *Jade Cipher's Book of Poisons.*

I walked to the sign for Gray Moor.

Dungeon School (Gray Moor)

Gray Moor focuses on strategy, management, and strength to ensure its graduates are well-equipped to command their peers on the battlefield. If you have a desire to be a true leader, then attendance at Gray Moor is mandatory.

Gray Moor's program offers three classes per semester, each designed to hone a student's skills and increase their tactical knowledge. As an enrollment bonus, each student receives a personal advisor who will help tailor their course load to their individual strengths.

Class Type: Soldier

Classes Per Semester: 3

Enrollment Bonus: Personal Advisor. Advising meetings last one (1) hour.

The descriptions of the other two towers were similar in tone to the first two: professional and clear-cut, without a single hint of personality. As I read them, I found myself missing the weirdness of the earlier descriptions, though not enough to ask Brynn to change them back.

"Should we finalize our choices?" Jocko said. He was staring at me, and I knew what he expected. "Crow, I assume you're thinking about entering Gray Moor?"

"Yes," I said.

"Then you're with me," Jocko said cheerfully. "Geeta? I think your choice is obvious. Unless you're considering something else?"

"Talon Lake."

"Brynn?"

"I appreciate you asking, but I think we all know I'm headed to Wicked Field."

We all turned our attention to Rayne. The undead librarian stood before the sign for Winter Ridge. She was so still I couldn't tell if she was breathing.

Then, she moved. It was like watching a skeleton come to life. One moment she might as well have been lifeless. The next, the charms in her hair jangled as she lifted a thin arm and extended a bony finger toward Winter Ridge.

Creepy.

If Jocko was at all bothered by his companion, he didn't show it. "I was wondering if you'd choose that one," he said. "Tell us what you find in there. I'm personally *dying* to know."

"Ha!" Spud said. "Dying to know! Get it? Because Rayne controls bone? That's how you make a pun. Nice one, Jocko!"

Our group stood in awkward silence. I'd always been bad with goodbyes. In the Dregs, where friends regularly died, you learned not to get too invested in relationships.

"I suppose this is it?" I asked.

"For now," Jocko said, surprisingly cheerful. "There's an old Thuin poem that I save for occasions like this. It's nice because it rhymes in translation: May your roads be lined with glory, your nights be free from rain, your dreams be sweet, your sleep be deep, until we meet again."

"That *is* nice," Perry said.

Jocko turned and started across the dock toward Gray Moor. Geeta watched him for a few steps, then shrugged and headed toward Talon Lake. Brynn moved toward Wicked Field.

"Wait!" Spud shouted. "All of you, hold on!"

My temporary companions stopped and turned to face us.

"Jocko had a nice poem, but I think the occasion needs a few more words," he said. "I thought Crow was going to make a speech, but since he didn't, I guess it's up to me."

He cleared his throat.

"I wish everyone the best," he said. "And I know we'll see each other soon. But if it takes five years, or ten, or a hundred, know this: no matter where you go, or what you do, you'll always be honorary members of the Spud Squad. Can I get a 'Spud Squad' on three?"

Jocko rolled his eyes, and Geeta coughed into her hand. I was also a little skeptical: Jocko had lied to me, and now he was asking me to trust him.

But if Spud noticed our hesitation, he didn't say anything. "One... two... three!" he said.

"Spud Squad!" came a chorus of voices.

I couldn't be sure, though I thought I even heard Rayne.

3

"Those were some nice words, *pacho*," Jocko said to Spud as we approached the door to Gray Moor. "Short and sweet, but inspiring. You've got the makings of a leader. If we get out of here, you can fight alongside me any time."

"Thank you, Jocko," Spud said. "Though when we make it out, I'm not sure how much fighting I'll be doing. I'll probably take a little time to myself. Put my feet in the sand and drink a few gallons of spicy cucumber margarita. But after that, who knows? Maybe I *will* take you up on the offer."

I wonder what will happen to Spud if we actually make it out. It's nice to imagine Spud on a private beach, licking salt from the rim of a glass, but is it possible?

Jocko interrupted my thoughts by rapping a hand against the wooden door that led into Gray Moor. "Here we are," he said.

Dungeon School (Gray Moor)

This is the entrance to Gray Moor.

WARNING: This is a terminal nexus on your path through Toroth-

Gol. Know that once you enter Gray Moor, you will NOT be able to choose a different tower.

I craned my neck to look toward the top of the tower. Now that we stood closer, I realized it didn't have any windows.

"Crow?" Jocko said. I glanced at him and saw that his hand rested on the door handle. "You coming, *pacho?*"

I swallowed. From here, there was no going back.

Do I trust Jocko? No. But of all the towers, Gray Moor seems best suited to help me get stronger, and Jocko appears to be acting on my father's wishes. I have so many questions for Sal. If going into Gray Moor means seeing him again, I'll do it.

We entered the tower. I was a little surprised to find myself in a pleasant atrium with a gurgling fountain. Stained-glass windows overhung two sweeping stone staircases, which was odd, because there hadn't been any windows when I'd looked at the tower from the outside. Light came in through the windows and cast the floor in dazzling hues of ruby, emerald, and sapphire.

Something else about the atrium looked odd, and it took me a moment to place it. "The tower is bigger on the inside than it is on the outside," I said. I turned around to look at the door behind me, but the door had melted into the wall, leaving nothing but stone at our backs.

"That's right, *pacho,*" Jocko said, though I could tell he wasn't really listening. Instead, he moved like he was in a daze, walking toward one of the staircases.

"Jocko?" I said. "Hey, Jocko. What's up?"

Jocko ignored me. He walked up two steps until he stood directly under one of the stained-glass windows, then stared up at it.

"Look at all that glass," Spud whispered reverently as I walked over to Jocko. "You ever worked with glass, Crow? Someone had to cut all those shapes without shattering them. Actually, never mind. You wouldn't know art if it was hanging from your bandolier."

"Shut up, Spud," I said. "Something is wrong with Jocko."

"He's in awe, is all," Spud said. "Whoever made these panels was a genius. I wonder what oxide they used to get that shade of ruby. It's exquisite!"

Jocko still stared at the window, but I was pretty sure he wasn't reacting to the artistry.

"Jocko?" I said again. "Are you okay?"

Finally, he snapped out of his trance.

"Hmm?" he said. He turned around. "Oh! Sorry. Yeah. Just expected something different, is all."

Different? I looked up at the window, which showed a serpent rising from a circular well. *What does he mean, different? I thought the first two levels of the dungeon were always the same.*

As if he could read my mind, Jocko flashed me a reassuring smile.

"Don't you worry, *pacho*," he said. "Everything is fine. I told you I'd take care of you, and I mean it. Come on! Let's get to these advising sessions."

We took the stairs two at a time. At the top was a landing, and Jocko led us across it. When we neared the door on the far side, he drew his blade and swished it through the air a few times.

"Spud, do you know any victory songs?" he asked.

I groaned. "Gods, no!" I said. "Jocko, I said I trusted you!"

"*So* glad you asked," Spud said, and then he burst into a tune: "Brave men of valor, brave men of might! Brave carbohydrates, fighting for right!"

"Ha!" Jocko said. "That's excellent. I love it!"

"Oh, that's only the first stanza," Spud said. "I have thirty-one more."

Jocko led us through the doorway on the far side of the landing. He stopped so suddenly I almost crashed into his back.

"Uh, Jocko?" I said. "What's up?"

The hallway we'd just entered looked normal enough to me. The walls were made of wood, and on the far side of the hallway was a large, ominous-looking door made of black iron.

"This doesn't look right," Jocko said, his voice barely above a whisper. "The last time, the door was smaller, and the walls were made of stone."

A chill ran down my spine as I realized what Jocko was saying. If the room had changed…

"We've got to keep moving," Jocko said, his voice shaking. "Now."

He dashed across the room, and I followed, my heart pounding in my chest. As we approached the strange iron door, the air grew colder. Jocko stopped before it, hesitating only for a moment before he took a deep breath and pushed it open.

The room on the other side of the door was massive. It had maintained the general shape of the tower, tall and skinny, and it must've been a hundred yards from floor to ceiling. The inside walls were perfectly smooth and made of the same gray stone I'd seen on the outside of the tower. Light came in through a translucent skylight high overhead.

In the center of the room was a shallow pool that contained the room's most obvious feature: a gigantic statue. It stood on a pedestal, its head nearly touching the ceiling.

"Is that—?" I started to ask, but Spud interrupted me.

"It's a trash panda," he said. "A raccoon!"

But it wasn't a raccoon. Not exactly. It had the face of a raccoon, but its body was that of a man. It wore chain armor and its hands gripped the crossguard of a greatsword that reached from the middle of its chest to the ground between its feet. On its shoulders were spiked pauldrons, and it held a helmet under one arm.

Statue of Sirax Sirco

Raccoon-kin.
General of the prey forces during the War of Fangs.
Founder of Gray Moor.
Father to a nation, leader to an army, hero to a people.

May he rest in peace.

"Huh," I said. I was starting to get a sense for what was happening on this level. Clearly, there'd been a battle here: the War of Fangs. A fight between prey and predators? After the battle, Sirax Sirco must've founded Gray Moor.

Or something like that.

I glanced at Jocko and noticed the Grass King had turned white. People say that all the time—*he turned white as a sheet! White as a ghost!* —but until it happened to Jocko, I hadn't realized it was something that could *actually* happen. But as Jocko stared at the statue above us, the color drained from his face and his knees buckled.

"No," he said. "It's supposed to have a human head. Sirax Sirco is supposed to be a human!"

The horror was clear on his features. My stomach dropped, because it could only mean one thing: whatever he'd expected to see, this *wasn't* it.

Internally, I panicked. "It's okay, *majoré*. Whatever is wrong, we'll figure it out together."

But this was one challenge too large for Jocko. He sank to the floor, leaned against the wall, and laid his sword on the stone beside him.

"I don't think so, *pacho*," he said quietly. "It seems I've made a terrible mistake. In twenty years, the dungeon hasn't changed, but I didn't recognize the entry, and the statue shouldn't look like that. The dungeon *is* different, *pacho*. Get it? I spent two decades preparing for nothing. Go on, if you want. I need some time."

Time? This isn't right. We split up because you told me to trust you. So I did, and this is what I get?

"Hey," I said. He didn't move. "Hey!"

Still, nothing.

I moved to slap him. I hadn't meant to, but his apathy made me angry. *No way you give me a speech like that on the platform and then give up.*

Right before my palm connected with Jocko's cheek, I thought, *He's not going to let me hit him. His eyes will open, he'll see my hand, and he'll grab my wrist before he gets hit.*

Crack. My slap connected with his cheek and the noise echoed in the hallway.

"I think he's in shock," Perry said. "Give him a moment."

"We don't have a moment." I reached down and hefted his sword. It was so light, with a long and thin blade, and yet it felt substantial. I glanced down at Jocko, curious whether he'd come alive now that I'd touched his weapon. Nope.

If what Jocko said earlier was true, he carried me through the whole first level of the dungeon. I suppose it's only fair that I return the favor.

I put the sword into my Inventory. Then I lifted Jocko. He was similar to his sword, light but with a curious gravity.

I'm going to get him through this. I'm making that vow to myself right now. I'm going to get us both through this, as well as anyone else who puts their trust in me.

With Jocko draped over my shoulders, I walked farther into the chamber, my footsteps echoing on the stone. A voice called to us: "Greetings! My friends! Over here!"

I looked up and saw a desk at the foot of the statue. I'd been so distracted that I'd originally missed it. Behind the desk was a creature I recognized but couldn't initially place, as I'd never seen one of them sitting behind a desk before. From where I stood, I could make out a long face and branching antlers.

"Is that a horse?" Spud asked.

"A buck, I think," I said.

"I can hear you guys," the buck said. "One of the advantages of these silken ears." The buck's ears twitched. "Come on over! Step right up and we'll get into the paperwork."

Paperwork? Since the buck didn't seem like it wanted to kill us, I approached the desk.

Armored Buck (Feng)

Although Feng wasn't old enough to have participated in the War of Fangs, he grew up listening to stories of the heroes who helped the prey emerge victorious. As a child, his idol was Fergus Cameron, the legendary sharpshooter who came out of the war with seventy-nine confirmed kills.

Before Feng had shed the velvet from his antlers, he was practicing with his clan's rifle. Since that time, Feng has grown into a keen sniper and dutiful supporter of Gray Moor.

"Trouble in paradise?" Feng asked as I set Jocko down; he'd gone limp as a child's doll. I actually had to prop him up against the desk and balance his head so it didn't flop over.

"You could say that," I said. I liked this creature already. He had amber eyes and his torso was covered by a tactical vest that held several clips of ammunition, a strange juxtaposition to the ascot tied around his neck. A sniper rifle lay propped against the desk, though Feng made no move to reach for it.

"What's your name?" he asked, his pen hovering over paper. When I told him, he gasped.

"Okay, wow," he said as he met my eyes. "You're him." His eyes darted to my chest. "Which means this is…"

"Yes?" Spud said. "Do go on."

The buck stared at Spud. "Spud," he said. "And that's Perry, and that must be Jocko."

"Yeah," I said. If the buck had been more threatening, I might've been worried. "How do you know who we are?"

Using his pen, the buck pointed at himself. "Uh, I don't want to make this weird, but I'm your *biggest fan*. Natives aren't supposed to talk to each other between levels, but we always hear things. And your reputation precedes you. I'd been hoping for the chance to meet you guys!"

"Yes!" Spud whispered. "This is awesome!"

I noticed the pin on Feng's lapel. It was about the size of an Empire mark and made from gold. It looked like…

"Is that a pin of *Spud*?" I asked.

"Oh *heck* yeah," Spud said.

The buck looked down at the pin. "Yes," he said cheerfully. "Like I said, I don't want to gush, but you've got a fan base down here. The Spud Squad, you know?"

"Don't tell me I'm dreaming," Spud said. "I mean that. Even if I am dreaming, don't tell me. I've got my own *fan club*? This is everything I've ever wanted!"

"Well, it's for all of you," Feng continued. "Spud, Perry, the whole crew. Uh, can I ask though, what's wrong with Jocko?"

I looked down at the Grass King. "Going through a bit of a rough time," I said. I hoped Feng would leave it at that, and he did.

"Bummer," he said. "But it happens to the best of us. Anyway, I'm glad you're here. You're early, too! We've still got space in all the classes and four of the five lodging types available. A big group recently cleared the Blessed Taiga, and a good many of them were soldiering types. It's first come, first served, so we should lock in what you want before they get here."

Feng slid a piece of paper across the desk. Although there was text written on the physical page, it appeared in my vision like the messages I received whenever I saw a new person or looked at a point of interest.

Gray Moor (Barracks)

The all-purpose quarters for students of Gray Moor. Barracks grant a twenty-percent increase in strength when fighting in groups of five or more.

Interesting. "So the room types we choose give us certain advantages?"

"That's right," Feng said. He looked around, then leaned forward and said in a conspiratorial whisper, "If I were you, I wouldn't take the Barracks. They're really a catch-all, used when the other lodging types get taken. Since you're here early, you still have your choice. Everything except for the Warmaster's Conference Room. We only have one of those, and it's not available right now."

"Got it," I said. I read the next available lodging type on the sheet.

Gray Moor (Field Soldier's Tent)

Capable of folding into a hunter's Inventory, the Field Soldier's Tent is the only portable lodging type offered by Gray Moor. The tent comes with an endless cauldron capable of producing one pound of vegetable stew per hour.

I glanced at Feng.

"Keep reading," he said, and I read the third lodging type.

Gray Moor (Strategist's Chambers)

Available in one- or two-room units. The Strategist's Chambers grant privacy of all types—not only from other hunters, but from outside broadcasts as well.

"That looks pretty good," Spud said. "Crow, it's like the dungeon *knows* you have a crush on Jocko. You guys can room together!"

I ignored him. "What do you think of this one, Feng?" I asked.

Once again, the buck glanced around, like someone might appear and catch him doing something naughty.

"Uh, I'm not actually supposed to give you any hints," he said. "Nope! Feng always follows the rules." But as he spoke, he flashed me a thumbs up.

"Right," I said. "Okay, one more to look at. Let's see what we've got."

Gray Moor (General's Quarters)

The General's Quarters come with a special ability that lets up to five graduates of Talon Lake place points of interest on your Map. While this might not serve you in Dungeon School, it will come in handy in later levels of the dungeon.

Talon Lake. That's the tower Geeta entered.

Now *that* was interesting. *Except you aren't currently in contact with anyone from Talon Lake. And you don't know the next time you'll hear from them.*

Spud arrived at the same conclusion. *"Boring!* I mean, we could definitely do worse. Who chooses the Barracks? But it says the special ability you'd get from picking the General's Quarters only comes into play much later down the road. We need something to help us *now*. I vote Strategist's Chambers. That lets us keep two members of the Spud Squad together. We can make secret plans!"

I glanced at Jocko. "What do you say, *majoré*? Should we be roommates?"

As expected, he didn't say anything.

Feng cleared his throat. "Again, I'm not supposed to direct you one way or the other, but I like the way you guys think. Now, if you could check the box next to the lodging type you'd like, and then sign here?"

Feng handed me his pen. I was about to put a check next to Strategist's Chambers when I stopped. "Out of curiosity, what do you get with the Warmaster's Conference Room?" It was the one lodging type we hadn't gotten to see, and the option hadn't been on my sheet.

Feng's mouth thinned. "I can't reveal that."

By the Dregs. Now I'm really going to wonder what we missed.

I filled out the rooming sheet and handed it back to him. Text flashed across my vision.

Your response has been recorded. You have been assigned to the Strategist's Chambers.

Classes begin once all portals from the Castle of 1,000 Doors are closed. Check your timer to see how much time is left.

So that's why I still have a four-day countdown. It's not four days until the Purge, but four days until classes. That's a relief.

Turning to Feng, I asked, "Can I fill one of these out for Jocko? I'm not sure he can hold a pen right now."

"Sure," Feng said. He handed me a fresh form and I signed for Jocko as well.

I was about to ask Feng another question when his nostrils flared. He sniffed the air, and then pinched his nose. "That group from the Blessed Taiga just arrived. Phew! I can smell them from here. Before I forget, let me give you this."

Feng reached beneath his desk and handed me a pamphlet. It was a trifold, like the kind the Empire printed and disseminated throughout Gomindor on game days. Except, instead of a picture of yours truly, this one featured the statue of Sirax Sirco.

"You'll need that once you get inside," Feng said. "It contains lots of useful information about the school, as well as the switching codes."

"Switching codes?"

"You'll see what I mean soon enough. You have some time before classes start, so use it wisely. I recommend getting to the commissary as soon as possible, as Fairlan has some deals that won't be available once classes start. She drives a hard bargain, so watch out, but you might be able to find something useful. And definitely take advantage of your advising session! It'll help you plan an optimal course of study."

Commotion from behind me caused me to turn around. Nine heavily armored people stood on the other side of the room.

"That's the group," Feng said. He motioned to his right, where the path curved around the small lake that held the statue of Sirax Sirco. "Get down there and choose your classes. The good ones fill up quickly, so you'll want to make sure you get in your preferences soon."

"Thank you," I said. I pocketed the map, then bent down and hefted Jocko. Once again, I was surprised by how light he felt.

"Go Spud Squad," Feng said. "I'm sure I'll see you all again soon."

"I'd like one of those pins, if you've got extra," Spud said.

But Feng didn't hear him. He waved at the group near the door. "Hello, welcome!" he said. "Over here. No, I'm not an antelope. I'm a buck. Yes, I'm a talking buck. It's not that odd down here. Right this way, please. Over here!"

4

Once I'd put the statue of Sirax Sirco behind us, I set Jocko down and pulled Feng's pamphlet from my pocket. I wasn't a person who cared about advertising, but I had to admit that the statue of Sirax Sirco made a pretty striking image for the cover. The way the light hit the stone made Sirco look grimly determined, and I doubted I would've wanted to meet him on the battlefield.

It's always the little guys who are the most dangerous, I thought, which was a maxim I'd tested numerous times on the lightball field. *They have the most to prove.*

On the inside of the pamphlet were a few paragraphs that gave a brief history of the school.

The History of Gray Moor

The story of Gray Moor began in the aftermath of the War of Fangs, a brutal conflict between predators and prey. As the dust settled on the war, it became clear to the survivors that the world needed tools to prevent another such conflict.

One of the key figures in this new era was Sirax Sirco, a veteran warrior who led the prey forces during the war. Sirax had seen the horrors of war up close, and he knew the prey needed a new kind of soldier: one who could think, strategize, and work with others to protect their communities. With this in mind, Sirax established Gray Moor.

Originally, the school was built on a rocky outcropping in the middle of a vast moor surrounded by mist, which made it difficult to find for those who didn't know the way. Its walls were made of gray stone, hence its name—Gray Moor—and it was designed to be impregnable, with narrow windows, hidden doors, and secret passageways. However, twenty years after establishing his school, Sirax joined forces with the leaders of three other institutions to found Dungeon School, a four-unit consortium that catered to the skillsets of different students.

Today, Gray Moor is one of the most respected institutions in the world, known for its rigorous curriculum, skilled teachers, and fierce commitment to protecting the innocent. Its students go on to become some of the most talented and respected warriors in the land, carrying on the legacy of Sirax Sirco and his vision for a better, more peaceful world.

I flipped to the next page, which was titled *Switching Codes*. It showed names of rooms, and each name was followed by four shapes of different colors. For instance, *Mess Hall* was a red circle followed by three blue squares; *Commissary* was two green triangles followed by a red square and a blue circle; something called *Sirax Sirco's Personal Armory* was on there, but it was followed by question marks.

The rest of the pamphlet contained more information about the school's various points of interest. I skimmed it, but it was the last page that truly grabbed my attention.

Sirax Sirco's Personal Armory

Calling all adventurers and treasure seekers. Do you have what it takes to find Sirax Sirco's fabled armory, hidden deep within the legendary tower of Gray Moor?

Sirax Sirco, the great general and founder of Gray Moor, was known for his strategic mind, leadership skills, and powerful weaponry. Rumors suggest that his weapons are still inside Gray Moor, waiting to be discovered by those brave enough to search for them.

The path to the armory isn't for the faint of heart. In order to find it, you'll have to get inside Sirco's mind. You'll have to solve riddles, navigate treacherous traps, and outsmart cunning guardians to reach the ultimate treasure. The journey will take you through hidden chambers, where ancient magic still lingers and danger lurks in every corner.

Sharpen your wits and your weapons. The treasure awaits, but only the bravest will find it.

"I like the sound of that," Spud said. "Jocko, do you see this? We've *got* to find this armory!"

Jocko didn't respond.

"Nice try, Spud," I said. I put the pamphlet back in my pocket, hoisted Jocko over my shoulders, and continued down the hall.

It was still strange to me that I was headed to *school*. As an orphan in the Dregs, I'd received a practical education, which meant I'd learned how to work an assembly line without getting crushed by an industrial gear. In those early years, I'd taught myself to read from old magazines I occasionally found lying in the gutters. From the time work ended until bedtime, the orphans in our tenement got an hour and twelve minutes of light, and I'd used that time to better myself.

This was probably how I'd managed to perform so well on Sal Valentine's aptitude test. One day I was living in the tenements, trying to avoid getting whipped by overseers, and the next I was brought to live in a mansion in Gomindor. I'd received private lessons there, though I'd never gone to school. The opportunity to learn alongside a group of peers was something I'd heard about, though I'd never thought it was something I'd get to experience.

I guess you're finally living your dream.

I couldn't help but laugh.

From the end of the hall came a strange noise, like the clacking of ivory gambling chips against a wooden table. I turned the corner and the room opened up.

Gray Moor (Switching Station)

Originally, Gray Moor was built to accommodate Sirax Sirco's hand-chosen group of fifty students. Over the years, as an increasing number of Gray Moor graduates achieved acclaim in their respective fields, more and more students requested the tower's services. To accommodate their demand, subsequent heads of school have plunged deeper into the earth to build more rooms. All the rooms in Gray Moor can be accessed via the school's various Switching Stations.

The chamber smelled musty, like it had been a while since someone had mopped the floors and dusted. Its far side was bisected by a track that entered and exited through dark tunnels, and the clacking noise came from inside the tunnels.

"Hmm," I said as I approached a chest-high wooden podium that sat beside the track.

Switching Station Controller

Enter your code.

The face of the podium resembled the one in the training room in the Electric Fortress, only this one was simpler. Instead of multiple buttons and dials, this one had four glass windows. Beneath each window was a wheel, and beneath each wheel was a large green button.

"I bet this is where you use those switching codes from the pamphlet," Perry said. "Feng recommended visiting the commissary first. I think it was green triangle, green triangle, red square, blue circle."

With Jocko still on my shoulders, I pulled out my pamphlet and opened to the page with the switching codes. Sure enough, Perry had nailed that one.

"How'd you remember that?" I asked.

"I have a good memory," Perry said.

"What'd you have for breakfast?" Spud asked.

"I don't need to eat to survive," Perry said. "Which you know, because you don't either."

"Ha!" Spud said. "You can't remember. Loser."

I twisted the first wheel. As I did, the white rectangle behind the first window changed to a green triangle.

"So that's easy enough," I said. I moved to the second wheel, switching the image behind the window above it to another green triangle, and then moved the third wheel, cycling through several colored shapes until I arrived at the one I wanted. I added a fourth shape, then pressed the green button.

"If you got the code wrong you'll summon a demon from an alternate dimension," Spud said.

"What?" I said. "Where'd you read that?"

"I didn't," Spud said. "I made it up. But can you imagine? That would *suck*."

The clacking grew louder, and then a cart shot out of the tunnel to my right. It was made of steel and shaped like a bullet, with three rows of benches covered in red leather. As it squealed to a halt before me, bars lifted from the seats, allowing me to climb down into it.

Transport Cart

A cart designed by Sirax Sirco's protégé, Nevis Lyveris, to bring students of Gray Moor from one section of the tower to another.

I set Jocko into one bench, propping him up so he sat straight, and then took the seat behind him. The moment my butt hit the cushions, the bar that had previously been covering the seat dropped across my lap. In front of me, the same thing happened to Jocko.

"Hold onto your skins, boys," Spud said. "We're going to the commissary!"

The cart shot forward. Wind rushed past me as I clung to the metal bar, and adrenaline pumped through my veins. Ignoring the fact that I was in a murderous dungeon, protecting a companion who currently didn't seem capable of independent motion, it was actually fun.

"Yippee!" Perry yelled as we barreled through the darkness. "This is the most fun I've had since... well, I can't ever remember having fun before this!"

After a few seconds, we shot out of the tunnel and entered a central cavern. I glanced over the edge of the cart and saw that it was illuminated by glowing crystals that grew out of the walls. Both above and below us, the tracks stretched out in all directions, forming steep drops, wild corkscrews, and hairpin turns as they branched off into smaller tunnels and corridors. Other carts flew by on different tracks, sometimes passing so close I could've reached out and touched them. That seemed like a really good way to lose a limb. Some of those other carts held passengers, their eyes as wide as my own, but others were empty. The air was filled with the sound of rushing wind, the distant hum of machinery, and the clacking sound the carts made as they tore across the rails.

When the cart finally stopped and the bar lifted from my lap, I climbed onto a platform. To my surprise, Jocko got out of the cart by himself.

Progress, I thought, summoning his sword from my Inventory. I slipped it into its scabbard. *Slowly but surely, I guess.*

I looked toward the far end of the platform, where there appeared to be an area set up like a general store. From what I could see, there were rows and rows of cases that held a variety of weapons: pistols, muskets, maces, and more. A case hanging from one of the walls contained nothing but rapiers. At the ends of each row were different types of armor, which ranged from chain mail and plate to lighter leather armor and flowing robes that I assumed provided magical protection.

I walked toward the store and Jocko followed. He moved with a slow, shuffling gait, but at least he was walking under his own power now.

Gray Moor (Commissary)

At the commissary, Gray Moor students can purchase gear, weapons, and healing items. The store is organized into sections based on the type of item for sale. The shelves contain a variety of swords, shields, wands, staffs, potions, and elixirs. In the back of the store are rare and powerful items such as enchanted armor, amulets, and ancient artifacts.

The store's operator, Fairlan, may be willing to negotiate prices and trade items.

WARNING: Steal at your own risk.

At the back of the commissary, beneath a chandelier containing roughly a hundred thousand lit candles, was a low counter, behind which stood a short woman with the body of a human and the head of a robin. She appeared to be playing some sort of card game. As she saw me walking toward her, she swept the cards into a pile and waved me over.

"New customers!" she said cheerfully. "Step right up. Let's see what types of deals we can make."

I approached the counter, making my way between a rack of spears and several deep bins filled with arrows and crossbow bolts. As I neared the woman, I realized she wasn't actually standing, but seated in a wheeled chair.

Bird-kin (Fairlan)

A graduate of Gray Moor and one-time captain of a platoon of bird-kin, Fairlan lost the use of both her legs when a routine scouting mission turned into a predator ambush. She has since become the proprietor of the Gray Moor commissary, where she helps the next generation of students prepare for future battles.

"Good day and welcome," Fairlan said, cocking her head to one side in a strange, bird-like movement. "Classes don't start for another few days, but I'm glad to have some visitors. Early bird gets the worm, as they say."

From his spot on my bandolier, Spud said, "That was an *incredible* pun. I like this woman already!"

Fairlan gasped and wiggled her fingers as she looked down at Spud. "What's this? A sapient potato?" She looked up at me. "Is it for sale?"

"You can have Perry," Spud said. "Don't need to pay us for him either."

"I bet Perry is the tomato," Fairlan said. "So he can talk too?"

I put my hand protectively over Perry. "Neither Spud nor Perry are for sale," I said. "Though I do have some other things that might interest you. Care to look?"

Fairlan sighed. "You hunters never want to sell the good stuff," she said. "But fine. I'll see what you've got."

Show Fairlan your Inventory?

Confirm. Yes or No.

I mentally selected *Yes* and waited a moment while Fairlan checked my wares.

"Hmm," she said. "Oh, you've got pickle juice! I'll give you three hundred thousand marks for that."

My heart soared. "Really?"

"No," Fairlan said. "It's worthless. Are you *sure* the sapient vegetables aren't available?"

"Take Perry," Spud said. "*Please.*"

"Neither of them is for sale," I repeated.

"Fine," Fairlan said. "Okay, how about Giant's Roar? I think I'd have a buyer for that. Sell me the skill and I'll actually give you three hundred thousand marks."

As she finished speaking, text appeared in my vision.

Sell Giant's Roar to Fairlan for three hundred thousand marks?

Confirm. Yes or No.

I considered the offer. I wasn't necessarily wedded to Giant's Roar, though it had gotten me out of some sticky situations. Still, I wasn't ready to sell one of my most important assets without knowing what I could get in return.

No. "Not yet," I said. "What could I buy for three hundred thousand marks? Do you have anything that could help a guy who shoots sapient produce?"

Fairlan nodded. "I have plenty of health items, which I imagine you've needed frequently."

"Sick burn," Spud said.

"Or, you could look at these." From beneath the counter, Fairlan lifted a small display case. Beneath the glass cover, two dozen orbs rested on a bed of black velvet, each of them glowing with a different-colored light. The light wasn't static; it danced and writhed within the orbs like living fog.

"What *are* these?" I asked, as no text had popped into my vision.

As if reading my thoughts, Fairlan said, "Your eye won't work on this display case. Helps keep me from getting robbed." She tapped the glass above the smallest orbs. "Down at the bottom here, we've got your minor soul cores. Then here, you've got your lesser soul cores." She moved her finger to hover over the slightly larger orbs. "They continue to increase in quality as they get bigger. Minor, lesser, common, broad, greater. I've also got a few grand soul cores, but I keep those in the vaults. I've heard of master cores, though I've never seen one."

"And what do these soul cores do?" I asked.

Fairlan pointed at Spud. "It's how you make those," she said. "At least, I *assume* it's how someone made those. Soul cores are literally souls that have been ripped from another body and kept in stasis for safekeeping. From there, they can be transferred to a new form, like a potato, or a tomato."

"Huh," I said. "I'd never thought about that. So if I had another soul core, I could make another type of ammunition?"

"That's one use for them," Fairlan said. "You'd also need the right training, though we have a specialist here in the tower. Grumpy old coot, but if you take his class, he might help you."

I was both intrigued and surprised. *How did I get to a point where I'm excited by the prospect of learning how to create sapient produce? I guess getting thrown into a murderous dungeon re-orients a person's priorities.*

"And how much do soul cores run?" I asked.

"Minors are twenty-five thousand. Lessers are fifty to a hundred thousand, depending on the quality. Commons are one hundred to two hundred, and broads get up to three hundred, if they're high quality. Greaters are five hundred, and grands start at a million." She pointed at my chest. "To make something like that, with full sapience, you'd need a grand or a master."

I whistled. "Good to know."

And it *was* good to know, though I didn't actually need a soul core at the moment.

"Still no trade?" Fairlan said.

"Not yet. I want to see what classes I end up taking."

Fairlan shrugged. "You know where to find me if you change your mind." She looked past me. "Oh! It looks like your friend has found something he likes."

With an electric hum, Fairlan's chair moved away from the counter.

"Jocko?" I said. I looked over my shoulder. "He's not…"

I trailed off. Something *had* caught Jocko's attention. He stood before a low table that held six swords, each with its own matching scabbard.

"And how can I help *you*?" Fairlan asked as she pulled up beside him.

Jocko pointed to one of the swords. It was a wicked-looking weapon with a grip wrapped in strips of black leather. It had a blade the color of obsidian, darker than Geeta's Stiletto of Silence. Although the scabbard wasn't ornate, there was something about its dark-gray metal that spoke of obvious craftsmanship.

The Sword of a Thousand Cuts

The Sword of a Thousand Cuts is a magical weapon said to be able to slice through anything. The blade is made from a unique alloy of metals, and its hilt is adorned with intricate runes that are said to amplify the sword's magical powers.

When swung, the sword makes a thousand cuts in a direct line before it. However, while the sword's power is undeniable, it's also said to be incredibly difficult to wield. Only the most skilled and experienced warriors are able to control the weapon's immense power without injuring themselves, and none in the last decade have proven themselves worthy. Because of this, it's often said that

the sword is cursed, as it can do more harm than good for its wielder.

Fairlan cocked her head to one side, her obsidian eyes glinting in the light of the massive chandelier.

"One of the best in my collection," she said. "What have you got to trade for it?" Fairlan let the silence stretch, then waved a dismissive wing. "I don't give anything out of the kindness of my heart. Later, if you think you've got something else, we can talk."

The bird-kin wheeled herself back toward the counter.

"Zero for two today," she said absentmindedly. "Ah, well. Some days are like that."

I laid a hand on Jocko's shoulder. "Come on," I said. "Doesn't look like we can buy anything yet, though it's been good to see what the commissary has. Let's get over to our advising sessions."

5

A cart dropped us off on a long platform similar to the one we'd recently left, only this one had a huge gap beyond the track. I stood on the edge of the platform and looked down, yet I couldn't see where the nothingness ended. Was it fifty feet deep? A hundred? A thousand? Then the cart that had dropped us off clattered away toward the far tunnel, so I realized it was time to keep moving.

"I'm not sure what's going to happen in the next hour, but I think it's going to be important," I said to Jocko, who stood beside me. "So I need you to take this seriously, okay?"

Still, Jocko said nothing. *What's wrong with him?* I didn't know, but I hoped he'd snap out of it soon. I turned from the track and walked toward the far side of the platform.

Instead of a shop area, this platform had two doors embedded in the wall. The first was obviously the more interesting. It was circular, twenty paces across, and made from gold. Carved into the stone on either side of the door were two soldiers with the heads of elephants. Each clutched a massive stone axe.

Treasure Door — Locked

Solve the riddle of this door to reveal the room beyond.

"Now that's interesting. Treasure Door. I wonder if that's hiding the armory?"

I looked more closely at the door. There was no knocker, knob, or keyhole of any kind, but there were letters painted across the surface.

dtgcvjg hktg wrqp og

"What language is that?" I hadn't been speaking to anyone in particular, and no one responded.

I stared at the door for another moment, trying to find an angle on the riddle, but didn't come up with anything. "Perry? Spud? What have you got?"

"Nothing from me," Perry said. "I'll think about it, though."

"Why'd you ask me second?" Spud asked. "Do you think I'm dumb or something?"

"I went alphabetically," I said, picking the first excuse that came to mind—then sighed internally with relief when I realized it was true.

"Oh," Spud said. "So you did."

I didn't have an obvious way to open the treasure door, so I resolved to give it some thought and come back later. Now I turned my attention to the more boring of the two doors, a simple piece of wood with a brass knob and a sign above it that said, **Advising Rooms**. I moved through it, Jocko behind me, and found myself in a hall that reminded me of the Sledgehammers' clubhouse. The walls were made of dark wood, and recessed lighting cast the hallway in a warm glow. There were doors on either side of the hallway and little gold plaques on each one. There was also a familiar object between the first and second doors on the right side: it was a Kinetoscope, similar to the one I'd used to talk to Elvis Madden back in Dark City.

"Nope," I said. "Not doing it."

During my last peek into the Kinetoscope, I'd gotten Perry, but the device was a reminder that the Empire was still watching—and that they still had some measure of control. When my face had been pressed against the pads, I hadn't been able to move until they'd released me.

I won't let them hold me hostage again. I returned my gaze to the first door.

Gray Moor (Advising Room #1)

A room in Gray Moor built for personal advising sessions.

I turned toward Jocko, who stood behind me, and motioned him to the first door.

"We'll meet back here in an hour?"

The Grass King pulled open the door, stepped inside, and shut the door behind him.

"Cool, *majoré*. See you later."

"That guy is *not* in good shape," Spud said. "Even my jokes weren't helping. I could be totally off-base—which I'm not, obviously—but I've been crushing it with the humor lately."

I sighed and moved to the door on the other side of the Kine-toscope.

"Let's see what classes we should take."

I should've known what I'd see when I opened the door, but I was still shocked to find my father. Or, not my father. Gatekeeper Valentine.

Gatekeeper (Sal Valentine)

A guide in the dungeon of Toroth-Gol. The Gatekeeper appears as a different person for each hunter who sees it.

"Hello, my boy," the Gatekeeper said. He sat behind a wooden desk in the middle of the room. On the desk was a small gong, and in one hand he held a mallet. On one side of the room was a fireplace, and the other side featured a floor-to-ceiling bookshelf filled with dusty tomes. "Long time, no see. I trust you've been well since we last spoke?"

"Gatekeeper Valentine," I said. "Good to see you. I don't believe you've met my friends, Perry and Spud."

"Spud and Perry," Spud said.

"Sure. Guys, this is Gatekeeper Valentine. He's a, uh, a simulation of my dad."

Spud gasped. "I'm sorry," he said. "I must've had potato in my ears. Did you say he was a simulation of your *dad*?"

"Yeah. Gatekeeper Valentine guided me when I first came into the dungeon. He's actually the reason I got you, Spud."

Perry glanced shyly at the Gatekeeper. "Hi, Mr. Crow," he said.

"Call me Sal," the Gatekeeper said. "Unless that's too weird? Then you can call me Gatekeeper. We only have an hour together and we need to be efficient with our time. So we'll get started, if that's okay?"

I shivered. The Gatekeeper's mannerisms were so similar to the real Sal Valentine's that I found myself feeling emotional, though I knew he was just a construct of the dungeon.

"I'm ready."

"Let's begin, then. Remember: the dungeon wants you to succeed."

"What does that mean?"

The Gatekeeper only winked at me. Then he lifted his mallet and struck the gong.

Bong. I blinked, and the Gatekeeper was gone. "Gatekeeper Valentine?" There was no response. "Hey, Gatekeeper?"

Still, nothing.

Bluish smoke rose from the floor. It was wispy, ethereal, and glowing. Within moments, the strange glowing smoke covered the entire floor. Where it touched my ankles, it felt cold. Goosebumps formed on my legs like I was standing outside in a blizzard.

"Um, that smoke is probably a good thing, right?" Spud said. "Because no father would want to hurt his son. Right?"

I didn't have an answer. The smoke continued to fill the room, the strange blue wisps curling around me.

You have activated your advising session. Over the next hour,

you'll be asked a series of questions, and you may be put into scenarios. Although these scenarios may feel real, they're part of the session. At the end of the session, you'll be advised on a course of study that best complements your innate and acquired attributes.

Proceed? Yes or No.

Yes. The smoke swirled as if disturbed by a breeze, and then it began to take form. Within seconds, the previously wispy strands of smoke had coalesced and adopted a humanoid shape. It had a toad-like face and a naked, hunched back covered in slabs of muscle.

A mulcher horde is attacking your village. You enter an alley and see a mulcher threatening two innocents: a puppy and a child. Which do you save?

"*What?*" I said as the ghostly creature—a mulcher, I presumed—opened its fang-filled mouth and beat its chest. "What kind of sick question is that?"

"We're saving the puppy, right?" Spud said. "Children are so sticky."

"The child," I said. "Final answer."

"Okay, puppy killer. That's going to sit on your conscience forever."

The mulcher dissipated, the smoke returning to wisps. Then it moved again, this time surrounding me. Within seconds, I was enclosed in a glowing box.

You find yourself trapped in a room with no visible exits. What do you do?

"I imagine that first, I'd look for a *hidden* exit," I said as I stared dubiously at the smoky walls. "If I couldn't find one, I'd try to climb up to the ceiling or check the walls for any cracks or weak spots I could break through. And if that failed, I'd try to create an improvised tool or weapon to break down the walls or pry up any loose stones. After that, I'd probably sit and wait until someone opened the door. I'd attack them, kill them, and get away."

"That's better than your last answer," Spud said. "I like the attacking part."

The box broke apart, the smoke dissipating, and this time it reformed into a massive, ghostly demon. The creature stood at least ten feet tall, the tips of its horns nearly touching the ceiling. It held a smoke-gray greatsword in both hands, the blade longer than my entire body.

You encounter a powerful enemy. What is your strategy for defeating it?

I considered my answer. "I guess it'd depend on the enemy. But if it's that thing, I'm *not* defeating it. I'm running away."

"Are you kidding?" Spud said. "Coward!"

"Final answer."

The demon blew apart. When the smoke coalesced, it had formed into a corridor that ended in two branching pathways.

You're presented with a choice of two paths. One path is easy, but leads to a dead end. The other is harder but could lead to great rewards. Which do you choose?

"The hard one. Unless it's going to result in sure death, like fighting that demon. If that's the case, I'd take the easy one, no question."

When the smoke started to shift again, I held up a hand. "Look, this is getting tedious. Are we building to something? Really, what are we doing here?"

This time, when the smoke coalesced, the result looked more *real* than it had before. The glowing, ghostly smoke solidified and I found myself staring at a door. It resembled the treasure door I'd seen outside, completely round and made from gold.

To my surprise, the door swung open. Behind it was a strange room.

"Whoa." I stepped inside. The room beyond was enormous, with high vaulted ceilings, but spartanly decorated. The only ornamentation was a platform in its center, atop which stood a man in a red robe. Set into the wall behind the man was another door.

"Greetings," the man said. His voice echoed through the chamber. Strangely enough, no text triggered when I looked at him.

"Uh, hi," I said. "What's up?"

The robed man didn't *look* like he'd hurt us, but it paid to stay on your guard. "Come closer," the man said. "I have a quest for you."

At the word 'quest,' Spud squealed with delight. "Oh, a *quest!* Get closer, Crow. The Spud Squad is always up for adventure."

"What sort of quest?" I asked without stepping forward. I'd been told this was a simulation, though I still didn't know if I could trust this man.

From within his robes, the man drew out a box and held it toward me. The box was wooden, about the size of a shoebox, and I could see a keyhole on the face. "Inside this box is a key," the man said. "It unlocks the door behind me. In the room beyond is a powerful artifact that has been stolen from my people. I need you to retrieve it for me."

"That doesn't make any sense," Perry said. "Why don't you get it yourself?"

"Don't ruin an opportunity for a quest, Perry!" Spud cried. "We don't get those often. In fact, this might be the first time!"

It was a good question. I raised an eyebrow at the man, and he looked sheepishly at his own feet. "I'm not capable of such a task," he said. "That's why I need your help."

"See?" Spud said. "Perfectly reasonable explanation. I think we should take the quest, Crow. And maybe leave Perry with this nice man while we're at it."

I grew frustrated. "Look. Not to ruin this whole thing, but this is silly. Can we get some advice on what classes to choose?"

The man glanced up at me, then lowered the box to his side. "Very well. I suppose I can help you with that. What are your strengths?"

I considered the question. "I was a professional athlete before this. My biggest asset was never my physical prowess, but my ability to strategize. When plans didn't come together, I was able to revise them on the fly. Here in the dungeon, I also have Spud and Perry, whom I can shoot at enemies."

"I cause chaos and light stuff on fire," Spud said.

"And I'm good at spraying things with acid," Perry said.

"He throws up on them," Spud muttered.

"I also have a club that I've used successfully in the past, and a special ability called Giant's Roar," I said. "When I use that, I can—"

"I'm familiar with Giant's Roar," the man said. He stroked his chin thoughtfully. "Hmm. I see how those make you powerful now, but if you don't specialize soon, you'll be at a disadvantage in later levels. Giant's Roar is for melee fighters, while your sapient ammunition speaks to a more strategic technique. You say that physicality was never your strength, and that at your core, you're a strategist. Is that true?"

I didn't need to think about it. "Yes," I replied.

"Then get rid of that club and your special ability, and focus on your true path," the man said.

I was about to ask what the man meant by 'true path' when I blinked and found myself back in the room with the gong. The smoke was gone, and Gatekeeper Valentine sat behind the desk.

"Welcome back," he said.

"I'm done?" I said. "That was it?"

Congratulations! You've completed your advising session. Based on your responses, we recommend the following option.

Path: The Wily Way

The Wily Way course of study includes two classes that take a total of three class spots. Students of the Wily Way learn how to analyze and manipulate situations to their advantage. This field of study also covers topics such as deception, improvisation, and adaptability. Students learn how to deceive opponents through misdirection and illusion, and how to improvise in difficult situations when faced with unexpected obstacles. They also study the importance of adaptability in a rapidly changing environment, as well as how to think on their feet and adjust their plans accordingly.

Overall, the Wily Way celebrates intelligence and resourcefulness over brute strength and force. It provides students with the tools and techniques to navigate complex situations successfully and emerge victorious through cleverness and guile.

"So what does that mean?" I asked.
The Gatekeeper only smiled.

Course Catalogue: Section 12.6. Bulletsmithing.
Mon. (3:00 PM to 6:00 PM)
Instructor: Justice Maron

This course provides students with a comprehensive understanding of the art and science of bulletsmithing, a specialized field within magical engineering. The creation of magical projectiles requires the use of soul cores, so understanding how to create, stabilize, and utilize soul cores will be integral to completion of this course.

Hands-on projects will allow students to apply their learned knowledge to practical problems. By the end of this course, students will have the knowledge to create magical projectiles for themselves.

WARNING: All students enrolled in Bulletsmithing must have an available soul core (grand or higher) by the first day of class.

I read and reread the course of study, and I had to admit I was intrigued. I'd already set myself up as a ranged fighter, and Perry and Spud had already shown me the value of magical ammunition.

This must've been the course Fairlan mentioned. How much more powerful would I be if I could create sapient bullets from scratch?

At the same time, I wasn't sure if this class was for me. It required me to equip myself with a soul core, which was something I didn't have at the moment. Fairlan had them, but even if I sold Giant's Roar, acquiring one would be prohibitively expensive.

Yet, I was willing to keep an open mind and took a look at the second course.

Course Catalogue: Section 104.6. Wisdom.
Mon. (9:00 AM to 12:00 PM)
Instructor: Mother Baganza

This course provides students with a unique opportunity to explore the mystical realm of meditation and to access the hidden truths of the world. Through meditation, students will develop a deep understanding of the fundamental nature of reality. Once per week, students will be able to use this understanding to enter a meditative fugue and gain the answer to a single question.

Through this course, students will develop a deep understanding of the nature of reality and their place within it. They will also learn how to access hidden truths through meditation and spiritual practice, and how to apply these insights to their lives. Ultimately, this course provides students with a unique opportunity to explore the mysteries of the universe and discover their own path to enlightenment.

WARNING: This course takes up two course slots.

I finished reading the description. "So, what is this?" I finally asked. "I take this course, and then once per week, I can meditate and see the future?"

"Assuming you master the lessons in question, you can learn the *truth*," the Gatekeeper corrected. "It's the perfect course for a man with questions."

I thought through the implications. I *did* have questions. Like, what *was* the dungeon? Why did it exist, and what had the Gatekeeper meant when he'd told me it wanted me to succeed? How could I get through it, and how could I bring my friends through as well?

Where can I find Sirax Sirco's Personal Armory?

"Wisdom can answer *any* question?" I asked.

"Any question," the Gatekeeper said.

"Hmm." On the one hand, I didn't love the idea of only taking two courses. Three would certainly make me more versatile, though both Jocko and the man from the vision in my advising session had encouraged me to specialize.

There was another consideration: as I re-read through the course descriptions, I felt a strange sense of familiarity. I didn't know why, but my gut told me to take these courses. Bulletsmithing seemed like an interesting field, and from my past practice with lightball gloves, I *was* uniquely equipped to be a ranged fighter—even if I hadn't originally planned on shooting sapient ammunition. Assuming I could master the skill taught in Wisdom, I'd gain deeper insights into the dungeon, and maybe the world beyond.

"We have enough time to run you through the test once more, if you're not happy with the results," the Gatekeeper said. "Though if you do want these classes, you just need to sign here."

He slid a piece of paper and a pen across the table.

Sign here to accept the proposed course of study.

I took a deep breath, then made my choice.

6

———

I came out of my advising session to see Jocko leaning against the Kinetoscope. If his own session had had any impact on him, it wasn't apparent.

"How was your session?" I asked. "Learn anything good?"

Jocko only shrugged.

"What courses did it suggest?" I asked.

"Give it up, *pacho*," Jocko said. "I don't want to talk."

Before I had a chance to call him a coward, he turned and walked down the hall toward the platform.

"Where are you going?" I called after him, but he kept walking.

Fine. Maybe Perry is right. He's in shock and needs some time to get over it.

Still, I ran to catch up with him. I was about to tell him about the Wily Way when there was a *crack*. I looked down the platform toward the source of the noise and saw that a rock had broken free from the wall. I held up a hand, worried I might've led us straight into the path of an avalanche, when I realized the rock was attached to another rock, and another, all of them connected to form a humanoid creature, fifteen feet tall and composed entirely of jagged, boulder-like fragments.

"I bet that thing is friendly," Spud said as another *crack* freed the creature's right arm. "The dungeon wants us to succeed, remember?"

"No chance," I said.

The creature's obsidian eyes smoldered with malevolent black light, and the air around it seemed to vibrate.

Rock Golem

The history of the rock golems is shrouded in mystery and legend. Some say these creatures were formed by powerful earth magic wielded by ancient sorcerers, while others believe they arose spontaneously from the natural energies of the earth.

Whatever their origins, rock golems are known for their immense strength and durability, as well as their anger and aggression toward humans. Though their numbers have dwindled over the centuries, sightings of rock golems still occur in remote areas of the world, always as a portent of greater evil.

"Uh, Crow?" Perry said. "What do you want to do?"

I could've activated Giant's Roar, though that would've left me weak for hours. I thought of that strange wizard's voice: *Then get rid of that club and your special ability, and focus on your true path.*

"I want to see what you boys can do," I said as I ripped Spud off my bandolier and set him to hover above my hand. The potato burst into flame. "Reverse alphabetical order this time."

"Rock might beat scissors, but—*arghhh*—potato beats rock!" Spud yelled.

I shot him at the golem and landed a hit in the dead center of the creature's chest. I might as well have slapped it with a feather. Spud bounced off the golem's rocky body and rolled away without leaving so much as a scratch.

"I probably could've predicted that," I said. "Jocko, a little help here?"

The Grass King stared at his feet like there wasn't a fifteen-foot-tall monster in front of us.

"That thing is about to charge!" Perry yelled. Sure enough, the golem beat its chest with both fists and roared. Then, it galloped toward us.

"Run, Jocko!" I yelled. I tore down the platform, hoping Jocko was doing the same. He wasn't. I jumped a small outcropping of rock, and as I did I twisted in the air and sent Perry shooting at the golem. *Maybe we can distract him.* Before Perry could release his acid, the golem turned and swatted him down.

"Perry!" I shouted.

The tomato hit the hard ground and bounced like a rubber ball. "I'm okay," he shouted. "Just a little nauseous."

"*Arghhh!*" Spud shouted from farther down the platform. He was still on fire. "What else is new?"

Although the tomato hadn't gotten a chance to spit his acid, he *had* succeeded in attracting the golem's attention. Instead of continuing to charge toward Jocko, the creature slowed itself in a spray of chipped stone and reoriented itself on me. Which wasn't great, though at least it wasn't headed at my friend, who didn't seem capable of defending himself.

You said you'd protect him. Let's see if you really meant it.

I turned and ran. Behind me, the golem crashed through the small pile of stone I'd put between us, turning it into a cloud of brown dust.

Now would be a great time to have a vegetable that could make vines that could grab the golem's legs or something. Anything to slow this monster down!

But I didn't have anything like that. Only Spud and Perry.

As I ran, I pulled Perry back into my hand and launched another shot. This time, the tomato spat his acid well before he came into the golem's reach, and his momentum—combined with the creature's charge—carried the liquid toward its chest.

"Nice shot!" I said as I pulled Perry back into my hand. I didn't wait to see what would happen. "Did it hit?"

"Dead on," Perry said. "And the acid is eating through the stone. Crow, watch out!"

I turned in time to catch a rock the size of my fist in the shoulder. The socket groaned. My shoulder held, though the hit spun me in a full circle, nearly sending me to the ground.

"Be careful, Crow!" Spud shouted from the other side of the platform. He'd turned off his flames, so he wasn't moaning anymore. "The thing throws rocks!"

"Thanks," I coughed. Gingerly, I probed my shoulder. *Nothing broken.* I knew I'd soon have a bruise that would make a blackberry jealous.

"There are crystals on its back, Crow," Spud said. "I think those might be a weak point."

Could that be useful information? From Spud?

When the golem dug into the earth for another rock, I ran through a gap between two large piles of stone. In a worst-case scenario, they'd provide cover, but my hope was that the creature would follow and I could use the stone to get around it and examine the crystals.

But as I pressed my back to the stone, the creature's roars went silent. In fact, the whole cavern fell silent, save for the clacking of carts that came through the distant tunnels.

"What do you think it's doing?" Perry whispered.

We got our answer when Spud yelled, "Crow, it's going after Jocko!"

"By the Dregs," I hissed. How had I forgotten about Jocko? I ran back through the gap in the stones in time to see the golem hurl a rock at my friend.

That's fine. Jocko is fast. And he has a sword that can cut through metal. The stone isn't moving that quickly. He'll see it coming and slice it to pebbles.

Only, Jocko didn't move. The rock hit him in the forehead and he dropped.

"No!" I yelled. I ran toward the golem, which must've heard me coming, because it turned to face me. When it saw me, it roared and scooped up another stone.

I slammed Perry against my bandolier and summoned the Clockwork Guardian's Club. The golem threw its stone, but I smashed it out of the air with the club. Then I brought Perry back into my hand and flung him at the monster yet again.

Third time is the charm, I thought as Perry released his acid. I watched with grim satisfaction as it splashed against the golem's face. The creature roared and swiped at its own eyes, trying to wipe away the acid.

Since I'd summoned the club, I hadn't stopped running. When I reached the golem's stomping legs, I dropped into a slide, slipping beneath one pounding foot and coming up behind it. There were the crystals Spud had mentioned. They jutted out from the creature's back in a single line like the ridge on a fish, translucent and glowing with purple light.

I didn't waste another moment. I still held the club, so I used it to smash the lowest crystal on the creature's back. The crystal popped as if I'd hit a lightbulb.

"Score one for the Spud Squad!" Spud yelled.

The golem made to turn around, but I shoved the tip of the club into the hole that had been exposed by the broken crystal. The creature's roar rose an octave, and it fell to its knees. I managed to break two more crystals before the golem finally turned to face me. I thought it might try to crush me beneath its stone fists, but instead it mewled and scrambled backward.

It's scared of you, I realized. *You can kill it.*

And I would. Back in the Castle of 1,000 Doors, killing Cravag had yielded the club I now held, as well as the Giant's Roar skill.

Maybe this golem will yield other resources.

I raised my club and growled my defiance at the downed golem. Only, before I could take another step, it crawled backward and threw itself over the edge of the platform.

"Get back here!" I shouted as it disappeared into the depths. I ran toward it and looked down over the edge. Part of me hoped a stone fist might reach out and grab me—anything to suggest that I hadn't lost my prey—but the golem was gone.

"You'll get the next one, Crow," Perry said. "Should we check on Jocko?"

His soft voice shocked me out of my bloodlust. *Jocko.* I turned and ran to my friend, who lay where he'd dropped. Spud sat beside him. There was a growing pool of blood near Jocko's head, but I exhaled with relief as I noticed the rise and fall of his chest.

Although his breathing was shallow, Jocko lived.

"There was an infirmary on the list of switching codes," Perry said. "Four blue circles. Think they can help him?"

"Good idea," I said. Yet another time that day, I lifted my friend into my arms.

7

The infirmary was little more than a long hall with beds on either side, each separated by thin curtains. From within its depths came the moans of those in pain.

"This is an odd place for medical care," Spud said. "Doesn't seem sanitary."

I couldn't argue, but I also didn't have the luxury of trying to find an alternative. On our harrowing, bumpy trip through the bowels of Gray Moor, Jocko had let out a little gasp, and his breath had started coming in quick rasps. I didn't know what that meant, but it didn't seem good.

I carried Jocko to the desk that clearly served as the infirmary's administrative hub. Behind the desk was a diminutive clerk in a blue cowl. When he saw me approaching, he hit a small bell on his desk.

Ding.

Two more blue-cowled figures appeared from around a curtain behind him and rushed to meet us, a wheeled gurney pushed before them.

Gray Moor (Infirmary)

Deep beneath Gray Moor lies a hidden infirmary, run by a mysterious group known as the Blue Medics. These skilled doctors and healers are known to possess mystical powers that allow them to cure the most dire illnesses and injuries. However, rumors abound of the dark payments required to gain access to the infirmary's healing, leading some to question the true nature of the Blue Medics and their practices.

"Welcome, welcome," the clerk said. "Lay your charge there."

He pointed to the gurney and I placed Jocko atop it. *Please be okay.*

The two attendants whisked him away, and I leaned against the desk. The fight with the rock golem and the harrowing flight through Gray Moor's tunnels had taken everything out of me. Although I felt like collapsing to the ground and putting my head between my knees, I forced myself to look into the clerk's eyes.

The clerk looked back at me from within the recesses of his blue cowl, his face shaded by the cloth. He smiled. For some reason, I didn't take any comfort in it.

"M'lord, the Blue Medics are here to serve," he said, and his wheedling tone immediately rubbed me the wrong way. "Have you heard of our little group? We're widely regarded as the best surgeons in the dungeon."

"I haven't," I admitted. "But if you can help my friend, I'll be in your debt."

"We are the best," he repeated.

"Will my friend survive?"

"Of course. Under the ministrations of my fellow acolytes, survival isn't the question. But we do ask for payment, as operations are expensive. What are marks compared to the life of a friend?"

I swallowed. *No one does anything for free. Why did I imagine Toroth-Gol might be different?*

"How much are we talking about here?" I asked.

The smile never left the clerk's face. "Maybe two or three hundred thousand marks," he said. "It depends on the scope of the operation."

I gasped. Outside the dungeon, that number wouldn't have been so exorbitant. But inside Toroth-Gol, where I didn't have so much as a single mark to my name?

"This is robbery," I said. I couldn't remember pulling Spud from my bandolier, but there he was, hovering above my hand. He moaned softly as his skin crackled with flame.

The clerk stiffened. "M'lord!" he said. "We have expenses!"

"Let's dip them in—*ugh*—oil and fry them up!" Spud said.

"M'lord," the clerk said again. "I beseech thee: don't bring violence to this holy place. I see you find yourselves tempted, but if you continue down this road, you won't enjoy the consequences. Look behind you, M'lord. Please."

But that was the oldest trick in the book. Pretend there was something behind a person, and then attack them the moment they turned.

"Yeah, right," I said. I didn't take my eyes from the clerk. Though, in case there *was* something important behind me, I held Spud over my shoulder.

"Oh," Spud said as his flames winked out. "Uh, let's forget the oil comment, yeah? I was joking about that. Crow, there's an army behind you."

Only then did I look over my shoulder, and the sight gave me goosebumps. Behind me stood at least a *hundred* figures in blue cowls, each of them clutching a mallet in one hand and a lantern in the other.

"Impossible," I breathed. "Where did they come from?"

"Let's be civil," the clerk said. I pivoted to face him. "We're not asking for anything other than what's due. If your friend can't pay, he'll labor for the Blue Medics. It's a worthy exchange for his life. Or, you can choose to labor for him."

I shuddered and glanced over my shoulder again.

The platform was empty.

Did I really see all of those people? Were they real, or was that some sort of illusion? If it *was* an illusion, I might be able to fight my way out of the infirmary. Though, that was a gamble. If I lost, it wasn't only my life that was at stake.

I felt sick to my stomach. "How long do we have to pay?"

"Payment should be rendered by the end of the operation," the clerk said. "You have twenty, maybe thirty minutes."

I grimaced. It wasn't like I could ask for my friend back. He'd been on the cusp of death when I'd brought him in, and the Blue Medics *were* healing him.

This is the cost of Jocko's life. It's either this, or he dies.

I didn't like it, though I knew where I could get three hundred thousand marks. "I'll be right back," I said. I turned and fled to the transport platform, where I punched in the code for the commissary.

"Ordinarily, I'd make fun of you for choosing diplomacy over violence," Spud said as a cart clattered to a stop in front of us. "However, in this case, I think we can all agree that most alternatives are better than fighting that blue-robed freak show."

I climbed into the cart and let the safety bar slam over my lap, and then we were off, tearing through the dark corridors of Gray Moor.

I'll get the money. I remembered the vow I'd made to myself a few hours earlier, at the entrance to Gray Moor. *Whatever the cost, I'm going to save Jocko.*

When we stopped, I jumped out and charged into the commissary at such speed that I ran straight into Feng, who'd rounded a shelf and stepped into my path.

"Sorry," I said as I bounced off him. "I'm in a rush."

He merely held up his hands. "No worries, Crow. Say, you okay?"

But I couldn't stop to talk. I didn't have time.

"He's not usually this rude," Spud called to the armored buck as I ran past him. "Our apologies, Feng! Please don't hate us!"

"Fairlan!" I yelled as I pelted toward her counter. "Fairlan, you've got your deal!"

The bird-kin still sat in her wheeled chair behind the counter. In one hand she gripped a dagger with a steel loop attached to the hilt. In the other, she held a bundle of black cord that was attached to the loop.

She set the dagger on the counter and looked at me, her head cocked to one side. "Deal? I'm not sure what you're talking about."

"Giant's Roar for three hundred thousand marks."

Fairlan sighed. "I'll give you a hundred thousand marks for it."

It was like I'd been punched in the gut. "What? You said three hundred before."

"Yes, and *now* I'm saying a hundred. You come running in here, panting like you're running from a pack of death hyenas, and demand a trade you've already refused. Clearly, you're in dire circumstances. You need money, and I know it. So now I have leverage."

I growled. "This is life and death, and you're trying to make a buck."

She shrugged. "You have the right of it. But that's my job. If it makes you feel any better, consider the two-hundred-thousand-mark difference an investment in your future. You'll never make this mistake again, will you? I can tell you with the utmost confidence: the bargains only get rarer from here."

"Understood. But I *need* that money. Make it two hundred thousand. Please. I'll do anything."

Fairlan's beak clicked in disgust. "You don't learn, do you? I'm a proprietor of the commissary and I also teach a class in dealmaking and negotiation. What did I say about giving me leverage? If I know the scope of your desperation, I'll give you less. Now, you just told me you'd do anything for the marks. Ninety thousand. Take it or leave it."

I saw red. "This isn't a game!" I grabbed the knife off the counter and stabbed it into the wood. The blade sank two inches into the soft material.

Fairlan looked at the quivering hilt, then calmly drew it out and laid it down again. She poked at the freshly made divot.

"Seventy-five thousand, and that's a bargain for the lesson you're getting," she said. "And because now I have to fix this counter. Keep going and I'll demand one of your vegetables instead."

I was about to lose it, but then text appeared in my vision.

Accept 225,000 marks from Feng?

Confirm. Yes or No.

I turned to see the armored buck standing behind me. I raised an eyebrow at him.

"Happy to help, Crow," Feng said. "It's not like I have much to spend it on down here anyway."

"Swallow your pride and take it," Spud hissed. "Then, when we're done here, we're going to have a talk on negotiation strategy."

I confirmed the transfer. To my surprise, it went through, and 225,000 marks appeared in my Inventory.

"Thank you," I mumbled to Feng. I think I was in shock. I turned back to Fairlan.

"You have a deal," I said. "Giant's Roar for seventy-five thousand marks."

Fairlan chirped joyously. "Seventy-five thousand, and you're lucky I'm nice."

I kept my mouth shut. Every word I'd said to this woman thus far had been used against me, so I didn't want to provide her with any more ammunition. Another message popped into my vision.

Sell Giant's Roar to Fairlan for 75,000 marks?

Confirm. Yes or No.

I confirmed the sale. I turned back to thank Feng, but he was gone.

"Weren't you in a rush?" Fairlan said. "Tick, tock."

I turned and threw her a rude hand gesture. In return, she blew me a kiss.

"You're lucky you're not in my class," she said. "I'd bleed you dry. Remember: blades win battles, but coins win wars."

I turned and ran from the commissary, eager to put as much distance between myself and Fairlan as possible. Her voice followed me down the platform: "You owe me one, Crow! That lesson was worth its weight in gold!"

8

I didn't see Feng as I reached the switching station; nor did I catch sight of him on the winding journey back to the infirmary.

You'll find him later. Whatever he wants, you'll give him.

I still didn't know why he'd chosen to help us, or what repercussions he might suffer as a result. For better or worse, I remained ignorant about so much of the dungeon's inner workings.

Are the dungeon natives actual people? Do they have lives down here that exist beyond the Hunt? Or do they simply go into stasis or something when the hunters aren't around?

At different points in my journey, I'd asked both Spud and Perry, yet neither knew the answer. For the first time, I found myself wishing I'd watched the Hunt. I knew why I hadn't: in the Dregs, I'd experienced so much real violence I couldn't bring myself to find entertainment in the suffering of others. But if I'd seen a season or two, I might've gained information I could've used to my advantage.

Jocko studied the Hunt his entire life, though, and look where that got him. I guess there's no use worrying about it now.

When I got back to the infirmary, I found the same clerk waiting for me at the front desk.

"M'lord!" he said as I approached. "Good news. Your companion is good as new. There was some swelling around the brain, and a chip in his skull, but never doubt the skills of my brothers and sisters in healing."

I scarcely trusted myself to talk to the clerk without reaching over the desk and wrapping my hands around his thin neck. "How much?" I croaked.

"Two hundred sixty-three thousand marks," the clerk said.

I ran some mental math and was glad I'd sold the club, as Feng's gift alone wouldn't have been enough to cover the bill.

Pay the Blue Medics 263,000 marks?

Confirm. Yes or No.

Yes. The coins were pulled from my Inventory. The clerk clapped his hands and flashed his obsequious smile.

"A pleasure doing business, M'lord," he said. "We'll have your friend out in a moment."

I didn't see how the clerk signaled his colleagues, but the curtain behind him parted and Jocko shuffled toward me.

"We should make sure he's okay and not like, a mindless zombie," Spud said. "I wouldn't put it past these clowns to return him with half his brains scooped out."

As the clerk had promised, Jocko looked fine. If there were any signs of the damage he'd taken, or the healing he'd gone through, I couldn't find them. There wasn't so much as a bandage wrapped around his head.

"Hey, Jocko," I said as he came around the desk. "You good?"

"Yeah, *pacho.* Thanks."

His words took me by surprise. *He's responding to questions now. Maybe the Blue Medics really* did *help him.*

Still, I was loath to give them credit for anything. I glanced at the clerk. "Is our business done here?"

"Yes, M'lord. Thank you for your patronage of the Blue Medics. You'll want to make sure he gets plenty of rest, and have him drink at least four liters of water every day until the start of classes. Do come see us again."

"Got it," I said, then took Jocko by the arm. "Come on. Let's go find our rooms."

As we walked toward the edge of the platform, the eyes of the Blue Medics followed us. I willed myself not to turn around. Instead, I pulled the pamphlet Feng had given me from my pocket and found the code for base housing.

"Blue circle, blue circle, green triangle, and red square," Perry said a second before I found it. "I could've told you that."

We reached the podium and I punched in the code. As we waited for the cart to arrive, Jocko spoke up from beside me.

"I'm sorry," he said.

I glanced over at him. *He looks so tired.*

I sighed. "It's okay, *majoré*," I said. "Let's focus on getting you better."

The cart stopped before us. We were about to climb inside when a voice behind us asked: "Hey. Did I hear you say you were headed to base housing?"

I turned to see a woman standing behind us. Her muscular frame was accentuated by a thin leather tunic that revealed her well-defined arms and hands, which were dyed the orange of an arsonist. A thick belt was cinched tightly at her hips, and from it hung a single dented metal flask. Her long, dark hair was tied back in a braid, and there was a hardness to her expression that suggested she'd experienced her fair share of difficult living.

Brewmaster (Devora)

For many years, Devora fought for the Empire as a soldier, rising through the ranks with her skill and determination. As she grew older, she yearned for a quieter life, one where she could put down roots and leave the battlefield behind. With her savings, she bought a small plot of land in the city of Ironwood and began construction

on a bar; she dreamt of serving travelers and locals alike with her homemade brews and hearty meals. When the bar burned to the ground, she was convicted of arson and sentenced to Toroth-Gol.

I couldn't help but wonder more about her story, and also why she carried that lone flask on her belt like a prized possession.

Probably something to do with her title? Brewmaster. I wonder what she can do?

But as she regarded me, waiting for my answer, I knew that it wasn't my place to ask. Not yet, at least.

"Yes." I felt like we could trust her. "Would you like to come with us?"

"Sure," Devora said. The cart screeched to a stop in front of us. Jocko climbed into the back, and I got into the middle seat. Devora didn't look excited to take the front, but I certainly wasn't letting a stranger sit behind me, and it was the only seat left.

"Take it or leave it," I said. She took it. As soon as she sat down, the lap bars fell and the cart surged forward into the darkness.

When I'd played lightball, I'd had teammates like Devora. I knew the type: quiet, shy, distrustful. What they all had in common was that they'd been hurt before. Their gruff exteriors were like scar tissue that had been built atop a wound.

There was only one way to win them over, and that was by putting yourself out there. Once they saw you extend yourself, they felt more comfortable letting down their own guard.

As our cart tore along the underground track, I leaned forward until my mouth was near her ear.

"I'm King Crow, the lightball player," I yelled. I wanted to make sure she could hear me over the sound of the clacking cart and rushing wind. "I didn't commit the crime that put me in here. And I can use the magnetism in my gloves to shoot magical projectiles."

Her meaty hand landed on the back of my neck, and she pulled me toward her so hard that the lap bar dug into my hips. It was an uncomfortable position, but this time my ear was by her mouth as she yelled, "That's nice. But you're about to be dead if you keep screaming in my ear."

So it was like that, then. She released me, and I sat bodily into my seat as the cart dropped.

Okay. Maybe not the easiest nut to crack.

The cart dropped us off on a new platform, which was long and had several podiums. We were the only ones in the space. About a hundred yards ahead of us was a tall arch.

Gray Moor (Base Housing)

All students at Gray Moor live in one of five different types of housing, each of which provides its own advantages.

"What room type are you in?" I asked Devora.

She studied me suspiciously. "Strategist's Chambers. You?"

"The same. Shall we?"

We walked across the platform and through the arch, blinking at bright sunlight. Somehow, we were now outside. But it wasn't the same outside as the platform from which we entered Gray Moor; the ocean and other towers were nowhere in sight. Instead, we stood inside a high stone wall that ran about two hundred yards in either direction before branching at right angles to create a large, rectangular yard. At even intervals, I saw towers topped with observation decks and mounted spotlights.

Located within the confines of the yard were several low stone buildings that looked like bigger versions of the block houses from the Dark City. The ground was made of hard-packed earth, and there were dry yellow grasses that grew in the shade.

Gray Moor (Barracks)

Originally built to house soldiers on campaign, the Barracks were eventually repurposed to serve as long-term housing for students in Gray Moor. Over time, the buildings grew in size and complex-

ity, as various additions were made to accommodate the changing needs of their inhabitants. Despite their age, the Barracks remain a vital part of Gray Moor's housing system, providing a communal living space for those who prefer camaraderie to isolation.

There was a signpost nearby, with various sections pointing the way toward the other types of lodging Feng had mentioned. As I read them, they appeared as text in my vision.

Field Soldier's Tents
Strategist's Chambers
General's Quarters
Warmaster's Conference Room

I gestured to the sign that pointed to our room type. Devora grunted again and we started down a path that ran between the buildings that comprised the Barracks. As we walked, my feet kicked up little clouds of dust. When we came to a fork in the path, we followed another sign for the Strategist's Chambers. In the near distance, I saw a long, multi-level building made from the same stone as the Barracks. There was a statue on a pedestal out front in the shape of a creature with the body of a man and the head of a horse. The man was dressed in flowing robes and was thoughtfully looking down at a book he held open between his hands.

Statue of Nevis Lyveris

A renowned scholar and protégé of Sirax Sirco, Nevis Lyveris helped implement the system of switching stations at Gray Moor. He personally used his magic to establish the base camp, further allowing students to differentiate themselves by their choice of lodging.

The building behind the statue was accessible via an arched doorway.

Gray Moor (Command and Control)

This single building houses both the Strategist's Chambers and the Warmaster's Conference Room.

Strategist's Chambers are in the East Wing. The Warmaster's Conference Room is in the West Wing.

Devora walked toward the building and I followed, noticing how much cooler the air got as I stepped through the arched doorway. I found myself in a rectangular lobby, unadorned and empty save for two doorways on either side of the room. Above the doorway to my left was a sign for the Warmaster's Conference Room, though of course the text appeared bright and bold in my vision.

Gray Moor (Warmaster's Conference Room)

The one to my right was labeled Strategist's Chambers.

We ducked through the doorway. A quick trip up a set of stairs led to a long hallway with doors on either side, each of which had a name or names written across a sign that hung from the knob.

"Guess I'll see you later?" I said to Devora, but she was already pushing into the room with her name on it. The door closed behind her, so I was left standing alone in the hallway with Jocko. Sighing, I found the door with our names on it and pushed through.

"I'm a little confused because I didn't see *my* name on the door?" Spud said as we walked inside.

"Probably a mistake with the registrar," I said. "I'm sure it was an accident."

The Strategist's Chambers were a circular room with high ceilings and a fireplace on one wall. There were floor-to-ceiling windows with frosted glass that didn't provide a view outside, though they did let in copious amounts of natural light.

Gray Moor (Strategist's Chambers)

The Strategist's Chambers are a unique and highly sought-after lodging type designed to house the brightest and most strategic minds at Gray Moor. With their spacious layout and abundant natural light, the Strategist's Chambers are the perfect place for privacy from prying eyes.

In the center of the room sat a long conference table covered in paper and pens. There were blue flowers in a glass vase, and a little notecard beside them. I walked over to the table and picked up the notecard.

To Jocko, with all best wishes for a quick recovery.

Your friends in both sickness and health,
The Blue Medics

"Wow, Crow, this is great," Spud said. "I don't mean that creepy note. I hate that! But our room is fantastic. It reminds me of Potato Hell, but different, of course. Down there, you sleep in quadruple bunkbeds, and that's *if* you get to sleep at all. There's a lot of burping, and the beds squeak when someone changes positions. And sometimes, the overlords come down and wake you all up with songs."

"Songs?" Perry said. "What type of music do they play in Potato Hell?"

"Yeah," Spud replied. "I remember one of them. It went, 'Rah, rah-ah-ah-ah, roma, roma-ma, blah blah, ooh-la-la,' over and over and over. It's an earworm, especially after you've listened to it for sixteen hours straight."

"That doesn't sound fun," Perry said.

"It's not fun, Perry," Spud said. "Obviously. It's Potato Hell."

On the far side of the room was a cork board on wheels with a little shelf that held tacks so that we could pin things up. Two additional doors led out of the room, one labeled with my name and another with Jocko's.

I pushed through the door with my name on it. On the other side was a small room with a bookshelf, a desk, and a bed. Over the bed hung a poster for the Steel City Sledgehammers, the city name in block letters above the team logo—two crossed sledgehammers—with the team name below.

It was strange to see a Sledgehammers poster in Toroth-Gol, and I felt a wave of homesickness. This time of year, we'd be welcoming our new players to the team.

I wonder what Frederic and Zorba are doing right now. Probably teaching our recruits the team handshake.

I shook off any thoughts of home. The only way I was going to see my old teammates again was by getting through Toroth-Gol, and I couldn't afford to let nostalgia distract me.

I ducked back out into the main room and found Jocko exploring his room, which mirrored mine. It had the same bookshelf, desk, and small bed. Instead of a poster, he had a small shelf over his bed that was covered in shells about the size of my palm.

Jocko looked up at me. "Hey, *pacho*," he said. He looked tired. "I'm going to take a little rest if that's all right."

"Yeah," I said. "Sure. You want me to get the door?"

When Jocko sighed, I stepped from his room, closing his door behind me.

"Let me know if you need anything," I said to him through the wood, but there was no response.

"You could probably do with a little rest yourself," Perry said. He wasn't wrong. I was exhausted. I took a seat at the table and put my head in my hands.

One foot after the other. I fell asleep instantly.

9

I awoke with a crick in my neck. A quick glance at my timer
showed me I'd slept for over ten hours.

My goodness. I must've slept through the night!

I sat up and wiped a line of drool away from my chin. Jocko's door
was still closed. I was about to stand when a voice in my ear whispered, "I think I know how to get into the personal armory."

"Gah!" I said. Spud sat on my left shoulder, and Perry was on my
right. It was Perry who'd been whispering. "What are you doing?" I
asked. "Why are you on my shoulder?"

"Sorry," Perry said. "I saw Spud sitting up here, so I thought it
might be fun to try."

"Copycat," Spud said.

"I prefer the bandolier anyway," Perry said.

It took me a moment to remember where I was and what was
happening. Then Perry's words finally registered and I sat bolt
upright.

"You know how to get into the armory?" I asked. Other than
surviving, that seemed like the most important thing I could do on
this level. "Where? How?"

Perry hopped from my shoulder to the table.

"Well, I should rephrase," he said. "I *think* I know how to get us through that golden door we saw near the advising rooms. I'm not sure if it'll lead to the armory, but that *could* be the way. I remember reading this book once—"

"When did you have time to read a book?" Spud asked.

"Before I met you guys," Perry said. "You have memories from a time before meeting Crow, don't you?"

"I have *flashes* of memory," Spud said. "But are they real? Am I real? *Is anything real?*"

Perry ignored the anxious outburst and continued. "I remember reading about a crew that found a door similar to the one we saw. The crew knew it was magic, because it glowed with a strange light and there was writing all around it. Most of the crew didn't know how to read the writing, but one of them was from Geth, and it turned out the writing was Gethi. When he translated it, it said, 'Only the worthy may enter.' So he said, 'I'm worthy' in Gethi, and the door opened right up."

"How does that help *us*?" Spud asked. "None of us speak Gethi. At least, I don't."

"I don't think we actually need to speak Gethi to get inside," Perry said. "But I think the mechanics might be the same. Locked magical door with strange writing? If we can figure out what the writing says, we might get a clue on how to open the door."

"You translated it?" I asked.

"Decoded," Perry said. "That was the key. At first, I thought it needed to be translated, but after a while I realized the text *wasn't* in a different language. There isn't a written language in the Empire that has the letters 'h' and 'g' next to one another. That's when I realized I wasn't looking for a translation, but a cipher."

"It's probably too much to ask, but could you, like, get to the point?" Spud said. "That's not even me being mean! I'm just saying."

I shot Spud a dirty look. "Let him explain," I said. "I'm curious."

Perry's cheeks turned a darker shade of red. "The words over the door were 'dtgcvjg hktg wrqp og,'" he said. "There are a few ciphers that are more popular than others, so I tried those first. I wasn't getting anywhere until I tried a simple variable shift, where each letter in a phrase is replaced by another one a certain number of letters away from the first. So take the phrase above the door: dtgcvjg hktg wrqp og. If you replace every letter with the one that comes two letters before it in the alphabet, you get a message. So the 'd' becomes a 'b.' The 't' becomes an 'r.' And so on."

My heart raced. "And it says something when you do that? Something that makes sense?"

"Yeah," Perry said. "It says, 'Breathe fire upon me.' The door is asking us to hit it with fire."

I stood up so quickly that I knocked over my chair. "Perry, you're a genius!" I said, scooping him up and setting him against my bandolier. My timer showed that I still had several days until classes started. "Let's go see what it does."

I knew it'd be irresponsible to go alone. I wasn't sure what I'd face, and neither my nerves nor my wallet could handle another visit with the Blue Medics.

Jocko, then. I started toward his room, but paused. Since we'd entered Dungeon School, Jocko had been a liability. He seemed better, though still not fully healed. And with him lying to me about Toroth-Gol's early levels and then leaving me to fend for myself, I wasn't sure if I could trust him.

Spud sensed what I was thinking. "Maybe we let the guy rest? Would be nice to have some firepower, but, uh…"

He trailed off, though he didn't need to finish the sentence. I turned away from the closed door. *But who else can I trust?*

Feng came to mind, but I didn't know where to find him. Then I thought of Devora. She *was* right across the hall. While I still didn't know what she could do, she'd certainly *looked* powerful.

Maybe I'm right to try and bring her into my confidences. Maybe I didn't go far enough.

I walked across the hall and knocked on Devora's door. The woman answered, staring down at me with the same suspicious look she'd given me earlier.

"Would you be up for a potentially deadly adventure that has the small possibility of a massive reward?" I asked.

Her questioning eyebrow lifted higher. "You're going for the armory?" When I nodded, her face split into a grin. "Say no more."

Devora walked back into her room. When she next exited, she had that thick belt strapped around her waist, the one that held the dented iron flask against her hip.

"What's the plan?" she asked.

"Tell her, Perry," I said.

The tomato explained how he'd solved the cipher. Once he was done, I said, "What do you think?"

Devora shrugged. "Sounds like a decent place to start. I'd certainly like to find that armory, so let's go for it."

"Good," I said. "If the dungeon is making the treasure hunt public and giving all of us the same challenge, I have to imagine we want whatever is inside."

"How do we split the treasure?"

"Fifty-fifty,"

"Fifty-fifty," Devora repeated. She spit into her palm and we shook hands.

To my surprise, we weren't the only ones at the switching station. When we got there, another group already stood at the edge of the platform. There were four of them, all human.

The man adjusting the wheels on the podium was absolutely ripped. He was even bigger than Devora, with a flat head and jaw so square I could've used his chin to draw right angles. His hands were dyed the dark brown of a smuggler. He wore a skintight red-and-yellow tank top with cutoff sleeves that showed off his thick arms, as well as—and I'm not kidding—*spandex short-shorts* that did the same for his muscular legs. If I didn't think he could punch me into yesterday, I might've laughed.

Colossus (Megathrion)

By day, Megathrion worked as a dockworker in the Crescent. But

at night, the mountain of a man served as a bouncer at Kamalu, the infamous nightclub. One night, an Empire guard who was visiting the Crescent for some rest and relaxation got a little too handsy with a dancer; that dancer was Megathrion's wife. The next day, the guard was found with a broken jaw and two missing fingers on his left hand. Megathrion was charged with smuggling and sedition and sentenced to Toroth-Gol.

Behind the man stood a tall, thin woman with a streak of white through her jet-black hair and the red hands of a murderer. Two blades were secured to her back, the hilts sticking over her shoulders. The hilts were attached to one another with a length of chain that was covered in frost.

Ice Witch (Esmé)

After her brother's death at the hands of a minor nobleman went unpunished by the Empire, Esmé took matters into her own hands. She secured a job at the nobleman's preferred salon and worked her way up to become his personal stylist. It was during a grooming session that Esmé used a straight razor to slit the man's throat. She was caught and sentenced to Toroth-Gol for murder.

Beside Esmé was another woman, this one also slender. Her hair was cut short, and she had green eyes that glinted mischievously. Freckles dotted the bridge of her nose, and she had the green hands of a thief.

Putty Lord (Robyn)

Robyn grew up in a family of thieves and swindlers, but her restless spirit led her to want a life of adventure and exploration. She left her family behind by joining a group of Empire archaeologists as a bodyguard and guide. While exploring an ancient Thuin ruin

in the Wastes, she was caught stealing a valuable artifact and sentenced to Toroth-Gol for thievery.

The final member of the group stood in Megathrion's shadow. Like Robyn, she had the green hands of a thief.

As I glanced down at her, I realized I was looking at a young girl. I gasped. I should've expected that the Empire wouldn't be above sentencing children to Toroth-Gol, but it still caught me by surprise.

Metal Masticator (Jinx)

Jinx was born into a family of street performers, who taught her the art of sleight-of-hand and misdirection. But when her parents died in a freak accident, Jinx was forced to fend for herself on the streets. Desperate to survive, she turned to pickpocketing and small-time scams. Her luck ran out when she attempted to swindle a wealthy merchant and was caught red-handed. Jinx was convicted of theft and sentenced to Toroth-Gol.

The hulking man lifted a ham-sized hand in our direction. "Greetings, friends," he said, his voice low and rumbling. "I'm Megathrion, but you can call me Mega." He nudged the small girl next to him. "Look, Jinx," he said. "More survivors from the first level."

From behind Mega's massive thigh, Jinx flashed me a shy smile and I saw that her teeth were covered in shiny metal.

"Hi there," I said. "Well met. Can I ask where you're headed?"

"We're off to our advising sessions," Mega said. He seemed to be the leader of the group. "Have you done yours already?"

I nodded. I wasn't about to tell them we were headed to the same place. If we found anything useful, I'd already be splitting it with Devora, and I definitely didn't need to add four more people into the mix.

"Anything we should know before we head in?" Mega asked.

I thought about what to tell them. *Be honest with yourself and accept what the dungeon gives you?* But I didn't yet know if that was a recipe for success, as it remained to be seen if the Wily Way would benefit me.

I decided to stick to the facts. "You'll have an hour, as you probably already know," I said. "You probably won't need all of it. For me, the advisor appeared as my father. I imagine it'll be someone equally personal for you. He gave good advice. Somewhat vague, but helpful."

The big man grunted. "Thank you," he said. Then he looked me up and down. "You really *are* him, aren't you? I heard rumors from some of the other hunters we met in the castle, but I didn't believe them. I watched so many of your games. You know Tamlin Muir?"

Muir was the King Crow of the Crescent's lightball team, the Necromancers. On the field, she was an absolute terror. Whereas my team focused on the technical aspects of the game, the Crescent won by injuring their opponents' players. It wasn't a strategy I advocated, though it was part of the game, and Muir was the best disabler of them all.

In response to Mega, I brought my hand to my side. "She broke two of my ribs in the Lightning Cup three years ago." I winced at the memory. "Ultimately, the Sledgehammers won that game, and I drank so much in celebration that I woke up the next morning with my entire head shaved."

"Ha!" Mega said. He clapped me on the shoulder. I'm a big guy, but the blow nearly knocked me over. "She was my hero. I saw her in the city once, but she wasn't breaking ribs then. Just throwing candy off the back of a cart to children."

I managed to keep my footing. "I liked her, too," I said. "Despite the whole rib thing."

A grin spread across Mega's square face. "Sorry to see you here with us," he said. "Maybe some good will come of it. I've always wondered what it'd be like to have King Crow on our team. Now, I might get the chance to find out." He winked at Devora. "And you, beautiful? You never introduced yourself. What's your name?"

Devora blushed furiously. "Devora."

There was a clattering as a cart arrived. Mega turned and climbed inside, and Jinx sat beside him. Robyn climbed into the row behind them, and Esmé got into the third and final row.

"Well met, King Crow and Devora," Mega said as the bar fell over his lap. "I've got a sense for the two of you. You have friends in us."

Before I could respond, the cart took off.

"Huh," I said as I watched them disappear into the distant tunnel. I liked the group, even *if* they were from the Crescent. "How about that?"

"He was cute, wasn't he?" Devora said as she leaned over the edge of the chasm to watch them go. I thought she was kidding, but the look on her face was deadly serious.

"Yeah," I said. "Really cute. Should we give them some time to find their bearings first, so they don't think we're following them?"

"Sure," Devora said. We passed the time idly, and after a few minutes, I stepped to the podium and punched in the code for the Advising Rooms. Our own cart arrived, and we boarded.

The cart shot into the darkness.

10

After several minutes of twists and turns, the cart pulled up to the platform. I didn't see Mega or his crew, though I wasn't really worried about them.

"The last time I was here, I had to fight a monster," I told Devora as I looked for any sign of the rock golem. I didn't see it. In fact, it looked as if someone had cleaned the platform in my absence. "Fifteen feet tall and made of crystal and stone. That's what hit my friend and sent him to the infirmary."

Devora whistled. "You kill it?" she asked.

"Nah," I said. "But we busted it up pretty good. It jumped over the edge of the platform to get away from us."

I jerked a thumb toward the chasm behind us and Devora clucked her tongue. "Shame," she said. "Never good to leave an enemy alive."

She was right, but what could I have done differently? I shrugged and walked over to the golden door. When we reached it, I lifted Spud from my bandolier and set him to hover above my palm. He floated in a slow circle, and when he faced me, I saw his eyes were narrowed in determination.

"This part might be a little disturbing," I said to Devora.

"Disturbing?" Devora said.

Spud burst into flame. "Oh *yeah*," he moaned. "*Arghhhh!*"

"Oh," Devora said. "Disturbing. Got it."

I held my hand to the door. Bright tongues of orange flame crawled over Spud's skin and licked the metal.

"I think it's working," Perry said. "Keep going, Spud!"

"I'm burning as hot as I—*ugh*—can," Spud said. "Check me out, Twinkletoes. I'm on *fire!*"

From somewhere deep below us came a *click*. There was another *click*, and I realized it was the sound of a lock disengaging.

Breathe fire upon me, the message had said, so I moved Spud around different areas of the door, trying to cover every bit of metal with his flames.

"Come on, baby, *burn!*" Spud yelled. "*Burn so good!*"

As I waved Spud over the bottom third of the door, there was a final *click*, and then a rumbling as the huge metal door slid to one side.

"We did it," I whispered as I found myself staring into the room behind the door. It was a classroom, the floors made of wood and the walls of cut stone. Two rows of desks ran through the room's center, and on the far side of the room was a chalkboard with writing on it, though I was too far away to see what it said. A set of stone steps behind the chalkboard led to another door.

Gray Moor (Chamber of Summoning)

A classroom built by the enigmatic wizard Aldor Ravenswood, the chamber was a place where gifted students could learn the most advanced summoning spells and incantations without fear of releasing any summoned creatures into the rest of Gray Moor. The room is surrounded by protective runes put down by Sirax Sirco himself.

One day, students found the chamber sealed from the inside. It has remained that way ever since.

"This doesn't really look like an armory," Perry said.

I had to agree with Perry: this *didn't* look like an armory. Tables lined the outer edges of the room, and books and papers sat atop them. Many of the books were open, as if we'd interrupted a lesson.

I extinguished Spud's flames, but a prickling along the back of my neck told me not to put him away.

"What do you think?" I said to Devora.

"I think we're about to get attacked," she said as she pulled a flask from her belt and unscrewed the cap. She took a swig, then belched loudly. "*Something* is watching us."

I got the same feeling, yet I couldn't see anything. Devora took another swig and belched again. This time, I caught a whiff of alcohol.

"I'm sorry, but are you drinking?" I asked. I wanted to look over to her, though I didn't dare take my eyes off the classroom. Now, I noticed something that I hadn't originally seen: a human skull sat on the ground under one of the tables.

I'd made a terrible mistake. I really didn't know Devora, and I found myself missing the Grass King at my side.

"Nah," she said. "Well, I am drinking, yes. But don't worry about it. Whoa. Do you see those? Human bones!"

By the Dregs. We're doomed.

Devora must've sensed what I was thinking, because she added, "Don't worry about it, Crow. This is my power. Trust me."

Trust me. Those two little words were so easy to say, but did I believe it when people used them? Not for a moment. My father had told me to trust him, and so had Jocko. But here I was, trapped in Toroth-Gol without either of them to help me.

I was about to reply when the door at the top of the stairs opened and a man strode out. At least, he had the body of a man. His head was that of a raven. The man wore green robes and his fingers were covered in jeweled rings.

"*Another* person with an animal head," Spud said. "They really do love a theme down here."

Bird-kin (Aldor Ravenswood / Sor'kodich)

Aldor Ravenswood was born into a family of prominent wizards, and showed a prodigious talent for magic from a young age. After mastering the basics of the magical arts, Aldor set out to explore the more esoteric and forbidden aspects of magic, eventually becoming one of the most skilled summoners in the world. With the help of his old general Sirax Sirco, he built the Chamber of Summoning as a place where he could teach the most gifted students the secrets of summoning magic.

As a teacher, Ravenswood was strict and demanding. Those who couldn't keep up with his increasingly difficult lessons were promptly removed from the class list. In the later years of his life, his reputation was tarnished by rumors of dark and dangerous practices. The rumors about him proved true when he lost control of a spell and was possessed by an ancient, powerful demon named Sor'kodich.

"So I liked everything until the bit about the demon," Spud murmured. "That doesn't sound good at all."

"Students!" the man said cheerfully as he extended a bejeweled hand toward us. I had no clue if I was looking at Aldor or Sor'kodich. "It's been such a long time since I've had students. At least, I think it's been a long time." He ran a hand over the jet-black feathers of his head. "Time seems to have slipped away from me lately. Anyway, come in. We should begin."

He started down the stairs, one hand on the balustrade. There was something wrong with the man. He looked kindly enough, but I sensed something evil lurking behind his cheerful façade.

"Do we go in?" Devora asked. Before I could respond, she said, "You know what? I'm going for it. Keep the thing distracted and let me get close. I'll handle the rest."

Her words might've inspired more confidence if she hadn't stumbled as she stepped past me into the chamber, or giggled when she landed in a heap on the floor. Or belched yet again as she took another swig from her flask, which she barely managed to cap and reattach to her belt.

"Oh wow," Spud said. "Should we, uh, leave her?"

But leaving Devora would mean abandoning her to whatever horrors lay inside the classroom, and I'd already vowed to protect those who trusted in me.

"Stupid promises," I said as I stepped into the room. I didn't bother turning as the door ground shut behind me.

"Excellent," Aldor said. "Now, have a seat. You must attend to your studies."

When I didn't move, he lifted a thin hand toward me. A bolt of green lightning jumped from his fingers and sparked off the door, missing me by inches.

"I said, sit *down*," Aldor growled.

Beside me, Devora grabbed one of the wooden desks and used it to pull herself to her feet.

"Did you *see* that?" she mumbled. "That looked nasty. But we're fine, Crow, we're fine." She looked at me over her shoulder, which meant taking her eyes off the strange professor. She winked. "Fine, fine, fine."

"Maybe focus on the enemy?" I said as I pointed to the man.

Devora didn't turn to follow my finger. "Remember what I said, Crow boy." Her eyes went wide. "Crow." She turned and pointed at Aldor. "Raven. Ha! We've got a room full of bird brains."

"Oh man," Spud whispered. "She's drunk as a skunk! This doesn't look good at all."

I scanned the room for anything I could use to my advantage. *If I flip the desks, I can use them as cover. Same goes for the tables along the windows. The books look heavy enough to do some damage, but certainly no more than I could cause with Perry or Spud.*

Spud had been right. This *really* didn't look good.

I needed to buy us time. Quickly, I walked to a desk and sat down. I hoped it would distract Aldor from Devora, who was mumbling to herself as she stumbled toward him.

"I'm sitting," I said to Aldor. "What do you want now?"

"What do *I* want?" the professor repeated. Once again, he ran a hand over his feathered head. "It's funny you ask that. I used to know what I wanted: a generation of students who could rise like I did, tempered in the flames of hardship for the battle to come. But lately, I'm not sure. It's been a while since I've felt like myself."

As the ancient professor spoke, he started to change. Smoke rose from beneath the hem of his robes, and before I could call out, his robe caught fire. The orange flames raced up his clothing and ate it away in the time it took me to blink.

"Look at him burn!" Devora said.

"I'm jealous," Spud said. "I'm gonna join the fun." His body lit with orange flame. "Oh, *baby!*"

I stared at the burning professor in horror, worried I'd soon see the bones beneath Aldor's feathers. I thought the man would scream as he keeled over and died. Instead, he stood taller than before. The orange flames added another two feet above his head, and I spotted eyes within the hood of flame, black and charred as lumps of coal.

Lesser Demon (Sor'kodich)

Aldor Ravenswood was the greatest summoner of an age, though his pride led him to summon an entity he couldn't control. When he did, he triggered the defensive runes built around the Chamber of Summoning that sealed the classroom from the rest of the school—with Ravenswood and his students still inside. The students are long dead, as is Ravenswood, but the summoned creature lives on, though it now inhabits Ravenswood's body.

"You ask me what I want," the demon said, his voice low and beastly. "I do know, actually. I want to *feast.*"

11

I didn't need to be a tactical genius to see what Sor'kodich was going to do next. He lifted a foot, and I dove to one side as he stomped on the ground. Tongues of orange flame erupted from his foot and leapt across the floorboards in a straight line, missing Devora by inches. If I hadn't moved, they would've hit me. As it was, they spluttered into the desk at which I'd been sitting and set it aflame.

I flipped another desk and crouched behind it. I had no clue if it would protect me, but something was better than nothing. "Devora, get down!" I yelled. I peeked around the desk to see her continue her stumbling walk toward Sor'kodich.

"Hey, you handsome, fiery beast," she said. She moved with the shuffling gait of someone well past the point of casual inebriation, which meant she was going to get herself killed.

"You're insolent," Sor'kodich said. "You'll suffer for it."

"I don't know what that means," Devora said. In her hand, she held her dented flask, and she took another swig. "Bird brain. Fire breath. Professor. Whatever you are. I have a question."

"Enough," Sor'kodich hissed. He lifted a hand toward her, like he'd done to me before he'd cast the green lightning. Devora waved her flask at him.

"Hey, now!" she said. "Wait a minute. You're a professor, and I have a question. Hold on."

To my surprise, Sor'kodich didn't unleash his lightning. He didn't lower his hand, either. But for the moment, at least, Devora continued to live.

"How much wood would a woodchuck chuck if a woodchuck could chuck wood?" Devora asked.

The demon's eyes narrowed as his fingers once again glowed green.

"We can't let her die," Spud hissed. "Save her!"

I wanted to help, but I couldn't see how. "You can't secretly shoot water, can you?" I asked.

"That's the weakest element," Spud said. "Actually, earth isn't great, either. We can argue about it later. Do something, Crow!"

I stepped out from behind the overturned desk, and Sor'kodich's black eyes darted toward me.

So did his outstretched hand.

"Wait!" I said as I held both my hands above my head. "I'm not trying to start trouble. I, uh, had a question, too. A real one, this time. I promise it's better than hers."

Sor'kodich narrowed his eyes at me. "What?" he hissed.

My eyes darted toward the chalkboard. Now that I was a little farther into the room, I could make out some of the writing. Most of the scribbles were notations and symbols, but there was writing across the top of the board.

I'm not alive, but I grow.
I don't have a mouth, but I eat.
I don't have lungs, but I need air.

"Uh, what's that?" I asked. I pointed to the chalkboard.

Sor'kodich turned to look. *This would be a good time to fire at him,* I thought, but I didn't have anything worthwhile to shoot. I didn't think Spud's flames would do anything to a flaming demon, and I didn't want to risk Perry. Besides, Sor'kodich still held his hand toward me, and I'd seen how quickly the green lightning had moved. By the time I pulled my hand back to shoot, I'd be burned to a crisp.

"You've found my predecessor's riddles," Sor'kodich said. "He'd often post them for his students. He's no longer with us, and I ate his students, too. But I admit I enjoyed the exercise. I'll give you five more seconds. If you can guess the answer, I'll make your death a quick one."

"Fire," Perry whispered. "That's the answer. What's not alive, but still grows? What doesn't have a mouth, but still eats? And what doesn't have lungs, but needs air? Fire!"

Sor'kodich grinned. "Bonus points for you," he said. "Remind me to include those on your final exam."

Before he could unleash his lightning, Devora leaned forward and pressed a palm against his chest. The brewmaster screamed as her skin sizzled with a sound like meat on a grill. A new smell filled the air, but I won't describe it. All I can say is that it was something I hope to never smell again.

"Devora!" I yelled.

Sor'kodich looked down at the drunk, who still had her hand pressed against his body. "It has been a while since I've touched a human," he said. "Have they gotten dumber in the last twenty years?"

Now, his fingers flashed green and lightning flew toward me. I couldn't have been more than thirty feet away. Still, the lightning crackled a dozen feet to my right.

Sor'kodich looked at his hand, clearly shocked that he'd missed. He tried again. Once again, the lightning crackled, and I ducked, but I needn't have bothered. A desk ten feet to my left exploded with green electricity.

"What's happening to me?" Sor'kodich asked. He looked back down at his hand.

"You said you were hungry," Devora said through clenched teeth. This time when she spoke, her voice was clear of any hint of a drunken slur. "I gave you a liquid lunch."

Sor'kodich roared and reached for Devora's head, but she jumped nimbly backward. Once again, she pressed her flask to her lips.

Sor'kodich missed her with a swipe of one fiery arm and crashed to the ground. Devora swallowed once, twice, and then pressed her ruined hand to the elemental's head.

This time, they both screamed.

"I think she's transferring her drunkenness to Sor'kodich," Perry said. "That's her power. She drinks, and then transfers her inebriation through touch!"

I wanted to help, but all I could do was stare. True to her word, Devora had the situation well in hand. With the flask still pressed to her lips, she stepped away from the demon. He tried to rise, fell over, and attempted get up once again. As he lifted his great fiery head, Devora leaned down to look into his black eyes.

"Please say something cool, Devora," Spud said. "School is over. Class is cancelled. *Anything*. This is the perfect time for a punchline!"

Devora didn't say anything. Instead, she leaned forward and spat a mouthful of spirits into Sor'kodich's face.

Whoosh. It was like Sor'kodich had been shot in the face at point-blank range. Flames and chunks of what looked like rock blew out from the back of his skull. He toppled backward and fell to the ground a moment before the fire that had sustained him guttered out.

Behind me, the door slid open. Then, as I stared at the body, familiar text popped into my vision.

Deceased Lesser Demon

Loot? Yes or No.

"Hey, Crow," Devora said, and I turned to face her as she collapsed bodily into a chair that sat behind one of the desks. Sweat plastered her hair to her forehead and she clutched the wrist of her right hand. The skin was a nasty shade of red, already suppurating and glistening with fluid. Her expression told me that it felt worse than it looked.

"By the Dregs, Devora," I said. "Are you okay?"

"Any chance you have a healing item?" she said through gritted teeth.

I didn't have anything in my Inventory that would help, and the healing items at the commissary were only marginally less expensive than the soul cores. I could take her to the Blue Medics, but that was a last resort.

"I'll look around," I said. "We'll find you a fix. Let me see what I can do."

"Loot Sor'kodich," Perry said. "He might have a salve or something."

It was a good idea, and I looted the demon.

Loot acquired. From the Lesser Demon (Sor'kodich), you've gained 50,000 Empire marks. Each mark weighs one ounce and was minted in the year 2337. The coins are of exceptional quality and bear the seal of Helios. The coins appear to be in excellent condition. Items sent to Inventory.

"Anything?" Devora rasped.

"You're twenty-five thousand Empire marks richer than before," I said. "Worst-case scenario, I'll throw in my half and we'll buy you a minor healing potion from the commissary."

"That would be appreciated," Devora said, but I was distracted from her words as more text popped into my vision.

Loot acquired. From the Lesser Demon (Sor'kodich), you've gained the Flameheart. This artifact appears as a small gemstone that pulsates with an intense red-orange light. The Flameheart is said to contain a fragment of the essence of fire itself, and those who possess it gain mastery over flame and heat. The gemstone is warm to the touch, and those who hold it for too long may find themselves feeling as if they are on fire. Item sent to Inventory.

"It's a special material," I said before she could ask. "Interesting, but not what we need right now."

"We could check the room Sor'kodich came from," Perry said.

It was the only other option. I ran toward the back of the room and took the stairs two at a time. The smell of smoke was still in my nostrils. Smoke and cooked flesh.

As I pushed through the door to the room beyond, a new smell hit me.

The room before me had four tables arranged in a line, each one covered with a human body. The bodies were in various states of decomposition, and each had been sliced open with a precision that spoke of the fire elemental's expertise, skin and sinew peeled back and pinned like a butterfly on a board. On a desk to my right was the hollowed-out chest cavity of a fifth body. Its organs had been removed and were displayed in glass jars that sat on the edge of the desk.

"Oh, for the love of all that's crispy," Spud said. "I don't have a joke here. This is terrible."

My stomach churned. I stayed long enough to verify there wasn't anything to loot before I fled the room.

"Nothing useful?" Devora said. She was pale, and her breath came in quick gasps. But she must've seen something in my face because she said, "Never mind. I don't want to know."

I breathed the smoke-tinged air of the Chamber of Summoning, never having been more grateful to have the scent of someone else's charred flesh in my nostrils. I would've taken anything other than the smell of those bodies.

"Can you hold out for ten minutes?" I asked. "Looks like it's going to be the commissary after all, because I really, *really* don't want to go back to the infirmary."

"Commissary, please," Devora said. "I'm great over here. Take all the time in the world."

12

After my last experience with Fairlan, I didn't want to see her any more than I wanted to see the Blue Medics, though desperate times called for desperate measures. And between her and the Blue Medics, she was definitely the lesser of two evils. With Fairlan, the worst-case scenario saw me losing all my money. With the Blue Medics... well, I didn't want to think about that.

"Once Fairlan fleeces you for the money we found, we won't have much to show for that battle," Spud said as our cart clattered toward the commissary. "But in my humble and always-correct opinion, the violent murder of a demon is its own reward."

"I think we got more than you realized," Perry said. "There's the Flameheart, and we also formed a new relationship. Devora seems like a good person to have on our side."

"You're saying our reward is *friendship?*"

Yet Perry was right. To that point, my success in the dungeon hadn't come from big explosions or powerful weapons, but my connections with other people. I wouldn't say Devora and I were friends, though I knew I could trust her to watch my back.

Still, it would've been nice to have walked away from the battle with something more than a few marks and the Flameheart. "Let's see what this will cost," I said as our cart pulled up to the platform.

As it turned out, negotiations with Fairlan cost me all 50,000 marks, as well as the Clockwork Guardian's Club. I was loath to let go of the club, but without Giant's Roar, it wasn't actually useful to me. My advising session had shown me another path, so if I was truly going to excel, I needed to commit.

"Do you want me to wrap this up?" Fairlan said as she held up the healing potion I wanted. I was about to respond when I realized she hadn't yet accepted the trade.

She's testing you. Prying for info to use as leverage. If you tell her to leave it out, she'll know you need it now, and she's going to push for a higher price.

I shrugged like I didn't care one way or the other. "Go ahead," I said. "Or don't. It's just going into my Inventory."

A huge grin split Fairlan's face. "I know you're lying, but you're clearly learning, so I'll let you get away with it," she said as she accepted the trade. "Maybe there's hope for you yet."

I considered that a minor victory.

I rode the cart back to Devora, and found her where I'd left her. She accepted the potion gratefully, tore the cork off with her teeth, and downed the contents. A second later, the angry red flesh on her hand turned as tan as the rest of her skin.

"Whoa," she said as she flexed her hand. "The pain is gone."

"Glad to hear it," I said. Then I summoned the Flameheart from my Inventory and held it toward her.

"What's this?" she asked.

"After expenses on the potion, this is all we've got to show for that battle," I said. I didn't tell her I'd also needed to sell my club. "You're the one who killed the thing, so I think you should have it."

Devora met my eyes. "You know the first thing that happened to me in Gray Moor?" she asked. "After I picked my room in front of that giant statue? I was standing at the switching station, waiting for the cart to take me to base camp, when two other hunters came up. They asked if they could ride with me, and I let them. But at some point during that ride, they knocked me out. I woke up in the infirmary and all my stuff was gone. Those idiots had stolen everything." She rapped her knuckles against the flask at her hip. "I used to have two of these, but I had to trade one to pay for my medical expenses. So now, this dented flask is my only weapon."

"I'm sorry," I said, not knowing what else to say. "Do you know who it was that hit you?"

"No. I think I could recognize them, though. If I see them again, they're dead. But that's not the point. What I'm trying to say is, for the past few hours, I thought trust was going to get me killed. Though, while I was waiting for you to come back, I realized trust isn't my problem. When I was a soldier, I trusted my friends, and they saved my life on countless occasions. The problem is putting my trust in the *wrong* people. But you're the right people."

She pushed the hand holding the Flameheart back toward me.

"You keep it," she said. "If we fight together again, I get an extra item."

I smiled at her. "You've got yourself a deal," I said.

After that, we parted ways. Devora wanted to visit the training rooms, while I needed to work on finding a soul core. Since I no longer had money for one, nor any items to trade, I didn't know how I'd get into Bulletsmithing.

You don't get what you don't ask for. That was my father's way of saying, 'shoot your shot.' Once, when I was younger, my father had taken me to a meeting with a supplier. He'd been buying industrial gears from the man, and if my father could get that supplier down twelve marks per order, he'd hit a thirty-percent margin on his steel. My father always tried for at least thirty percent. Before he got into promises or negotiations, he bought the man a coffee and then he'd asked for what he wanted. The man said yes. The meeting had lasted seven minutes.

I took a cart to the machine shop, which was where my Bullet-smithing class was supposed to be held. When my cart stopped, I walked toward the door on one end of the platform. I pushed inside to a deafening cacophony.

Most of the noise came from the machines that sat in a row before a set of frosted windows. I didn't know what the machines did, but they clattered and banged as wheels and gears turned. And they were hot. Molten metal poured out of pipes in the wall, running through chutes and into the various machines.

I waited for text to explain what I was seeing, though nothing came.

"Uh, this is the machine shop, isn't it?" I said aloud to myself. I pulled up my Map. Sure enough, I stood in the machine shop.

Only when I'd closed the Map did the text finally appear.

Gray Moor (Machine Shop: Unglamored)

The machine shop's history dates back to the earliest days of the school, when Sirax Sirco recognized the need for weapons to protect his people. Over the years, the machine shop has evolved, integrating the latest technology and magic to produce not just arrows and bolts, but bullets and rockets. Today, the shop is run by Justice Maron, a dwarf bulletsmith who found his way to Gray Moor after the Great Exodus.

"That's odd," I said, looking again at the word 'unglamored.' "I wonder what that means."

I scanned the shop, but I didn't see Justice. For that matter, I didn't see anyone; the machines ran on their own. I walked over to one of them and tried to get a better sense of what it was doing. As I watched, molten metal poured out of a pipe in the wall and spilled onto a chute that ran into the machine. From there, the metal filtered through the machine's internal components, directed by metal flaps into a mold. When the mold was full, one of the metal flaps stopped the flow, and a belt fed the mold into another part of the machine. The mold came out the other side. It was empty, but I could hear the *plink, plink* of metal dropping into some central container.

"I think it's making bullets?" Spud said. As soon as he said it, text appeared in my vision.

Justice Maron's .45-Caliber Bullet Machine: Unglamored

Designed and built by the legendary dwarven bulletsmith Justice Maron, this machine is the pinnacle of bullet-making technology. The machine's output is exceptionally high, and it can produce hundreds of bullets in a single hour. However, despite its popularity, the designs remain a closely guarded secret. Only a select few were ever allowed to see the machine in action, and fewer were granted the privilege of using it.

"I guess we're now among the rarefied few who have seen the thing in action," I said. "But I'm still wondering about this 'unglamored' thing."

In response, Spud cleared his throat. "Uh, Crow? Behind you."

I turned and found myself looking at a dwarf. Although the man only came up to my stomach, he had a grizzled look and imposing aura that suggested years of hard-earned experience. He wore a leather apron that let me see his biceps, which looked like they belonged to someone a third of his age. Between his lips, he clutched the stub of a lit cigar, the glowing tip framed by strands of white mustache that ended in golden caps. His arms were crossed and he stared at me through one gray eye. The other eye was a glassy milk-white.

"What are you doing in my shop, deglamoring my glamors?" the dwarf growled. He pulled the cigar out of his mouth, dropped it to the floor, and stomped it out with his boot. Now that I'd seen him do it, I realized the floor was littered with the crushed ends of cigars and much more besides: scraps of wire, hunks of metal, and empty shell casings. "And don't plead ignorant with me, boy. I wasn't born yesterday. Give me a good reason why I shouldn't feed your fingers into that bullet machine right now."

The truth was, I had no idea what he was talking about. But the dwarf had already told me he wouldn't buy that answer.

"Are you Justice Maron?" I said, taking an educated guess.

Instantly, text popped into my vision.

Dwarf (Justice Maron: Unglamored)

A one-eyed dwarf with a penchant for brilliant inventions. One of the most talented machinists of his generation, Justice combines metalworking with magic to create enchanted objects. After his last apprentice abandoned him to work for his enemies, Justice became dejected, lonely, and increasingly paranoid about outsiders learning too much about him or his inventions.

"Bah!" the dwarf growled as he threw up his arms. "What did I say about ruining my glamors?"

"I'm sorry!" I said. "I really don't know how this works!"

Justice spat on the floor. "New students. Do you have any idea what you're interrupting?"

"No! That's what I'm telling you!"

Justice gave a short, dismissive grunt. The next time he spoke, I realized he wasn't talking to me, but to himself. "There's a war coming. I feel it in my bones. Feel it as sure as I felt the last one. The preds won't stop. See? They can't help but kill. It's part of them."

From his apron, he removed another cigar. He bit off the end, spat it onto the ground, and let the tip hover over the chute of molten metal.

"We stopped the preds last time, but now they're back," he continued. "I've got scouts working around the front lines. From what they tell me, the preds are gathering, sure as metal melts in a furnace. Sure as tobacco catches flame."

The tip of his cigar started smoking. He brought the other end to his lips and gave it a few puffs until the smoking tip burned bright orange.

"That was *awesome*," Spud whispered. "Can you light me a cigar from a stream of molten metal?"

"We don't have time to be fooling around with new blood," Justice said. "I've told the administration a hundred times. 'I've got work to do,' I say. 'Leave me in peace,' I say. 'Disconnect me from the switching stations,' I say. But they ignore me."

Justice puffed on his cigar, which caused smoke to wreathe around his head. It smelled smoky and sweet, like a mix between leather, old wood, and spices.

"It sounds like you don't want any new students, but I signed up for your class," I said. "I'd like to learn from you."

"Do you have a soul core?"

"Ah, no. But if you could find it within you to give us one, I know we could be a great asset in the war to come."

For a while, Justice didn't say anything. He stared at us and puffed on his cigar. Finally, after a silence that stretched a bit too long for comfort, he said, "No."

"No?"

Justice laughed. "You know what happened the last time I took on an apprentice?"

"Sure." I'd read as much in the description: the last student he'd taken had abandoned him for his enemies. "I'm not like that."

"Aye," Justice said as if I hadn't spoken. "But he was stronger than you. Didn't need to beg a soul core. He walked into my office with *three* of them, plus the schematics for a machine that produced enchanted rockets. Best bulletsmith I'd seen in an age. And now, he works for the preds."

He fell silent. The only sounds in the room were the humming of machinery and the *plink, plink, plink* of bullets falling into the central basket of the nearest machine.

"I'm sorry," I said. "I know what it's like to feel betrayed. But I really think if you trust me, we can help each other."

"Bah," Justice said. White smoke rose into the air above his head. "You seem like a nice kid. And your vegetables are cute. But trust me when I say this, boy: one hunter isn't going to do anything against the predators. You don't understand what they're like. Not yet. It doesn't matter how strong you get. They're coming for us, and if we don't stop playing games and start preparing, the war isn't going to go our way."

"If I get a soul core, will you teach me?" I asked.

Justice snorted. "That's your takeaway from all that?" he said. He shook his head. "I suppose if you got one before the first class starts, I wouldn't be able to stop you from taking the course. But I wouldn't like it. I wouldn't spend much time on it. The war is too close, and I've got too much to do to be training whelps. I'm doing this to protect this tower. And not only this one, but the other three as well. I'm done training anyone. Best of luck."

He gave a mock bow and walked down the row of machines, the sweet-smelling white smoke trailing behind him.

"He said we were cute," Spud said. "Was that a compliment?"

Sighing, I turned around. If I didn't want to waste my class, I only had a few more days to find a soul core.

13

On the morning of my first class, I awoke to see that my timer had changed, the numbers having shifted in the night to give me three more months of life. I still hadn't found a soul core.

But Wisdom is all about answers, I thought as I made my way to the classroom. *Maybe I'll find an answer there.*

My Wisdom class was held in a forest. Or rather, it was held in what *appeared* to be a forest, because there was no way a forest could grow inside Gray Moor. Still, the ground was covered in soft grass and wildflowers, pink and purple intermingled with vibrant green. Tall oak trees stretched as far as I could see. Twenty yards away, a statue in the shape of a turtle channeled a trickle of water down its bent neck into a small pool.

Gray Moor (The Glade)

The glade is home to a variety of native flora, including black oak, spreading aster, and thimbleberry. The artesian waters of the glade's turtle-shaped fountain are known to have a soporific effect on humanoids, as well as an explosive effect on the undead.

"I could get used to this," Spud said from my shoulder. "Reminds me a bit of where I grew up. Wait… nope. I can't remember that."

"I grew up on a farm," Perry said, waking up with a yawn. As so often happened when attached to my bandolier, he'd fallen asleep. "Cows and chickens and all that. Oh, look! Purple aster! They're beautiful."

I approached the fountain, hoping it was a Fountain of Wishes, but of course it wasn't. This was a regular fountain: pleasant, but without any true power within.

Don't count on the dungeon for any favors. It's not like you have a Gold Coin anyway.

Beyond the fountain was a stump, the top sanded and worn so it formed a seat. With a resigned sigh, I sat atop it. I didn't regret my decision to take Wisdom, as the Gatekeeper hadn't steered me wrong yet, but I still wondered if it was the right course of action.

"What does 'soporific' mean?" I asked Perry.

Spud clicked his teeth. "I got this one, Crow." He turned to face the tomato. "Soporific! S-o-p-o-r-i-f-i-c. It means that if you drink it, it'll make you want to sleep. Not to be confused with sophomoric. S-o-p-h-o-m-o-r-i-c. Childish or juvenile. Like Perry."

A voice cut through the glade, low and comforting and seemingly everywhere at once: "That's right, my child."

I looked around but didn't see anyone.

"Hello?" I said as I got to my feet. "Is someone there?"

Something hit me on the head. I looked down to see an acorn land at my feet. I glanced up, expecting to see someone overhead, but there was nothing among the branches.

"Are you an acorn?" I asked as I looked back at the small nut. Considering my primary weapons were a potato and a tomato, it was a reasonable question.

I leaned over and lifted it into my hand. The wood of the nut was smooth and polished, the cap a darker brown with a rough, knobby texture that reminded me of snakeskin. There was a little stem where it'd once connected to the tree.

I expected to see text pop into my vision, though none was forthcoming.

"We're all acorns," the voice said.

Another nut bonked me on the head. I looked up, then dodged to avoid taking a third acorn to the eye.

"Stop that," I said, rubbing a hand across my scalp as I tried to find the source of the voice. "What are you? *Where* are you?"

The voice laughed, and I swear the sound came from all around me. "You can't see me because you haven't been taught to see. We will get there, child. Welcome to Wisdom. I'm Mother Baganza. You must be my new students. King Crow, Spud Spuddington, and Peristopheles Magnesis IV. A powerful team if I've ever seen one. And I *have* seen you. In my visions."

I waited for Mother Baganza to continue, but she wasn't forthcoming.

"Do we get to see *you*?" I asked.

Mother Baganza hummed thoughtfully. "You will see me once you've been taught to see," she replied cryptically. "But enough of that. This is not a class for your questions, though I know you have many. We have much to cover in a short amount of time. If we don't start, we won't finish. What do you know of wisdom?"

"The class? Or do you mean more generally?"

"Wisdom," Spud said. "W-i-s-d-o-m. The application of knowledge earned through experience."

Mother Baganza hummed again. "That's a good definition, child," she said. "But it's only that: a definition. Vibrations used to convey what is, at best, a limited understanding. Strung syllables. Connected phonemes."

"If you're talking about wisdom in general, it seems that—"

Mother Baganza interrupted me. "It starts with *patience*. Close your eyes."

I had a sinking feeling I'd chosen the wrong class. *Before you write it off, you might as well try what she's telling you. Maybe something magical will happen.*

So I followed Mother Baganza's instructions. Green and purple splotches floated against the darkness behind my eyelids. But the harder I tried to focus, the more they evaded any type of shape.

I scrunched my eyes shut tighter and caught three vertical green lines that looked like claw marks. What did that mean? My left eye itched, as did my right shoulder blade.

After a few moments, Mother Baganza still hadn't said anything, and my back hurt from sitting on the stump.

"Mother Baganza?" I asked. There was no answer. I stood up and stretched, working the tightness out of my lower back with my thumbs. An acorn hit me on the head.

"Ow!" I said. "Okay, I'm sitting again!" I sat back on the stump. "Now what?"

"This is the only time we will meet each other," Mother Baganza said. "After today, we will not meet again. We will not speak again. I have seen this."

"What?" I said, jumping to my feet. I held up my arms to block the inevitable slew of acorns. "What do you mean? This class is on my schedule twice per week, and it's taking two of my three spots."

"Sit *down*," Mother Baganza said, and her voice was so loud and forceful that I couldn't help but obey. When she spoke again, her voice had returned to its normal volume.

"I teach *wisdom*," Mother Baganza said. "The ability to answer a single question once per week by looking over the twisting braids of fate and seeing the most likely path. This isn't the future, but what will probably come to pass. It's an imperfect magic, though a useful one. If it can be mastered."

"And you're a master?" I asked.

"Yes," Mother Baganza said. "It's why I teach."

"Can you answer one question for me, then?" I asked. "One question, and then I'll do whatever you say."

"Go on."

"I'm looking for Sirax Sirco's personal armory," I said. "Can you tell me where it is?"

The voice made a sound that I can only describe as a snort. "You already have the answer to that question, as you have the answers for so many others. You must plumb the depths of the mind. *That's* what I'm here to teach. Tell me: do you know what the dungeon is?"

I sighed. It'd been worth a shot.

"A place to keep prisoners."

Mother Baganza laughed. "As correct as Spud's definition of wisdom, and similarly inaccurate. I'm not asking about the definition of the word dungeon. I'm asking…" She trailed off.

"Mother Baganza?" I said, after a moment.

The voice hummed. "Ah," Mother Baganza said. "I can't go that way. Let's try something else. This might work. In order to gain wisdom, you need to see. To see, you need to become present. Then, you need to offer up a truth."

"A truth?"

"Exactly. A truth for a truth. Like for like. You see?"

"Not at all." I was growing increasingly frustrated. What did it mean to become present? To give a truth for a truth?

"You will," Mother Baganza said.

This wasn't making sense. "I'm still a little concerned about what you said earlier. That this is the only time we'll see each other? Wisdom takes two of my three class slots, and I have class twice per week. If we're not going to meet, what am I supposed to do?"

"Practice," Mother Baganza said.

"Practice *what?*"

"How to see."

My face grew hot with anger. "How to see *what?*"

There was no answer.

"Mother Baganza?" I opened my eyes. "Mother Baganza?" I said again, more loudly this time.

Still no answer. "She told you to become present and trade a truth for a truth," Perry said quietly. "Maybe try that?"

So, I did. I tried for over an hour. I sat there and attempted to focus on the truth, but maybe I was too distracted, because all I could think about was how I'd been robbed.

It takes up two class sessions and we're not meeting again. All I've got to show for it is some mumbo jumbo. Jocko doesn't want to fight, yet he gets to teleport in that spray of leaves. Devora can pass on her drunkenness through touch. And what have you got with your powers, Crow? A sapient potato and a sapient tomato who won't stop arguing with each other? And some spiritual advice?

I knew I was moping.

I sighed. *One foot after the other. You're going to get through this.*

"Come on," I said. "Let's get something to eat."

14

The mess hall was similar to the assembly hall in its grandeur, only more cheerful, with panes of frosted glass at one end. The walls were strung with pennant flags, each a different shape and color, with blue-and-green tassels that hung between them.

Devora and Jocko sat at a table with Mega and Feng. The armored buck was the first to see me, and he waved enthusiastically. I returned the gesture and got into the buffet line.

"Don't get the mashed potatoes or I'll be really upset," Spud whispered as I made my way through the line.

I loaded my plate with roast chicken, green beans, and absolutely no mashed potatoes, and then I walked over to their table and set down my tray.

"How was your first class?" Devora asked. I put Spud and Perry on the table and hung the bandolier over the back of my chair before taking a seat.

"Good," I said. "Fine." I really didn't want to talk about it. "You?"

"Great," Devora said. "Right now, I have to touch someone to pass on my intoxication, but the class I'm in will teach me how to spread the effect across a wider area without contact, and between multiple people."

I glanced over at Feng and Mega, who didn't look up from their food. Jocko didn't seem to be eating, but he used a fork to push a green bean back and forth across his plate.

I never would've thought he'd turn out to be a coward, falling apart at the first sign of trouble, I thought, but I didn't say anything to him.

"Mega, what are you taking?" I asked. "And where's the rest of your crew?"

Mega swallowed a huge mouthful of food and washed it down with an entire glass of water. He wiped his mouth with the back of one hand.

"My people are still in their classes," he said. "I'm sure they'll catch up with me later. As for the class…"

Whatever he said was lost the moment the chicken hit my lips. After subsisting on little more than pickle juice and ham, the food tasted heavenly. Prior to that first meal in the mess hall, my only reference point for distributing food to a large number of people was the system the Empire used to feed us in the Dregs. Three times per day, the Empire dropped pre-measured doses of nutrient glop into proffered bowls through tubes that ran down from the city's second level. In our tenement, where we ate breakfast and dinner, the glop came in a single flavor: Honey Wheat, which we not-so-affectionately called 'Sawdust.' However, for lunch, which we ate in the warehouse, we got our choice of *six* different flavors, and praised be the rare day when ownership introduced a new flavor to the line.

This was food. The best I'd eaten since my arrest, and it rivaled what I'd eaten in my father's mansion.

Say what you will about Dungeon School, but someone behind the buffet counter knew how to cook.

I snapped back to the conversation in time to hear Mega talking about his professor, a dwarf named Don Cortes.

"For thirty years, he wandered the wilds around the towers," Mega said. "He was in a city called Kortaj when the War of Fangs broke out. He was one of a hundred civilian volunteers who took up arms when a thousand predators threatened to overrun the causeway that led into the city. After the war, he accepted a teaching position at Gray Moor."

"Wouldn't that make him super old?" Devora asked.

"Oh, he's ancient," Mega said.

"Sometimes, between Hunts, he puts on expos for those of us who live here," Feng said. "One time, he asked my friend Jorn to stab him in the throat with a fork." Feng lifted his fork, licked it clean, and tapped the tines against his ascot. "Right here. When it was done, Don Cortes was fine, but the fork was bent at a right angle."

"The class is called Reinforcement," Mega said. "My power is that I'm pretty much indestructible, but this class will teach me how to project a shield in a bubble around myself in a ten-yard radius. So I won't only be able to protect myself, but other people as well. For twenty seconds every hour, at least."

"Right," I said. "That's awesome." I turned to Jocko. "And you?"

Jocko stopped pushing around his green bean and looked up at me. His eyes were still hopelessly emotionless, but he seemed better.

Maybe?

"The class was good, *pacho*," he said. "I'm specializing in blade work. We started with basic stuff. Went through a few forms. Sparred a bit. The instructor simply wants to get a sense for where each of us is."

"The instructor is a *pro*," Feng said. "The shooting range is right next to where they hold blade practice, and we finished a bit early today, so I got to watch the end of Jocko's class. What this guy isn't telling you is that he agreed to participate as part of a demonstration. I think the instructor just wanted to pick on someone, but Jocko gave her a run for her money. The two ended up in a full-on battle. Lynn won, but I got the feeling Jocko wasn't really trying."

Jocko mumbled something. I thought it was, "She was better than me," but I couldn't be sure.

I glared at Jocko. *So he won't help me fight a rock golem, but he'll show off in front of his class? That doesn't make any sense.*

Feng probably didn't know why I was upset with Jocko, but he clearly sensed some tension, because he cleared his throat and said, "Uh, Crow. Tell us what you're taking again."

I continued staring at Jocko, but didn't press the issue. After a moment, I turned to Feng.

"Wisdom," I said. "I spent the last hour and a half with my eyes closed, trying to offer a truth to the universe."

"And that taught you something?" Devora asked. "What are you supposed to be learning?"

"We learned some definitions," Perry said. I thought he'd been asleep. "So that was interesting."

"I knew those definitions already," Spud said proudly. "I'm the one who taught them to Perry. But other than that, I'm not really sure. Apparently, we're supposed to be able to look into the future once per week and see a path that might happen, but isn't guaranteed to happen. Mother Baganza didn't say too much. Just dropped a ton of acorns on Crow's head. Oh, and we won't get to see her again. She told us that, at least."

Mega stopped eating and stared at me. Or not at me, but at the produce on the table before me.

"Did that tomato and potato just talk?" Mega rumbled.

"Oh," I said, then realized Mega didn't know about my weapons. "Yeah. Mega, this is Spud and Perry. Spud and Perry, this is Mega."

"Pleasure to meet you," Spud said. "Wow! You're really big. I bet you could punch Perry into yesterday."

"Hi, Mr. Mega," Perry said. "I bet Spud would go to Potato Hell if you stepped on him."

The big man blinked. "Uh, hello," he said, the confusion still clear on his face. "Hi there."

Now it was Devora's turn to look confused. "Are you sure you picked the right class? Getting acorns dropped on your head is probably something you could do without wasting a class session."

"*Two* class sessions," Spud said. "That single class takes up two spots."

I sighed. "It's what was recommended to me in advising," I said.

"I wish you were still able to switch," Feng lamented. "That used to be an option. I don't know why they stopped it."

We talked idly for a while longer until Devora pushed back from the table and lifted her tray.

"I hate to leave a stirring conversation, but Jocko and I were going to hit the training rooms before our next class," she said. "Anyone want to come?"

"I'll let you two handle this one," Feng said as he pushed aside his empty plate and lifted up a bowl of what looked to be blueberry cobbler. "I have a date with this little lady."

"Mega?" Devora said. "Crow?"

"Sorry," Mega said. "I'm, uh, busy."

His answer was suspicious, but I barely noticed. Instead, I stared at Jocko.

He's back to training? It didn't make any sense. One day, he was too distraught to defend himself, and the next he was sparring his professor, and training with strangers. When it came to dealing with others, he was healed.

But not with me.

I was so mad I wouldn't have been surprised if steam had started coming from my ears like it did in those old movies.

"I'm really running out of patience with you," I said.

Jocko shrugged. He kept pushing that stupid green bean.

I'm not proud of what happened next. All I can say in my own defense is that I'd had a rough day. Heck, I'd had several rough days, and I really wasn't in the mood for Jocko's attitude. So when Jocko shrugged at my comment, I lost it. I reached across the table and flipped his plate, spraying him with chicken bones, little clumps of mashed potato, and the cut ends of green beans. Some of the detritus stuck to his shirt, and other bits ended up in his lap. The plate hit the ground behind him and shattered.

A hush fell over the mess hall.

"You and I made a deal!" I yelled. My voice echoed in the now-quiet room, but I didn't care. "You agreed to help me, but you're not lifting a finger. You're a coward!"

I dared him to shrug. To say something blasé. To do anything to stoke my anger and make me throw a punch. Then, we could fight it out and be done with all the tension.

Instead, he met my eyes.

"You're right, *pacho*," he said quietly. "I guess I'm not as strong as I thought."

That was worse than any of those other options. Before that moment, I'd secretly hoped that Jocko would snap out of his funk. I wanted him to remember that he was the leader of the Thuins, the Desert Blade, a thorn in the side of the mighty Empire and one of the world's greatest living swordsmen. I mean, I was a professional athlete, and it'd taken all of my strength and skills to beat Metalhawk in the training room beneath the Electric Fortress. Jocko had not only beaten Metalhawk, but the creature's two brothers as well.

He'd done it all without breaking a sweat.

It was crushing to watch this larger-than-life hero admit his limitations. Instantly, I regretted flipping his plate, but it was too late. The damage had been done.

"Fine," I growled. "Run away, little baby. I don't need your help to save anyone. I'll do it all myself."

A hand settled on my shoulder. "Come on, man," Feng said quietly. "Let's get out of here. I think you need a break."

I didn't look away from Jocko, who returned my stare with a calm gaze.

What more could I say? Nothing seemed adequate. So instead I grabbed my bandolier, holstered Spud and Perry, and stomped out of the mess hall, Feng at my back.

15

<hr>

The ride wasn't long, but it angled upward sharply, without the dips and twists that had characterized all of my previous trips. The entire time, gravity pushed me against the cushion at my back.

"Where are we going?" I asked Feng.

"Just a place I like to visit when I need to think," Feng said. "Trust me on this one."

Trust me. I laughed. Trust was what had gotten me here in the first place. At least, trust in the wrong people. But who *could* I trust? I'd always considered myself a strong judge of character, though with my father's lies and Jocko shutting down on me, I wasn't sure if I still believed that about myself.

Still, Feng had only shown me kindness. And what else was I going to do? Go sulk alone in my room like a petulant child? That was certainly an option, though it didn't seem like the right move.

When the cart stopped, we didn't exit to a long platform but a small, circular one, barely wide enough for Feng and me to stand side-by-side. A ladder rose from the platform, so I let my gaze follow it upward, past beams and turning gears to a trapdoor in the roof high overhead.

"You're in for a treat," Feng said as he started climbing. He moved with an easy dexterity. His rifle, strapped tight against his back, barely swayed with his motion. He looked back down at me. "Come on!" he said.

I followed him up the ladder, the iron surprisingly warm beneath my gloves. By the time I reached Feng, he'd pushed open the trapdoor and was leveraging himself through the hole. I climbed after him and emerged into bright sunlight. The sky above me was a deep, vibrant blue, with fluffy white clouds scattered across it like cotton balls. The salty scent of the ocean filled my nostrils, and the distant sound of seagulls reached my ears.

"Is this…" I trailed off. The view answered my question. We were standing on top of Gray Moor.

I could see for miles. Beyond the crenellated edge of the tower, I spotted the other three towers: Talon Lake, Wicked Field, and Winter Ridge. Beyond them stretched the sea, glinting like a vast expanse of blue glass. In the distance, I made out the silhouette of land. Farther still, on the horizon, were the purple humps of distant mountains.

"Not bad, right?" Feng sat on the edge of a reclining chair someone had left on the roof. A second chair sat next to it, so I took that one. "I brought you up here for the view, but also because no one can hear us up here. You get it?" He tapped his eye. "No one."

"No one," I repeated, before realization dawned on me. "Oh! The broadcast doesn't get through?"

"Nope," Feng said. "I don't know why. Some type of magical inter-ference, I think."

A can appeared in his hand.

"What's this?" I asked as he cracked the can. There was a hiss of carbonation.

"Try it," he said, handing me the can.

Feng Goa's Local Soda

A refreshing drink made with ingredients grown in the basement

**greenhouses of Gray Moor. Brewed by the armored buck
Feng Goa.**

I took a sip and the cool, refreshing taste of citrus spread across my tongue. It was like nothing I'd ever tried. The drink had a bitter-though-not-unpleasant aftertaste that made me want to take another sip.

"Feng, this is delicious!" I said as he cracked a can for himself.

"Thanks." He lifted the can and looked appraisingly at the label. "It took me a while to perfect."

I took another sip. "I don't mean to be rude," I said. "But do you have a life down here? Between Hunts, I mean?"

Feng gazed toward the horizon. "As long as you survive a wave of hunters, you live until the Hunt comes around again the next year. I can't say it's a great existence, but it's certainly preferable to the alternative."

The way he said 'alternative' made me feel slightly queasy. "And what's that?"

"My memory of the experience isn't too strong," Feng said. "That's done on purpose, I think. Because what I can remember isn't pleasant. We go to a lab of some sort. Whoever runs the dungeon takes us apart and puts us back together in whatever form they need for the next year."

"That's terrible!" I said. "Why do they do that?"

Feng shrugged. "No idea. Like I said, my memory is hazy, but I have the vague recollection of having more arms, at one point. Anyway, I've figured out how to survive. It's been four years now. Four years since I became this, and every year I watch hunters come through Gray Moor and face its challenges. I've spent that time puttering around, finding places like this. I've trained with my rifle, and learned how to make soda. I had a girlfriend for a while, though she died last year. I used to think I'd be content with survival, with learning skills and building a personality, but I'm not."

I didn't think Feng was done talking, so I stayed silent until he continued.

"Last year, something strange happened. Do you know those golden devices, the ones that allow you to communicate with people outside Toroth-Gol?"

I groaned. "The Kinetoscope. I hate those things."

"Right," Feng said. "Well, I was walking past one near the mess hall and it popped open. I'm not sure how familiar you are with the device, but if you look closely, you can see hinges on the front, and they open up a little door. I hadn't known about that, so when the thing opened, I was surprised. In hindsight, I wish I'd left it alone, but I was curious."

"Did someone send you something?" I asked.

Feng nodded. "Not to me, though. Not specifically. It was a note written to anyone who found it. I don't still have it. Whoever wrote the note asked me to destroy it, which I did. But I memorized the text."

"What did it say?"

"It was a plea. It said, 'If you find this, you're my only hope. Soon, a woman named Miranda will come through Gray Moor. Help her and I'll help you. If you need to reach me, drop a message into this container at 12:00 PM every third day. Only use this container. No names. Burn this note.' That was it."

I was surprised, though I probably should've expected it. I'd known people on the outside were able to communicate with those inside Toroth-Gol. Hadn't Elvis Madden done this exact thing when he'd sent me Perry? But until now, I hadn't thought that someone in the Empire might use the Kinetoscope to reach a Toroth-Gol native.

"Did you find her?" I asked. "Miranda?"

"I did," Feng said. "And I helped her, too. I don't know everything about the tower, and I don't know where Sirax Sirco's Personal Armory is, so don't ask. I imagine she's dead by now, but I fulfilled my end of the bargain. I helped her through Gray Moor."

"And did you find out who was sending you the messages?"

"No. But I got to make a request of them. When I helped Miranda, I wasn't sure if it would pay off, but I trusted. And when it was done, I got a message that asked me what I wanted. And the answer is obvious, isn't it? I want out, Crow. I want to get out of this stinking, god-awful mess of a dungeon that takes me apart and puts me back together again on a whim. I want to be able to build a life without worrying that one wrong move will send me to that lab. I'm as real as anyone else, and I deserve that. Right?"

He asked it like a question, though I knew it was a statement, and I could only offer affirmation.

"Yes," I said. "Yes, you do."

Feng took two long glugs of his soda and threw the can over the edge of the tower. He burped. "I wrote back with a request to help me escape the dungeon. I knew it was ridiculous. I don't know what this place is, or how long it's been running, but I feel like I would've known if a native had ever escaped. That kind of word would get around, because all of us feel the same thing. The sane ones, at least. I've been up here with a dozen natives over the years and we've had the same conversation. If we could have one thing, we'd have a life. We'd get out of this place and just live. So I made my request."

I was on the edge of my seat. "Did you hear back?"

Feng laughed. "I didn't think I would. I thought that would be the end of our correspondence. But three days later, I came back to the Kinetoscope and saw the little door had popped open. There was a message inside. You know what it said?"

It was a rhetorical question, because I knew he was about to tell me.

"It said, 'In the next hunt, King Crow will come through Gray Moor. Attach yourself to him and you have a chance.'"

If I'd been surprised before, now my head was truly spinning. "Me? The note mentioned me by name?"

"Yes."

"But you don't know who sent it?"

"Nope. But you can help me, won't you? You'll try?" Nervously, he touched the ascot that was tied around his neck. "I understand if it's too much. Either way, I'll still help you however I can."

I thought of all the things I wanted to say. *Why me* or *I'll get you killed* or *I'm nothing special.* But there was so much *hope* in Feng's eyes.

And hadn't I vowed to get myself out of the dungeon? And not only myself, but anyone who trusted in me?

A question occurred to me then, one that had been quietly eating at me since I'd entered the tower. I hadn't asked it before, but now, safe on the roof and drinking Feng's soda, I felt like it was time.

"Do you know what's wrong with the dungeon?" I asked.

"Everything," Feng said, then scratched his bristly chin. "Or is that not what you mean?"

I ran a hand over my head. "I could be mistaken here, but things seem to be breaking. There are creatures getting past the school's defenses that aren't supposed to be here. The entry looks different for the first time in twenty years. And this whole animal-head motif... that's new, too, isn't it? So, is it me? Or is the dungeon sick?"

Feng cocked his head to one side. "What? The monsters that get inside the school are part of the level. Same as it's been the whole time I've lived here. I mean, it's only been four years, but there's nothing new here. The entry is the same as always. So is the animal motif." He ran a hand down his equine nose. "I mean, I think I'd know if I had a different head, wouldn't I? To my knowledge, the only thing that ever changes from year-to-year is the location of Sirax Sirco's Personal Armory." He shrugged. "Which is why I can't tell anything about it. It's usually the first question I get asked."

"I guess you would be the expert on your own head," I said.

At the same time, it didn't make any sense.

Jocko told me the dungeon was different for the first time in two decades. He said the entrance didn't look the same as it did a year before. Heck, I watched him scream about Sirax Sirco's head being a raccoon instead of a human before his collapse. I'm not making this up, am I?

All of that had happened. I remembered it because that's when I'd started taking the lead: when I'd vowed not only to get myself through the dungeon, but anyone who trusted in me.

Thinking of my companion made me sad. *Poor Jocko.* I hadn't really meant to flip his plate. *I guess he was right about me. If a problem looks insurmountable, I really do rise to the occasion.*

A thought occurred to me, and I felt like I'd been punched by a plated gauntlet. Was it possible Jocko had pretended to fall into shock? That he'd purposefully taken a blow from the rock golem's projectile?

I knew the answer instantly: *Yes.* Of course Jocko would do something like that. He'd already lied to me once, hadn't he? And for the exact same reason.

To make me step it up. To make me come into my own.

I laughed at his audacity.

"Crow?" Feng said. "Are you okay?"

I couldn't stop laughing. I laughed until tears streamed down my face. Jocko was likable, a leader, and one of the most talented fighters I'd ever seen. Yet, a scheme this intricate required a patience and cunning I didn't believe he possessed. In fact, in my entire life, I'd only met one person who I thought might be capable of such a plan.

"Crow?" Feng said. "You're, uh, scaring me."

I looked over at the armored buck, tears still streaming down my face.

"Just realizing something," I said. "It's fine. Don't worry about it. Say, how handy are you with that rifle?"

"This?" Feng reached over one shoulder and wrapped a hand around the barrel of his rifle. "I'm good. *Really* good." He pointed to my soda. "You finished with that?"

I brought the can to my lips and tipped the last drops of homemade liquid down my throat. It really had been delicious. "Done," I said as I held out the can.

"Crush the can and throw it over the edge. Give it a nice arc. Actually, wait!" Feng pulled his ascot off his neck and tied it around his eyes. "Now do that."

I did as Feng instructed, crushing the can and tossing it over the edge of the tower. Because I was looking at where I was throwing, I didn't see the rifle appear in Feng's hands. Instead, there was a *crack*, and then the can simply ceased to exist. When I looked back at Feng, he stood with one leg behind the other, the rifle in his hands and the barrel smoking.

He was still blindfolded.

"I got it, didn't I?" he said.

I exhaled a slow breath. "Yeah," I said. "Okay, that's good enough for me. If you trust me, and you'll fight with us, you're in. Welcome to the Spud Squad."

Feng tore off his blindfold. "You mean it?" he said, notes of disbelief and concern mixed with hope in his voice. "You'll take me with you when you leave?"

I nodded. "You're coming to the next level, buddy."

16

I wanted to confront Jocko. But as I climbed back down the ladder, Spud interrupted my thoughts by saying, "I think I know where the armory is."

I didn't want to respond, because there was a zero-percent chance Spud was correct. Yet, I'd already pursued one of Perry's hunches, and I knew Spud would take it personally if I didn't respond to one of his.

I sighed. "What are you thinking?" I asked.

"Glad you asked," Spud said. "Being with Feng made me think about it. Hear that, Feng? You're the man!"

"Thanks," Feng said from above me. He pulled shut the trapdoor and started climbing down the ladder. "I'm excited to get to know you."

"*That's* how you treat a celebrity," Spud gushed. "Anyway, do you remember when we first came into the tower and Feng told us that there was only one Warmaster's Conference Room and it had already been taken?"

"Yes," I said.

"And he couldn't tell us anything about it, right?" Spud said. "Other than that it existed?"

"Right."

"What if it doesn't exist? What if the doorway in our building that *says* it leads to the Warmaster's Conference Room *actually* goes to Sirax Sirco's Personal Armory?"

"I feel like there's a pretty easy way to clear this up," I said. "Hey, Feng, did anyone grab the Warmaster's Conference Room before we got there? And if they did, did they look like a hunter or a dungeon native?"

"I honestly don't know," Feng said. "A few of us take shifts at the front desk, and it was booked when I got there."

"Hmm," I said. It actually wasn't impossible. I considered my options. I could barge into the training room, accuse Jocko of what I already knew was true, and then what? Shake his hand? Hug it out? Our reconciliation wasn't particularly pressing. On the other hand, I could follow up on Spud's hunch. I'd avoid listening to him complain for hours.

Maybe he'd even be right.

It was an easy decision. But I wouldn't go alone. I dropped to the platform and turned to Feng, who climbed down beside me.

"What's your schedule like?" I asked. "Up for a little adventure?"

He grinned, the expression strangely predatory on his face. "With the Spud Squad?" he said. "It would be my pleasure!"

I plugged in the code for base camp and a cart took us away. When we reached the platform, Spud said, "Oh man, I can't wait to see the look on Perry's face when I'm right."

"Shut up, Spud," Perry said. "You're always so mean."

"And you're always so annoying," Spud said. "So *you* shut up!"

One time, in the shopping mall at the Stadia, I'd watched a kid throw a tantrum because his mother wouldn't buy him a bag of candy. The kid had gotten so upset he'd started pulling the bags of candy off the shelf and throwing them around the store. At the stricken look on the poor mother's face, I'd put my head down and walked away, as I'd wanted to avoid being party to her shame. I'm sure the flush she'd felt was similar to the one that crept up my neck as Feng cleared his throat.

"Hey," I said. I grabbed the produce from their respective seats, one in each hand. "Knock it off. We've got company."

Both Spud and Perry had been preparing to hiss at each other, but now they stopped. Their eyes darted to Feng.

"Sorry, Mr. Feng," Perry said.

"My apologies, bud," Spud said.

Feng scratched awkwardly at his neck. "Uh, it's cool, guys. No worries."

We walked in silence to the Command and Control building. Instead of turning right for our room, we made a left and passed under the arch that led to the conference room—or what we'd been told was the conference room, but what was hopefully an entrance to Sirax Sirco's Armory. I still didn't think it was likely, though I crossed my fingers we'd find what I hoped to find.

"Here we go," I said. Just in case, I pulled Spud into my hand and set him to hover above my palm.

Around the corner were several interesting things. Spud had been right: at the far end of a long hall was a circular golden door like the one that had led into the Chamber of Summoning. Several figures stood before it.

Wait a minute. I stared at the figures. *I know them!*

It was Mega and his crew. They were gathered around Robyn, the woman with the short-cropped hair, as she ran her hands over the door's surface.

"It's working?" Mega asked.

"Nearly done," Robyn said.

I thought Robyn was caressing the door, but that wasn't right. Well, she was rubbing the door rather awkwardly, but it was only because the golden door was covered in a hundred different keyholes. As she moved her hands over the holes, her skin melted into them. The locks turned and clicked as if her hands were the keys themselves.

So that's *what a Putty Lord can do.* I'd been wondering about her power ever since I'd read about her back on the platform.

I extended a hand behind me, stopping Feng in his tracks, and clamped a hand over Spud's mouth. If anyone was going to give us away, it was the fast-talking potato. I inched back around the corner.

"Four people already there," I whispered to Feng. "One is unlocking the door."

"Do we jump them?" he asked, already reaching for his rifle.

"It's four against two, even if we have the element of surprise. But also, I know them, and they've seemed friendly enough. We could show ourselves, but with the armory at stake, I don't know how they'd react."

"We don't know it's the armory," Perry whispered. "The last golden door we found didn't lead to the armory."

"No, it didn't," Spud said. "Even though someone said it would."

Perry ignored Spud. "Mega and his crew may or may not know that. If they think we'll ruin their chances at the armory, I bet they'll attack. Wouldn't you attack, Crow, if the situation was reversed?"

"Crow wouldn't do that!" Spud hissed. "And not only because he's been virtually useless in all of our fights. He's a man of honor! Something you wouldn't understand, Twinkletoes."

Thankfully, a second argument was avoided as we heard a loud *bang*, and then... screaming?

I poked my head back around the corner. The bang hadn't come from the door sliding to one side, but the floor falling away, which had dropped Mega and his friends. A hidden trapdoor had split down the middle and left a pit directly in front of the door, roughly a dozen paces across.

All thoughts of a surprise approach were discarded as I ran toward the edge of the newly made gap and peered over the edge. Thirty feet below me were Mega and his friends. They lay on a square platform surrounded by a metal railing, dazed from the sudden drop. All of them seemed to have had the wind knocked out of them, but their fall had been lucky. If they'd fallen differently and missed the platform, they would've plunged through the floor and kept falling into a pit so deep that it simply looked like a yawning black maw.

The Valves (Secret Entrance)

The Valves are a labyrinthine network of tunnels beneath Gray Moor. Some say they were once the home of an ancient civilization, while others believe they were built in recent times by Sirax Sirco and his fellow generals to transport goods between the towers. However, no one disputes that the Valves were eventually abandoned and have since become a haven for the strange and the dangerous.

Those who venture into the Valves do so at their own risk. The creatures that lurk in the darkness are not of this world, and they will stop at nothing to protect their domain. Some of these creatures are said to be able to change their form, while others possess incredible strength and speed. Many adventurers have made efforts to map the tunnels, but few have returned to the surface with their sanity intact.

Despite the danger, some brave souls continue to explore the Valves, seeking treasures beyond measure or hoping to unravel the mysteries that lie hidden in the depths. But those who enter the Valves should beware, for once they are inside, they will likely never find their way out again.

WARNING: Entering the Valves will end your admittance to Gray Moor.

"Mega!" I called. "Are you okay?"

At the sound of my voice, Mega groaned and sat up. His eyes widened when he saw me.

"Hey!" he said. "King Crow! Get us out of here. I broke our fall with my shield, but I can't see how to—"

Whatever he was about to say was cut off as the floor folded back up under my feet. The two panels snapped back into place so quickly that a puff of displaced air hit my face.

"Crow, we've got to help them!" Perry cried. "Press something. There must be a mechanism on the door."

I examined the door. It was similar to the one we'd seen on the platform outside the advising rooms, golden and circular, though instead of writing on it, this one had those hundred keyholes in the shape of a six-pointed star.

"Let's not be hasty," Spud said. "They *did* try to pursue the armory without us. Remember at lunch, when Devora asked Mega to train, and he said he was busy? He could've told us what they were doing, but he didn't. Besides, I'm not sure you want to touch anything here. Mega did, and his group got dropped through the floor. You could find yourself with them. Or there might be other traps."

"You're talking about people's lives," Perry said. "I knew you were mean, Spud, but I didn't think you were heartless."

"I'm *realistic*, fertilizer-for-brains," Spud replied. "Grow up."

I considered my options. *I could leave them. Leave them, come back later, and loot their bodies. Steal whatever treasures they had.*

But leaving them wasn't actually an option. At least not for me, and certainly not with the promise I'd made for myself.

If you help them, maybe you'll end up with more than the armory could provide. You've already earned Devora's trust, and Feng is on your side. With you and Jocko, that's currently a team of four. Mega, Esmé, Robyn, and Jinx make eight.

That settled it. I put Spud on my shoulder and glanced at Feng, who held one end of a length of rope.

"I keep this in my Inventory for emergencies," he said. "Think we could fish them out?"

I considered. *That's helpful. But how do we do this? If I open the floor again, and we drop the rope, how do we pull them out before the trapdoor closes up again? With the way it closed, it would probably cut through the rope, or crush anyone who was halfway through.*

The first step was to see if I could get the floor back open.

"Maybe," I said. "Feng, take another step back, just to be safe. If you look closely, you can see the outline of the trap."

I pointed to the floor, where I could make out a thin seam that outlined the trapdoor.

Feng followed my instructions, and I walked around the outline until I reached the golden door. There was a small shelf between the trap and the door, and I balanced on it. Then I braced my hands against the door.

"I'm going to try and open the floor again," I said. "Feng, if I do, I don't want you to do anything other than count. We need to see how long the doors stay open before they slam shut again."

"Got it," Feng said. "Smart thinking."

I rubbed my hands over the keyholes. That was what Robyn had been doing when the door opened. Sure enough, as I moved a hand over the bottom point in the star, there was a *click*. The doors swung open. It happened so quickly that I nearly tipped backward, though I pressed myself against the door and closed my eyes.

"Do it, Feng!" I said. "Start counting!"

Behind me, the armored buck counted evenly. "One one thousand. Two one thousand, three one thousand…"

From within the pit, Mega and his team yelled at us to help them. Trying to stay focused, I kept my eyes closed and my body pressed against the golden door. I was up on the balls of my feet, my heels hanging over the edge of the trapdoor. One step backward and I'd fall into oblivion.

As Feng reached fifteen, the doors slammed shut.

I exhaled and opened my eyes. "Fifteen seconds. Hardly long enough for us to drop the rope and let someone climb out."

"If they had some agility skill, maybe," Perry said. "Or Jocko's teleportation. The little one might be able to do it. But Mega definitely isn't built for speed."

I looked down at the keyholes that comprised the bottom point of the star. Which one had activated the trapdoor? If I could find that, maybe I could keep my finger on it. Perhaps that would keep the door from slamming shut.

I told Feng what I was thinking. "But I'm not sure if it'll work, so don't throw the rope down yet," I added. "Let's make sure we can keep the door open first."

"Understood," Feng said. "Go for it."

This time, instead of running my hands over the door, I pressed the keyholes in the bottom point of the star one-by-one. It was like that game I had as a little kid, which was shaped like the head of a desert crocodile. You started the game by pulling open its jaws, and then you pressed each of its plastic teeth. Most teeth went down, but if you hit the wrong one... *snap!* The jaws would close on your finger.

That had been a game, the stakes nothing higher than surprise and a light pressure. The toy's gums had been lined with felt. This, however, was life and death.

There was a *click* as my finger pressed one of the keyholes, then a louder noise behind me as the floor fell away.

Yes! That's the one!

I put my finger back on the keyhole that had triggered the trapdoor and felt its slight give.

"Okay, Feng," I said. "I've got this pressed. Start counting. If we get past fifteen and the floor hasn't closed, we'll know this works. Then we can drop the rope and pull them out."

"Um, Crow?" Feng said from behind me. "I'm not sure it's going to matter."

I realized then I couldn't hear the shouts of Mega and his friends. With one finger still on the keyhole, I looked over my shoulder. The platform that Mega and his crew had been standing on was gone, and so were the hunters themselves. I found myself staring into nothing but a yawning black pit.

"Where did they go?" I asked.

"I don't know," Feng said. "Get off of there and we can talk about it. I don't want you falling in there with them."

I released the button. As I did, I pulled up my Map. In that first glimpse I'd gotten into the pit, my eye had told me that I wasn't just looking into an endless hole, but a secret entrance into another area of the dungeon. Would my advanced Map have any additional information as to the fate of Mega and his crew?

I found the room in which we stood, but even on a three-dimensional map, I couldn't see the shaft that had swallowed the other hunters.

The text had called it a secret entrance. Maybe it's a secret to the Map, too.

A few seconds later, the trapdoor closed behind me. I tiptoed off the ledge and jumped to safe ground. Even knowing the trigger, I didn't trust the trapdoor not to open beneath me.

"Do you know what the Valves are, Feng?" I asked.

The armored buck shook his head. "Rumors only," he said. "They predate my time here. Sirax Sirco and the generals built the towers above them, though I'm not sure why. I'm not sure anyone knows."

"Is there any way to help them?" I asked. "Mega and his crew?"

Again, Feng shook his head. "I don't think so," he said sadly. "I think they're on their own, now."

I sighed. This wasn't what I'd wanted at all. How could Mega and his friends be gone?

Feng put a hand on my shoulder. "Come on," he said. "We should get out of here. There's nothing we can do, and I don't think it's healthy for us to stick around. Keep the rope. I have another length in my room."

I looked down at the barely visible outline of the trapdoor.

"Good luck," I whispered. Then I put the rope in my Inventory and followed Feng around the corner.

17

That afternoon, after I'd tried and failed to 'gain wisdom' through an hour of useless meditation, I went to find Jocko.

I still didn't know what I'd say to the Desert Blade. On the one hand, I was furious. Jocko had lied to me about the Castle of 1,000 Doors, and then, before we'd gone into Gray Moor, had told me he was done lying, only to mess with my mind again.

On the other hand, he was right about what would motivate me.

We were waiting for the cart to the training rooms when Perry said, "I had another idea."

I groaned. "Not again. Guys, I want to find Sirax Sirco's Armory as much as the next person, but could we let it rest for a bit? We watched four people get swallowed by the dungeon in their pursuit, and I don't want to be the next to go."

"Well, we are two for two on finding doors that *might* be the armory," Spud said. "Though it pains me to admit, Vomit Boy did help us find some decent treasure that first time. I mean, that would've been a serious haul if Devora hadn't plunged her hand into the body of a flaming fire elemental."

I rolled my eyes. "She saved our lives," I said. "Spud, tell me honestly: would you have known how to fight that thing?"

"No," Spud said. "But that's not the point. The point is, we're on the right track. I mean, we're hot on the trail. Why not hear what Perry wants to say?"

I lifted both of them, one in each hand. "Okay, what's going on?" I said. "You two never agree on anything. Why so chummy all of a sudden?"

Perry glanced over at Spud, his eyes wide. Spud looked down at my palm and mumbled something.

"What was that?" I asked.

Spud looked back up at me. "Okay, hear me out," he said. "What if you're wrong? About Jocko, I mean? What if he's really as confused and scared as he's acted for the past few days?"

"I'd be crushed," I answered honestly.

"Right," Spud said. "We don't want to see that, Crow. Our feeling is that if you confront Jocko and it turns out he's *not* faking, it's going to destroy you. So maybe we, uh, don't do that."

"You don't think he's faking it?" I asked.

"I don't *know*," Spud said. "But why poke the bear? We're on a good path here. Let's keep it rolling."

I stared at them. Now I felt conflicted in a different way. On the one hand, Spud and Perry hadn't agreed on anything since they'd met, so a unified front was nice.

On the other, they'd unified against *me*.

"When did you have time to talk about this?" I asked.

"Sometimes we whisper to each other when we're both on your bandolier," Perry said. "Usually it's Spud insulting me, but I thought he had a good point with this one."

I sighed. I hadn't considered that Jocko might not be faking, but now that I did, I realized they were right. If it turned out Jocko really *was* messed up, it would send me back into a spiral.

"What are you proposing?" I asked.

Perry glanced at Spud again, then met my gaze. He licked his lips.

"Well," he said, and his voice cracked. He cleared his throat and tried again. "I think I might know where to find Sirax Sirco's Armory. For real this time."

"Go on," I said.

"I really like games," Perry said. "I don't remember too much about my time before I joined up with you guys, but from what I *can* remember—"

"Skip the exposition, Twinkletoes," Spud said. "Come on, man. Really."

"It's necessary!" Perry cried out. "I'm saying that before joining you guys, I remember playing a lot of games. I liked puzzles the best. So when we got here and I saw the switching codes in the pamphlet, and Sirax Sirco's Personal Armory had those question marks beside it, I started thinking about what they could mean. At first, I wondered if we could plug the question marks into the podium. But the podium didn't have any question marks, so then I started wondering if the shapes or colors it did have were some sort of code. I thought that if I could figure out why one switching code was three triangles and a circle, while another was three circles and a triangle, it might provide some clue as to why the armory was four question marks."

"And did you figure it out?" I asked.

Again, Perry shook his head. "No. I'm pretty sure it's nonsense. A false trail. But that's okay. Because when you read about the armory in your pamphlet, what did it say? I mean, it said a lot. But I want to remind you of one line: 'In order to find it, you'll have to get inside Sirco's mind.' Do you remember that?"

"Sure."

"And when we were in Wisdom, and you asked Mother Baganza about the armory, what was her response? She said, 'You must plumb the depths of the mind.' Not, 'your mind.' *The* mind."

"So what's your point? That the treasure is in Sirax Sirco's mind?"

"Exactly," Perry said.

"In the name of all that's—wait. Is he saying the treasure isn't tangible?" Spud said. "Maybe the treasure is friendship!"

"What?" Perry said. "No, I was going to say it's probably inside the head of the statue in the school's entrance. Get it? The treasure is *literally* in Sirax Sirco's mind."

"Oh," Spud said. "That makes way more sense."

My heart beat like I'd finished running a lap of the Stadia. *It makes sense. But how do we check? We couldn't move Mega and his crew thirty feet out of a trap. How are we going to get a hundred feet up the side of a slick statue?*

I realized the answer to both my problems lay in the same solution.

"Okay, now hear *me* out," I said. "That statue is over a hundred feet tall. The only one of us who could possibly reach the head is Jocko."

"But we don't want to approach Jocko right now," Spud said. "On account of him potentially being mentally broken and you being crushed when you realize it."

"Look at it this way," I said. "If I'm right, and he's faking, we get our friend back, and he can check the head and see if it's hiding the armory."

"And if you're wrong, and he's not faking?" Spud asked.

"If I'm wrong, and he's genuinely in a bad spot, the chance of finding the armory might give him hope," I said.

"What if he's in a bad way and we don't find the armory?" Perry asked.

"Then we're no worse off than we are right now," I said. "But in two of the three scenarios, we've got a pretty good chance of a positive outcome. What do you say?"

Perry glanced over at Spud. But to my surprise, Spud had turned to look at Perry.

"What?" Spud said. "I'm merely the brawn of this team. And the face. And the sex appeal. You're the nerd, Twinkletoes. It's your plan. If you like it, go for it."

Perry turned back toward me and his eyes narrowed in determination. "Fine," he said. "Let's find Jocko."

I plugged the training rooms into the podium and hit the green button. A cart arrived and took us on a wild, looping ride. When we got to the hall that led to the training rooms, it took us a few tries to find the one that Jocko and Devora were in, but eventually we got it right.

The training room was simpler than the one in the Electric

Fortress: just a large, square chamber with a concrete floor and a circle marked off in the center with red paint.

Gray Moor (Training Room #3)

The training rooms in Gray Moor are places where novice and veteran soldiers alike come to hone their skills. The rooms produce magical constructs, which can take the form of anything from dragons to golems to simple wooden targets. The constructs are imbued with magical energy that allows soldiers to train against them without fear of death, though many soldiers have been caught off guard by a particularly clever construct and found themselves battered and bruised.

This is the third of the forty training rooms in Gray Moor.

Jocko stood outside the ring and provided tips to Devora, who sparred against an animated skeleton wearing navy robes. In one hand, the skeleton wielded a foot-long staff with a crystal on the end that glowed a sickly green. In the other was a bone-handled sword.

"Watch your left foot, *pacho*," Jocko said as the skeleton feinted. He was animated. Excited. My heart leapt, though I was ready to punch him in the back of the skull for lying to me.

Again.

"No, not that one," Jocko howled. "Your other left!"

Devora didn't have time to react before tendrils of black smoke shot from beneath the skeleton's robe and wrapped around her right ankle. A tug sent her tumbling, and the skeleton stood over her, the point of its sword hovering above her heart.

"What the heck?" Devora said as the skeleton stepped back. From experience, I knew the tumble had probably hurt, though not worse than her wounded pride. "You told me to watch my *left* foot. That didn't help at all!"

The skeleton stood a few yards away with its hands clasped behind its back. The bone-handled sword that it had pointed at Devora's heart only moments before was back in the scabbard at its waist. Small lights in the hollow sockets of its eyes glinted with amusement.

From where he stood on the sidelines, Jocko shrugged. "In a real battle, you won't have the luxury of a trainer to call out directions. In war, there'll be a thousand other distractions. The sounds of war horns and siege engines. Metal against metal. The screams of your friends dying around you. You need to learn to tune it all out."

"Playing mind games with more than one of us?" I said. I couldn't help myself. But Jocko was *fine*. He was fine!

Jocko glanced at me over his shoulder as if he'd been expecting me all along.

"Oh, hey, Crow," he said. "I was wondering when you'd figure it out. You done being frustrated?"

"Sure," I said. "I know I can trust you to have my back, even if you lie to my face."

Jocko smirked at me. "If you can trust in anything, trust in that! If it makes you feel any better, I wanted to motivate you. I know you know that already. But congratulations! Consider yourself motivated."

In those simple words, I also heard the ones he didn't say, so as not to reveal his plot to an Empire that was watching our moves through our mechanical eyes: *your father spent the last twenty years planning this, and he's more cunning than you could possibly imagine. However angry you are, don't blow our cover.*

"This is kind of crazy," Perry said. "Is this normal?"

"No."

"But you're okay, Jocko?" Perry said. "You're really fine?"

Again, the Grass King shrugged. "I can't say it was much fun taking that boulder to the head. But yeah, *pacho*. I'm golden. A true leader knows how to motivate, no matter how unpleasant accomplishing that motivation might be. You want a turn in the ring?"

"We're here because I need a favor," I said. "After everything that's happened, you owe me one."

I told the group about what had happened to Mega and his crew. Then I told them about Perry's idea, and what we needed from Jocko. When I was done, the Grass King tapped his chin thoughtfully.

"Interesting thinking, *pacho*. Probably worth a look. Though it sounds like you're doing *me* a favor if you turn out to be right."

We walked to the platform and took a cart to the switching station at the tower's entrance, then made our way up the ramp that led to the massive statue. After a few minutes, we emerged from the depths to see the statue towering above us; I was glad to see that I'd been right: there was no way I could've climbed it. The tip of Sirco's great sword touched the ground, but the sword itself was a single smooth piece of dark stone without a handhold in sight. The armor that covered Sirco's shins looked like it might provide some decent holds; however, in order to reach it, one would need to scale the warrior's boots, which were as smooth as the blade of his sword.

I craned my neck, looking for any sign of a door in the statue's head, but couldn't see anything.

"You wouldn't be able to spot it from here, *pacho*," Jocko said. "That would ruin the fun of a good treasure hunt. I've got to get close. Maybe up the nose? Or through the ears. That seems safer. I'll check one, and then the other. The nose will be a last resort. Wish me luck!"

Jocko disappeared, leaves drifting to the ground in the spot where he'd been standing. He appeared on the tip of the statue's left boot. If I hadn't been watching for him, I never would've seen him. There was another explosion of leaves, and I let my eyes climb up the statue's ankle to where Jocko was now dangling by his fingertips from a link that made up the armor of the statue's shins. A third jump, and he appeared a little higher. Then a fourth jump, and a fifth. That's how it went, all the way up, until he disappeared into the statue's right ear.

"I like Jocko, even if he did lie to us," Perry said quietly. "We don't have to hate him, do we?"

"No, we don't have to hate him."

There was an explosion of leaves as Jocko appeared beside me.

"Jocko!" The Grass King bent over, his head down and his arms pressed against the low wall. His chest heaved like he'd run a dozen miles. "Jocko, are you okay?"

Jocko struggled to get air into his lungs. "I'm... sorry, it's... I can't..."

I put a hand on his shoulder. He'd manipulated me, though I still felt a fraternal bond with the guy, and I hadn't realized how much teleporting took out of him.

"Catch your breath. It can wait."

With a great gasp, Jocko stood. "I can't wait," he said, and even as he wheezed, I could tell that he was laughing. "It's there. Perry was right. It's there."

18

Once we were done celebrating, we had to figure out how to get the rest of us into the ear. The armory had more treasure than Jocko could carry even if he took a dozen trips.

Or, not the rest of us. Just me. As it turned out, Devora was scared of heights.

"It's really my only fear," she said casually. "Some people don't like spiders or snakes. I'm not big on heights."

"It's fine," I said. "I'll make a few extra trips."

"A few?" Jocko said. "More like many, *many* extra trips. We're talking an entire room full of treasure up there. Weapons, armor, old scrolls. Beautiful oil paintings."

"Oil paintings? Do we need those?"

Jocko shrugged. "What would the Crow who was raised in the Dregs say if he found out this new Crow was leaving anything behind? I say we take everything and see what's useful later."

Getting me into the ear was easier said than done. Jocko had searched for a trapdoor that might lead to a ladder or spiral staircase down. However, if it existed, he hadn't been able to find it.

The obvious solution was to give Jocko a rope and have him use his little teleporting trick to make his way up the statue, periodically tying off the rope so that I had something to climb other than the slick statue. But when I suggested it to Jocko, he gave a sharp laugh.

"No can do, *pacho*," he said. "When I do that trick, I go incorporeal. You hand me a rope, and the moment I jump it falls to the ground. I can't take anything with me."

"Could you put it in your Inventory?" Perry asked. "Get to the top, tie it off, and then drop it down?"

"Good thinking, *pacho*," Jocko said. "That's our best bet."

"Well, you *could* do that," Spud said. "Or you could put the rope in my mouth, have Jocko get to the top, and fire me up to him. That would be great. Good idea too, right?"

"That seems needlessly complex," I said. "Why would we do that when Jocko can carry the rope the entire way?"

"Give me this one, Crow," Spud hissed. "Perry was the one who found the armory. I *need* this."

I wanted to help him, yet it made absolutely no sense to endanger him or Jocko by doing something so stupid.

"Sorry, man," I said. "I'm not risking our lives so you can look awesome. Jocko, take up the rope!"

Spud grumbled, but Jocko was in the statue's ear again, and the rope came spiraling down. It hit the ground with a loud *smack*.

"See you soon," I said to Devora.

During lightball training, we'd often had to do rope climbs. I'd thought I was pretty good at them. But as I put one hand after the other, inching my way up the coarse rope, my muscles screamed, and my hands felt burned and raw. Finally, as I was truly starting to question whether I'd make it, I reached up and didn't grab the rope, but Jocko's hand. He pulled me into the ear and I gratefully accepted his help. I'd never been scared of heights, but the distance from the ground was making me queasy.

"Step this way, *pacho*," Jocko said. He guided me farther into the ear. "You'll feel better when you can't see the ground."

I let Jocko lead me through the smooth tunnel of the statue's inner ear and into the room at the center of the head. The door that had kept the room secure was already open. I stopped in the doorway, and my breath caught at the sight of the room. Although Sirax Sirco's Personal Armory was much smaller than the statue's head, it overflowed with all types of weapons, armor, and other items.

Gray Moor (Sirax Sirco's Personal Armory)

You've found Sirax Sirco's Personal Armory!

Sirax Sirco was the leader of the prey forces during the War of Fangs and the founder of Gray Moor. The items you see inside this room were part of his personal collection. During Sirco's lifetime, they were kept in a warded chest in his personal chambers. With every new wave of hunters into Toroth-Gol, they're moved to protect them from falling into the wrong hands.

Unlike the orderly displays in the commissary, the items in the armory were strewn about the room haphazardly. The only orderly part of the whole room was a small dais on the far side. Raised a few steps above the rest of the room, the dais supported a much smaller statue of Sirco. It appeared to be made entirely of silver, and it showed Sirco in a seated position, his right hand on the hilt of a truly massive sword that lay horizontally across his waist. Sirco stared down his long nose in quiet contemplation at the object in his left hand: an orb about the size of Spud. Lime-green light swirled inside the orb, providing enough of a glow to illuminate the entire room.

Jocko took a step into the room, but I stopped him with a hand to the shoulder. I couldn't help but think of the yellow strings I'd seen in Dark City, the ones that Metalhawk had triggered, which had blown both of us to smithereens—or would've, if Rayne hadn't used Brynn's special item to protect me. I winced at the memory.

"There aren't any traps or things like that?" I asked.

"Good thought, *pacho*," Jocko said. "But no. None that I can see, at least."

I remained cautious as I followed Jocko into the armory. The Thuin headed straight for the dais, eschewing the chests, weapons, and armor piled on the floor. I already knew what he wanted: the sword that lay across Sirco's lap. I followed.

Unlike the rest of the statue, the sword wasn't made of silver. Rather, it glowed a faint green. Near the cross guard, it was the lighter green of healthy mint, though the hue got richer and darker toward the end of the sword until it was turquoise. At first, I thought this was a reflection from the orb in Sirco's other hand. As I followed Jocko, I realized the blade glowed of its own accord.

Jocko mounted the dais and slipped the sword from Sirco's silver grip. It came free without so much as a whisper. As he lifted the weapon before him with both hands, a description of the sword appeared in my vision.

Sirax Sirco's Greatsword (Severance)

Severance was the personal weapon of Sirax Sirco. Personally crafted for Sirco by an eldritch wizard summoned with magic long since lost, Severance is capable of taking the soul of anyone it cuts and using their power to augment the blade. After creating a Soul Bond with Severance, a wielder is capable of utilizing captured power to augment their own body. Infinitely durable, Severance can't rust, tarnish, or chip, and it will never lose its edge.

As I watched Jocko stare lovingly at his new weapon, I found myself wondering how much it weighed. The sword was *colossal*. If Jocko had turned the sword upside down and rested the tip on the ground, the blade would've reached the base of his neck. The blade didn't taper to a point but actually widened so the tip looked like a shovel.

"It's beautiful," Jocko whispered. The sword disappeared into his Inventory.

"You're taking that?" I asked.

He winked. "You let me keep the sword, and I'll let you have that," he said, gesturing to the statue.

I suspected I knew what it held, but it was still nice to have confirmation as I gazed at the glowing orb in the statue's left hand.

Master Soul Core (Xenandor of Kratha)

This item contains the soul of Xenandor of Kratha, one of Sirax Sirco's sworn enemies, whom Sirco struck down in single combat during the War of Fangs.

Combine with additional Special Materials and a Schematic to create a Special Item.

"Whoa," Spud said. "That's a big pickup. I guess that angry dwarf has to train you now, right?"

I smiled. Justice wouldn't be happy about it, but I had a soul core. And not any soul core, but a *master* soul core. The kind that Fairlan had said was priceless.

I was about to reach for the orb, but I stopped myself. Moving forward with Jocko's plan would mean lying to Devora. Or, not lying exactly, but obscuring the truth. We'd promised to split the treasure, and if she didn't know about these items, her haul would be smaller.

"She didn't really do anything to *earn* the treasure," Spud whispered in my ear. "I mean, it was Perry who found it; Jocko got us up here; and you're the one who's going to get it down."

"You should do the right thing, Crow," Perry said.

I'd given Devora my word, and she trusted me.

"No deal," I told Jocko. "I'll back you up if you try to claim the sword, because you're the one who can do the most with it, just like I'm the one who can make the best use of the soul core. But I won't lie to her."

Jocko smiled at me. "Would you believe me if I told you that was a test, *pacho*?"

"I don't believe a word out of your mouth."

The grin didn't slip from Jocko's face. "Well said, *pacho*. Let's load up and get this stuff out of here."

Since the treasure was stored haphazardly, there was no rhyme or reason to where items were located. Armor lay atop piles of swords and shields, and potions had been stuffed into drawers, seemingly at random. Empire marks and gemstones spilled out of overflowing burlap bags. A group of framed oil paintings leaned on one wall. Not only were they awkwardly shaped, but they looked heavy.

Everything I could carry went into my Inventory.

I groaned under the weight of my first load, and it didn't look like I'd made a dent in the piles of treasure scattered throughout the room. Taking *everything* would mean multiple trips up and down the statue.

"Maybe we should get all the stuff organized, and then we can prioritize what to bring down first," I said.

"I'm with you," Jocko said. "Let me tell Devora what we're doing."

So began the process of trying to sort out what the room contained. As we did, we came up with an organizational system: weapons and armor went in one corner, enchanted jewelry went in another, and scrolls and potions went into a third. Within those corners, we further separated the piles into items that spoke specifically to Jocko's skillset and style of fighting, items that spoke to mine, neutral items, and things that didn't benefit either of us.

"Look here," Jocko said after a while, standing over the open drawer of a wooden desk. He reached inside and pulled out what looked like two rings. "You might like these."

I leaned the painting I was moving against a nearby wall and wiped the sweat from my forehead. I walked over to Jocko and looked down at the rings in his palm.

Ring of Teleportation (Trigger and Anchor)

The Ring of Teleportation was forged from moonstone by an ancient wizard who sought to make travel across great distances more efficient. The ring is split into two parts, the trigger and the anchor. When the trigger is activated, it creates a powerful magical portal that will transport the wearer to the location of the anchor. However, the trigger can only be used once every ten minutes, and

the anchor must be within 1,000 yards of the trigger for the tele-portation effect to work. To use, hold the trigger ring and think *activate.*

The utility was obvious. "That'll allow me to get into the armory without the climb," I said. "You can get down, drop the anchor, and I can join you. Then you can come back up, leave the anchor in here, and we can bring the first load of treasure to our rooms. Once we've dropped everything off, I can use the ring to teleport straight to the armory again. You come the long way, meet me here, and we can do the whole process over again until this place is empty."

"Here." Jocko dumped the trigger ring into my palm. "I'll go set the anchor. See you at the bottom?"

"Yeah," I said. "I've got about as much as I can carry, so I'll see you down there."

19

Although we saw several other hunters as we walked to our rooms, we held the armory's treasure safely in our Inventories, and no one we passed was any wiser. I had no doubt that if they knew what we had, at least one of them would've moved against us.

Best keep this a secret, I thought as I raised a hand in greeting to a nearby hunter. *This would put a target on your back.*

I imagined I knew what my father felt like, keeping a dangerous secret from the rest of the world. In recent months, I'd started to realize something was odd about his frequent "business trips," though I was still amazed Sal had worked with the Thuins for over twenty years without raising suspicion, and only then because he'd *wanted* to be caught.

Don't think about your father. You have more important things to worry about right now.

It took just over two hours to move all the treasure to our room. When we were done, I said goodbye to Jocko and Devora.

"You don't want to see how we split up the rest of this loot?" Jocko asked as he motioned to the pile of assorted weapons and magical items spread out across our room.

"If I hurry, I might be able to make my first bulletsmithing class," I said. "The instructor told me not to come back unless I had a soul core. But now I've got one, so I'm going to make him teach me."

"Good luck!" Devora said. Then I was out the door. I ran from the building and down the path, feeling lighter with every footfall. I felt great. Heck, I felt giddy. Since entering Dungeon School, not everything had worked out the way I wanted. But now, I'd found the armory, and I had a master soul core.

Ten minutes later, I pushed my way into the machine shop. Once again, I was hit with the sound of clacking gears and the scent of sulfur.

It smells like the inside of a gun barrel in here. I only knew what that smelled like because of my father's insistence on self-defense training. I searched the area, though I didn't see Justice.

"Skipped out on us, did he?" Spud said. "I knew he wouldn't keep his word. I could tell that dwarf had a cowardly streak from a mile away. Oh, hello Justice Maron, sir! Great to see you."

I turned around to see Justice step from his office, a hammer held against one shoulder. He brought his other hand to his cheek, where a streak of soot stained his skin right where it met his beard.

"What's this about a *cowardly streak?*" he growled.

"I wasn't talking about you," Spud said. "We have this other friend who's a coward. Awful guy. Stole Crow's cookies and blamed it on Perry."

"Hmm." Justice turned his gaze from Spud to me. "I told you not to come back."

I reached into the pouch at my waist and pulled out the master soul core. It was still oddly heavy and warm to the touch, and the strange smoke swirled within the glass.

"You told me not to come back unless I found a soul core," I said, holding it out to him. "So I did. Sir."

Justice reached a gauntleted hand toward the proffered orb, his fingers stopping before they brushed against the glass. He looked back to me as if trying to decide whether I was trying to pull a fast one or not, then snatched the object from my hand and held it to the light. A look of surprise spread across his features.

"Where did you get this?" He glanced to the door like someone might walk in. Then, he pulled a lever on the wall, and with the hiss of hydraulics, the door slammed shut. A plank of wood that I hadn't noticed before descended from the lintel by chains, one on each end, and fell across the inside of the door.

"I found Sirax Sirco's Armory," I said. "This was inside. So now, I'm going to ask you to hold up your end of the bargain."

Justice looked back at the soul core, opened his mouth like he was going to say something, then closed it again and licked his lips.

"Come." He turned on his heels and strode into his office.

I followed Justice into the office, which might've been the messiest room I'd ever seen. The tables were cluttered with papers, and the shelves were crammed with tools, canisters of screws, and scraps of metal. To walk from one side of the room to the other involved stepping on a book, schematic, gear, or tool. That's what Justice did, hanging his hammer from a hook beside the door and making his way across the room, heedless of the detritus that crunched beneath his boots.

Gray Moor (Justice Maron's Office)

The office of master bulletsmith Justice Maron.

Justice stopped on the far side of a desk and motioned for me to join him. As I did, he swept the schematics off the desk with a hairy forearm, the papers falling to the ground like Jocko's leaves, then set the soul core in the now-cleared space.

"Now look at this," he said. He turned to a shelf behind the desk and pulled out a leather-bound book. The shelf looked strange, and it took me a moment to realize why: in the messy room, it was the *only* thing that was organized. There were a dozen books, each held vertically and pressed against one another by two orbs of veined marble that served as bookends.

Justice set the heavy book on the desk with a *thump*. As he did, a description popped into my vision.

Book of Prophecy

One of only seven copies in existence, this book contains the collected prophecies of the Seer, one of Sirax Sirco's companions and the founder of Winter Ridge. Held as gospel by the group of Winter Ridge students known as the Believers, the Book of Prophecy tells of a renewed war between good and evil and the circumstances under which the Heart of the World will be removed from Toroth-Gol.

"You understand that Toroth-Gol is connected to great magic," Justice said as he riffled through the pages of the book. Although it was upside down, I could see lines of careful script, the slightly raised and textured letters indicative of someone putting pen to paper with high-quality ink. The penmanship was neat but small, the letters squeezed together in even lines. I tried to catch some of the text, but Justice was flipping the pages too quickly.

"You're talking about the Heart of the World?" I asked.

"Yes," Justice said. "Different people are able to harness its magic in different ways. Back when Sirax Sirco walked these lands, he had a friend that history simply calls 'the Seer.' A creature of disturbing contradiction. The histories can't agree whether it was a man or woman, or a human at all, as some say the Seer was a dwarf, and others say they came from elven stock. Have you heard this name before?"

"I don't think so."

"The Seer founded Winter Ridge," Justice said. "We all know that. But the records only agree on two other things: that the Seer channeled prophecies from the Heart of the World, and that the Seer left those prophecies behind in a book. *This* book. This is a direct copy of the original *Book of Prophecy*, which is held in Winter Ridge. Every copy is written by hand, by acolytes of Winter Ridge who memorize the text word for word. Each page is checked by the tower's elders, and if so much as a letter is out of place, they burn the whole page and make the acolyte start over. In this way, the words have been passed down from generation to generation as completely accurate copies of the original."

The scope of the work was mind-boggling. "That must take a very long time."

"Each copy takes nearly two years of daily work," Justice said. "But it's the only way to ensure that inaccuracies don't get introduced to the text over time. This copy here reads like the original, as does every other copy that exists. Here, read this poem."

Justice turned the book around and pushed it toward me. The chapter was called 'The Gardener,' so indicated by the text that appeared in my vision.

The Gardener

He cultivates the fallow fields!
Riotous life from empty husk.
He tills the soil, makes it fecund,
Growing gems amongst the rust.
Boon and plague upon this world:
Tuber, nightshades, berry, drupe.
Eight in total mean the end—
A cut upon the loop.

"I like the bit about the tuber," Spud said. "That sounds like me."

"That's what I'm thinking," Justice said. "You have two, and you have six more to go. And then, a cut upon the loop, like the poem says."

"What?" I said. I flipped the page, hoping for more, but the next page was a poem called 'The Beginning.' *The World was once a lonely place... nothing was that couldn't be... all that was, was empty space... stretching to Eternity...*

"If I'm correct, you were seen long ago by the Seer," Justice said. "I think this poem references you. It means you're going to play a role in the battle to come."

I flipped back to 'The Gardener' and read it again. I wanted to share Justice's enthusiasm, but it didn't make sense.

"I'm not really sure about that," I said. "I guess 'tuber' could refer to Spud, and 'nightshade' could be Perry, but otherwise I don't see how this refers to me. Wouldn't it mention any of my distinguishing features?"

Justice sighed and pulled the book back toward him. "You'd need to read the full book to understand. The point is, with my teachings, you can bring the rest of your arsenal to life. See this bit here? 'Riotous life from empty husks.' Do you know many other people who are running around with talking vegetables made from soul cores?"

"I'm *not* a vegetable," Spud said. "As the poem says, I'm a tuber. A sapient, electromagnetically charged tuber with elemental powers. And technically, Perry isn't a vegetable, either. He's a fruit."

"The appearance of the Gardener portends a battle that will make or break the world," Justice said. "That's why I reacted the way I did when you first came in here. We had a scare a few years ago, when another hunter entered the dungeon with sapient produce, but he died in the castle. When I saw your talking, uh, *tuber*, I suspected you might be the Gardener, but I was hoping we might have another couple hundred years before we faced the apocalypse. Maybe there's still hope."

He opened the book again and flipped through the pages until he apparently found the one he wanted. "Here, look at this," he said as he turned the book back toward me. "Does this make sense to you?"

This poem was a single line. I read the text that appeared in my vision.

The Sword

In a time of confusion, the Gardener will carry a sword from the desert.

"I don't have a sword," I said.

"Wait, isn't the 'Desert Blade' our friend Jocko's nickname?" Perry said. "Could that be what the poem means? The sword from the desert? The Desert Blade? You carried him through the entrance of the tower."

"And you were *definitely* confused while you were doing it," Spud said. "Then again, you're pretty much always confused. Maybe that's what the poem means when it references a time of confusion?"

I winced. "Maybe?"

Justice blanched. "By the Seer," he whispered. I was about to say something, but paused when he lifted the core from the desk and closed his eyes.

"*D'anzachai,*" he said, the word guttural and unfamiliar. Concentration furrowed his brow. As he drew the fingers of his right hand away from the orb, they trailed a glowing blue light, ethereal but at the same time solid and sticky, like tree sap. When he brought his fingers back toward the orb, the sap was reabsorbed.

"Yes," he muttered to himself. "Yes, this would work." He opened his eyes and met my gaze. "Do you know how soul cores are used?" he asked.

"In part," I said. "At some point, a great creature was killed and their soul was trapped in that orb. After that, the soul can be drawn out and placed into another object?"

"Crude, but yes," Justice said. "Each soul has a different weight, which affects the size and quality of the core needed to store it, as well as how much of its original personality and power gets transferred into its new form. That's why you have different grades of soul core: minor, lesser, common, broad, greater, grand, and master."

"So you could fit, say, a rabbit's soul into a minor soul core, and when you pull it out, it would still have the memory of being a rabbit?" I asked. "But if you shoved a human's soul into that same minor core, it might not fit?"

"Yes. You'd lose memory or power during the transfer." Justice held up the core in his hand. "The soul in this core comes from something exceedingly powerful. Exceedingly *dangerous*. Because of the size and quality of the soul core, whatever was placed inside here is guaranteed to have the same personality and power it had during its life."

"Is that something we want to let back out into the world?"

"As long as the transfer is done correctly, it shouldn't be able to act against your intentions. Do you have some sort of vessel? Something that could be imbued with the soul core?"

"What about that eggplant?" Spud said.

I was about to ask him what he was talking about when my eyes fell on a basket that sat on a table to my right. It was filled with food: a hunk of cheese, a crusty loaf of bread, and a large purple eggplant.

"I'm a tuber," Spud continued. "Then you have Perry, who's a nightshade, but that poem mentions night*shades*, plural. Remember the poem? Tuber, nightshades, berry, drupe."

"By botanical definition, an eggplant *is* a berry," Perry added. "Then again, so am I. But an eggplant is also a nightshade, so either of us could be one or the other."

Justice looked from me to the basket of food with an expression that could only be described as horror. "You have a master soul core, one of the most coveted and powerful objects in Toroth-Gol, and you're planning on putting it into an *eggplant?*"

I shrugged. Before Toroth-Gol, I wouldn't have chosen produce as weapons, but I'd seen what Spud and Perry could do, and I was curious about the powers of an eggplant imbued with a soul from a master core. And once again, I remembered the words from the man in my advising session: *If you don't specialize soon, you'll be at a disadvantage in later levels.'*

I've already got two pieces of sapient produce. A third probably makes sense.

"You're the one who gave us the poem," I said to Justice. "Do you want me to fulfill my destiny or not?"

Justice turned green. "Sirco help me," he said, but he plucked the eggplant from the basket.

"What do I have to do?" I asked.

"This class isn't like the others," Justice said. "There's no studying.

No homework. No practice. The test was in acquiring the core. Now that you have it, you need a vessel and the right words."

"The right words?" I asked. "Like, a spell?"

"Yes," Justice said. "The vibrations channel the magic from the Heart of the World into a desired effect. But this is risky business, and it's not something to be taken lightly. The prophecy is clear. If you're determined to go through with this, I'll teach you."

I felt a glimmer of hope. "What are the words?"

20

At first, I didn't know if the spell had worked, because nothing changed.

"Justice?" I asked.

Then I blinked, and Justice was gone. The office wasn't there, either. One moment, I stood before the desk; the next, I was in the center of a rocky clearing ringed by huge boulders. They were ten feet tall, their height augmented by stone slabs laid horizontally across their tops.

"Justice?" I said again. There was no response. "If you're out there, this isn't funny. Can you bring me back to your office, please? Or tell me what's happening?"

Around me were snow-covered peaks. The sky was an ominous gray and the wind howled through the boulders, biting and cold.

"Maybe you didn't say the spell correctly," Spud said from my shoulder. At least he was still with me. "I don't know for sure, but maybe you, like, trapped us *in* the soul core instead of drawing out the entity that it held. Or perhaps you banished us to some frigid realm between realms."

"Why do you sound excited about that?" Perry asked.

"I'm not," Spud said. "Just trying to keep you both from panicking."

An altar sat before us, a stone table carved with the likenesses of writhing serpents and segmented millipedes. As I studied it, the wind picked up, the gusts carrying flakes of peppery snow. Lightning flashed, making me jump, and I had Spud hovering above my hand a split-second later. I pressed my back to the standing stone behind me.

"Uh, Justice?" I called, though I knew he couldn't hear me. "If you're there, we need help!"

My words were snatched away. The howling wind intensified and the lightning grew more frequent, now accompanied by peals of rolling thunder that shook the clearing and made my teeth rattle inside my skull.

Is this supposed to be happening? Something on the other side of the clearing moved, and I raised my arm as I planned my next moves. *Shoot Spud, duck left, put the stones between myself and any attackers. Get ready to pull back Spud or load up Perry, depending on what happens next.*

Another blast of howling wind cut the clearing, this time carrying a curtain of snow that blocked the altar from my view. In a second, we'd gone from flurries to a complete whiteout. But I sensed something in the distant snow. With any luck, a potential attacker would have as much trouble seeing through the storm as I did.

"Who's there?" I called. I moved in a low crouch toward the last place I'd seen another standing stone. My face found it before my hands. "Whoever is out there, show yourself!"

"Come, now," said a voice that cut through the snow, audible over the howling winds. It was low and husky, but feminine. "Put your toys away. There's no need for violence. Not among those who would benefit from each other's power."

The wind and lightning stopped, and the snow stopped falling. I found myself crouching in two inches of snow, some ten feet from where I'd originally been standing. I stood, brushing the snow from my scalp, and stared at the creature that sat atop the altar.

It was an eggplant, its purple skin the same color as the smoke that had now dissipated. I figured it must've had lips, because it'd been talking to me, but they blended against its skin. I could see its eyes. The expression in them was a mix between condescension and amusement, like I was an adorable but muddy dog trying to get into its master's bed.

Xenandor of Kratha, Empress of Pain, Master of the Necromantic Arts, and Maestra of the Seven Exquisite Tortures (Xena)

Xenandor of Kratha was a legendary necromancer known for her incredible power over death, as well as her ability to command armies of the undead. During the height of her power, it was said that she could raise entire cities from the dead and that her magic was so potent it could turn the living into undead thralls with a single word. Yet, her power came at a terrible price, and her soul was forever stained by the horrors she committed in the name of her craft. Xenandor's soul was trapped in a master soul core by Sirax Sirco during the War of Fangs.

By combining esoteric magic, the prophecies of an ancient cult, and one of the most powerful soul cores ever created, you've placed Xenandor's soul into an eggplant.

"You have freed me from my prison, human," Xena said. "For that service, I will not submit you to my wrath. But we have enemies to conquer and I shall need your power."

I pointed my glove at Xena and pulled. She hovered above my palm, spittle flecking her lips as she struggled to get free.

"Unhand me, you fatuous ape!" she screamed.

With my other hand, I spun her to face me. "Happy you're feeling powerful enough to conquer some enemies," I said. "But let's get one thing straight: this is my show. You're on my team."

"Technically, it's *our* team," Spud said. "Maybe even my team. It's called the Spud Squad."

"That's right," I said. "*Our* team. Which you can join when you've proven yourself."

Xena continued to struggle against the magnetism, but she didn't have any arms or legs.

It's a good thing I put her soul into an eggplant and not, say, a fifteen-foot-high robotic killing beast. Justice had said that any entity I freed from a soul core would be bound to my intention, though that wasn't something I wanted to test yet.

Xena hung limply above my palm, turning in slow circles. "You've made a terrible mistake," she hissed. "I will murder you. Oh, how I'll end you!"

I felt sorry for her. Not *too* sorry, as anyone nicknamed "Maestra of the Seven Exquisite Tortures" didn't sound like a nice person, but I knew what it was like to feel helpless. At the same time, it was absolutely critical that I set the tone for our relationship.

I started to say something else, but when I blinked, I found myself standing back in Justice's office. It was as we'd left it, right down to the mess, only now I had a sapient eggplant floating above my hand, and the light had dimmed from the soul core on the desk.

"You did it," Justice whispered. "By the Seer. The end of the world is upon us."

"Slow down," I said. "What are you talking about?"

But Justice pushed me toward the door. "Sorry," he said, our feet crunching over the detritus that littered his floor. "There's another poem in the book that says once the Gardener gains an awareness of his role, the Bulletsmith needs to abandon him. Goodbye, Crow. This is the last time we'll speak to each other."

"You idiots," Xena hissed from my bandolier. "You pathetic peons and bumbling halfwits. You feeble-minded fiends! I'll slice your veins open and use your blood for soup."

I ignored her, as Xena was the lesser of my two problems.

"Come on!" I said. "You'll be the second teacher to abandon me. I need answers, Justice!"

But as I ignored Xena, Justice ignored *me*. He pulled a lever on the wall, and the wooden bar that secured it shut was pulled upward. The door swung toward us.

"Goodbye, Crow," Justice said as he pushed me toward the open doorway. "Goodbye and good luck."

Before I fully knew what was happening, he'd shoved me outside and slammed the door to the machine shop. There was a *bang* as the wooden bar came down on the other side.

I stared at the closed door. *And yet again, more questions than answers.*

I sighed as I walked to the podium and punched in the code for base housing. I didn't have anything else to do for the day, so I figured it'd be nice to have a private place to speak with Xena.

"I *guess* that could've gone worse," I said. "At least you're with us, Xena. Can you tell us about your powers? Spud can light himself on fire, and Perry can spit acid. I'm wondering what you can do."

"I'm also handsome," Spud said. "A king in the art of seduction."

My words only caused Xena to increase her vitriol. "You miserable miscreants! You witless wretches. Oh, how the blood will flow when I'm done with you."

Again, I sighed. If Xena was half as powerful as Justice had told me, she'd be a tremendous asset. But nothing I said worked to sway the mouthy eggplant, and she continued yelling as I pushed into our room.

"I'll burn your hair and sprinkle the ashes in my whiskey. I'll skin you alive and use your skin for carpets in a house made from your bones!"

"That whiskey would taste terrible," Spud said.

"And I don't think Crow's bones would make a big house," Perry mumbled. "Unless you were using it as a house for something small. Rodents, maybe."

21

After a strange and bumpy start, my life at Dungeon School fell into a rhythm. Every day, I meditated, though I didn't receive any answers from the universe. I spent most of my time in the training rooms learning from Jocko, Devora, Feng, or sometimes even random hunters I found honing their skills. As the weeks passed, I became a more confident fighter, capable of throwing solid punches and kicks and wielding a variety of weapons, including swords, shields, and staves. I learned how to anticipate attacks, which came slowly and resulted in several bruises before the moves lodged themselves in my muscle memory and dodging became instinct.

One evening, I came back to our room and found Jocko entertaining two guests. The first was a man with purple hands, which meant he'd been sent into Toroth-Gol for slavery. He wore a skirt of brown leather and sheepskin-lined boots that came to just below his knee. A tribal tattoo ran up his thigh from the top of his left boot to under the skirt. Around his neck, he wore a leather girdle decorated with the pale claws of some strange beast, and he had on a helmet that looked to be the skull of a bull. Three burlap bags hung from his belt; I wouldn't have been surprised to find out that they contained something weird, like dead birds.

It was an altogether creepy get-up, and he looked like he belonged in Winter Ridge more than Gray Moor, but I didn't know anything about his capabilities, and his description wasn't forthcoming.

Mind Witch (Adam)

?

Beside Adam sat a woman who also had purple hands. Although she wasn't reptilian, something about her reminded me of Geeta. She had black leather pants with buckles that held a baton strapped to her outer thigh. She also had a cape to match the pants, and she wore a black cowl that stopped above her eyes. Most striking were her nails, which extended an inch past her fingertips and were the rich scarlet of the poppies that grew in the flower beds at the entrance to the Pleasure Gardens.

Night Stalker (Lyra)

In the Nightlands, slavery is just as illegal as it is in the Empire. But that doesn't stop ambitious entrepreneurs from trying their luck. Born to a powerful merchant family in Kelfraito, Lyra used her family's caravans to move more than spices and demon hide. She was captured in a raid off Aramel and sentenced to Toroth-Gol for slavery.

"Crow!" Jocko said cheerfully. He was the only one smiling. The other two watched me with narrowed eyes. "Welcome back, *pacho*. I was telling Adam about the Endless Cup of Coffee we found."

The Endless Cup of Coffee was one of the many treasures we'd removed from Sirax Sirco's Personal Armory.

"I see," I said. "And why are you doing that?"

"Adam was addicted to coffee before he came into Toroth-Gol," Jocko said. "He's got debilitating headaches! This should help him."

"I'd be most appreciative," Adam said. His voice was monotone, so he didn't sound appreciative at all. "Been trying to get my fix since I got down here."

Lyra's eyes darted toward my bandolier. "Are those sapient?" she asked. "Did you imbue them with soul cores?"

"You're mistaken," I said, though I looked like a liar when Xena yelled out: "What is this, the parade of pathetics? More grist for the mill, I suppose."

We still weren't on good terms.

Lyra looked curiously at Xena. "Is that for sale?" she asked. "Or would you be willing to trade it? I've been looking to experiment with a sapient weapon for one of my classes."

"It's *not* for sale," I said. I turned to Jocko. "Hey man, can I talk to you for a minute?"

"Ah, sure," he said. "Let me finish up." He shrugged apologetically at Adam. "Sorry about that, *pacho*," he said. "Roommates! Where the rent is split, but the bathroom isn't." When no one laughed, Jocko cleared his throat and said, "Are we doing this deal?"

"Yes," Adam said without taking his eyes off me. He held a small square of fabric toward Jocko, and the Grass King made it disappear into his Inventory before I could read the description. In return, he passed Adam the Endless Cup of Coffee.

"A pleasure doing business," Jocko said. He smiled like this wasn't a terribly awkward interaction. "Until next time!"

He ushered Adam and Lyra out the door, and I felt a palpable sense of relief when it shut behind them.

"What was that?" I asked. "Why were those people in our room?"

Jocko raised an eyebrow at me. "You told us to do what we wanted with all the items we didn't want," he said. "I traded Adam the Endless Cup of Coffee for something called the Patch of Cleansing. Once per day, it automatically cleans any piece of clothing that it's touching. Thought it might be useful for you, actually."

"He's saying you stink, *pacho*," Spud said.

Jocko shrugged. "But that's neither here nor there," he said.

"I don't want slavers in our room," I said. "Do I really need to say that?"

Jocko blinked at me. "You want the truth? I invited him because of what they are: not nice people, *pacho*. Did you notice how nothing showed up about Adam when you looked at him? I think that's an item, and I thought it'd be helpful. We could've bartered for it, or bought it, but I'd rather pry it from his cold, dead hands. So I invited him here with the hopes that he'd see our stash and try to rob us. The eggplant spoke up at just the right time! That was icing on the cake. They won't be able to help themselves, now. I saw Adam do something funny to our door, and when they break in here to rob us, we'll kill them."

I sighed. "Okay, Jocko," I said. "Have fun with that. I don't want to argue."

"Sorry, *pacho?* I did this for us. We need an item they have, and if they attack us and we take it, it'll count as self-defense. It's all part of my plan."

"*Your* plan," I said. "What about me? I'm tired of feeling like I don't know what's going on."

When Jocko didn't respond, I walked into my room and closed the door behind me. Only once I got there did I realize I had no idea what to do next.

"Crow?" Jocko said from outside my door. "I'm sorry, *pacho*. I should've talked to you first. Can we start over?"

"I'll meet you on the field of battle," Xena hissed. "I'll kill all of you."

I sank to the ground and rested my back against the bed. Then I undid my bandolier, set it on the ground beside me, and closed my eyes.

I was exhausted.

"I see you looking at me, tomato boy," Xena said. "Don't even think about it. I'd turn you into sauce."

I heard a quiet *eek* I guessed was Perry.

"Do *not* talk to Perry like that," Spud said. "Don't you dare. Only I get to make fun of Twinkletoes Magnesis IV."

Xena cackled cruelly. "Isn't that precious! The little potato is standing up for the tomato. You want a slap fight, you can both come at me. Hit me at the same time, for all I care. But you're gonna look silly when I make a salad from your skins."

I cracked one eye and saw Xena glaring at me.

"You have something to say, big man?" she said as she narrowed her eyes at me. "Come at me, then. In a fair fight, I'd burst your stomach like a balloon and hang you with your own intestines."

Maybe it was because I was already on edge, but I'd had *enough*. I reached down and tore a length of fabric from the cuff of my pants. It was so worn and frayed that it ripped easily. Then, I reached into my Inventory and drew out the rope I'd gotten from Feng.

"Perry, cut me off a foot of that, please," I said as I laid the rope on the ground beside him.

"With pleasure," Perry said. He gagged and acid spilled from his mouth, cleanly eating through the rope and separating a foot-long strand from the larger coil. I lifted the smaller segment and put the rest back into my Inventory.

"Spud, if you'd fix the frayed end for me?" I said.

"Of course, my athletic prince," Spud said as he burst into flame. "*Yearrrrrgh!* Burns! So! Good!"

I held the rope toward him, and flames caught the loose threads, fusing them together. After another moment, I blew on the smoldering end, then set the rope down.

Xena glared at me. "What are you doing? You're not making something to hurt me, are you?"

I didn't answer. With my thumbnail, I poked two holes through the length of cloth, one on each side. Once that was done, I threaded the rope through the holes. Then, I set the rope and the cloth on the ground and looked at Xena.

The eggplant must've seen something in my eyes that she didn't like, because she started rolling away.

Where does she think she's going? I pointed my glove at her and pulled, which didn't do anything. I turned on my battery pack, which started with a hum, and tried again. This time, she flew into my hand.

"Get off me!" she screamed, fighting against my grip. "You're not fit to be *near* me, you great ox! You disgusting lummox! I'll revel in eating your *brains!*"

But like I said, I'd had enough. "Stop it," I said. "Stop it right now. I understand you might not be entirely happy, and that you've probably experienced some trauma in having your soul placed into a gem and then transferred to an eggplant. I won't demean your experience by pretending to know how you're feeling. But if you can't participate in the Spud Squad, or keep your mouth shut when it matters, I need to take more drastic measures. This is your last chance. Can you be a team player?"

She *bit* me, which was pretty much all the answer I needed.

"Oh no she *didn't*," Spud said. "That was the *wrong* move, princess."

I was done trying to reason with Xena. From the way she talked, I could tell she was a bully, but I knew how to handle bullies. I'd been doing it all my life. Without another word, I forced the length of cloth into her mouth. Then I pulled on each end of the rope and tied it tightly behind her.

"*Mhm!*" she grunted through the makeshift gag. "*Mhmgooahkilla!*"

I didn't understand what she was trying to say, but I could guess, and it wasn't nice. The gag muffled the sound of her cries, though it didn't stop them completely. For that, I needed to take another step.

"Last, *last* chance," I said.

Even with the gag, she snapped at me, hate visible in her bright eyes.

I sighed as I removed a jar of pickle juice from my Inventory. I popped the lid, my eyes watering the moment they were hit by acidic fumes.

"Um, Crow?" Perry said. "You're not gonna kill her, are you?"

I shook my head. Although I wanted to teach Xena a lesson, I wouldn't kill her. While I was sure she'd have no qualms drowning *me* in a jar of brine, there was clearly a wide gulf between what each of us saw as morally appropriate. For the sake of my soul, I wanted to keep it that way.

With both hands, I lifted the jar to my lips. *For old times' sake.* I took a sip. Then, I poured the remaining liquid into the nearby vase. I'd get rid of it later. The vase was about the size of the jar, so the juice filled it to the brim, but it left me with an empty jar. When all the liquid was gone, I dropped the screaming Xena through the top and closed the lid. Only then did I finally cease to hear her screams.

For the first time since I'd summoned Xena, there was quiet, joyful silence.

Spud, Perry, and I sat there, staring at the jar. Finally, Spud said, "You know, for a guy who loves to hear myself talk, sometimes it's nice not to hear anything at all."

"Amen to that," Perry said.

2 2

With the room finally silent, I sat on the floor with my back to the bed and my legs crossed in front of me. I wasn't happy about what I'd done. Was it cruel? Probably. But was it necessary? Absolutely.

"Okay, guys," I said, intentionally trying not to look at the jar that contained Xena, which I'd pushed into a corner. "I didn't do that for fun. I need *quiet*. Can you give me half an hour?"

"You got it, *pacho*," Spud said. "Oh, we're mad at Jocko right now, aren't we? Sorry, Crow. Quiet. You got it."

He stopped talking and I closed my eyes. *You got this. Step one, done. Now you need to focus on the breath. Focus on the truth, whatever that means.*

I breathed slowly: *in, two, three, four. Out, two, three, four.* The action was strangely calming to me. When I'd completed one cycle of the breath, I repeated the process. *In, two, three, four. Out, two, three, four.* I did it again. And again. When my mind started to wander, I brought my attention back to my breath.

Focus. In, out. In, out. What did I want to understand? I returned to my original question: *What do I need to reach the Heart of the World?* My mind crept away, so I brought my attention back to my breathing.

In, out. In, out. What do I need to reach the Heart of the World?

As I breathed, the question held in my mind as tentatively as the last wisps of a dream before full wakefulness, I offered the universe a truth. It came to me unbidden, just like my question.

I'm mad at Jocko, and I hate that he's manipulative, but I still want to trust him, because that piece of him reminds me of my father, who is the strongest and most manipulative person I know.

It was that last bit that echoed through my mind like words shouted into a canyon.

Your father is the most manipulative person you know.

There was a *ding*, like someone had just struck a chime, and I found myself staring down a long corridor. Spud and Perry were nowhere to be seen. The floor of the corridor was made of cobblestone, and the walls contained stained-glass windows, six on each side. The window to my right showed a huge serpent rising from some type of circular well, while the one to my left was of a monstrous spider.

"By the Dregs!" I said aloud. "Where am I?"

I blinked, but still found myself in the corridor. As I looked more closely at the windows, I realized the monstrosities in both scenes were under attack. The snake was shying away from a floating woman with glowing hands outstretched, long brown hair streaming behind and around her, while the spider appeared to be running toward distant cliffs at the head of an angry army. Light coming through the windows cast brilliant, multi-colored shapes on the floor.

Hallway of the Final Ascension

This hallway features stained-glass windows made by master artisan Qu'wan Li. The windows show Alkastone's twelve generals as they were vanquished by the forces of man.

Did the power I learned in Wisdom just work? Because what else could this be? And then, with a sense of giddiness: *I wanted to know what I needed to reach the Heart of the World, and this must be the answer!*

In my excitement, I attempted to step forward, though my body wouldn't respond. I forced myself to take slow, steady breaths.

So I'm a passenger here. Interestingly enough, when I glanced up and to the right, I saw a timer, which would make sense if the dungeon was presenting the same thing to each hunter.

My view shifted. Whoever's body I inhabited approached the start of the multi-colored path. Before the first splotch of color, I stopped, and an axe swung down from a gap in the wall before the first window, slicing through the air across the corridor an inch in front of my nose.

Gah! That had been *close*.

I took a deep breath. *This is only a vision. And if it weren't, there's nothing you can do. You're along for the ride.*

Still, it was little consolation as the body I inhabited stepped forward, placing one toe on a green triangle formed by the light that came through the windows.

Swinging axe before the colored cobblestones, I thought, committing the path to memory. *Then step on the green triangle. Got it!* My host hesitated, waiting for a second axe to drop the other way, then leapt forward and landed with their opposite foot on a green rectangle. Again, I walked through the directions in my head: *pause, axe, then green triangle to green rectangle. Easily done.*

But it wasn't easy. Despite my athleticism, I'm sure I would've fallen. The person whose body I inhabited not only stuck the landing, but ducked as something—an arrow, maybe—shot through the space above our head. It passed by so closely I felt the displaced air.

If only I could learn to move like that!

My host leaned forward and placed one hand on another green rectangle, then continued moving down the hallway at a crawl. Halfway through the corridor, the body I inhabited pressed down with a palm against a green circle and leaned against one side of the corridor. I held my breath as a spinning buzz saw roared past, and then my host continued down the corridor's length.

Green again, I thought as they placed a hand on a green oval. Although the windows cast many multi-colored shapes on the cobblestones, the body I inhabited only touched the ones where the green light fell. I felt that if I touched a stone of another color, something *bad* would happen. I didn't know what it was, and there was no way I should've known it, but I did. I knew it on instinct, the way one sometimes knows things in dreams.

My host continued crawling down the hallway, and I memorized our movements as I silently prayed that we wouldn't touch an incorrect color. Because just as I knew that I should only step on the cobblestones touched by green light, I got a sense that, vision or not, touching a stone *not* illuminated by green light would hurt me. Not only the body I inhabited, but *me*, the passenger along for the ride.

Please be safe, please be safe, please be safe. I needn't have worried. A few more acrobatic dodges brought us to ten square feet of safety beyond the light of the stained-glass windows.

My host straightened, and I found myself staring at an ornate door.

Treasure Door — Locked

Solve the riddle of this door to reveal the room beyond.

The door was circular and made from greenish-gray stone. At various points along its surface were discs the size of salad plates, each etched with one of the monsters depicted in the windows. There were twelve discs, as well as a thirteenth that didn't feature a monster, but a red, rectangular gemstone embedded in its face.

The Heart of the World, I thought as my host reached toward it, though this was clearly only a representation. When my hand reached the plate, I grasped its edge and slid it toward the center of the door. The plate moved smoothly across its surface as if sliding along a hidden track.

Once the plate with the gem was in the center of the door, the body I inhabited set about rearranging the other plates. They formed a wide circle around the center, like spokes on a wheel or the numbers of a clock. At twelve o'clock went a plate with a monster that looked like a dragon, and at one o'clock I put one with the etching of a soldier in plate-mail armor who carried a club over one shoulder.

Then there was the serpent from the first stained-glass window, as well as the giant spider; a tree-like creature with branches for arms and a loincloth around its waist; and a skinny man with his entire face covered in shadow except for a pair of fangs. There was a woman with snakes for hair; a grinning boulder that looked as if it was releasing gas through craters that pitted its surface; and a cheerful man with pointed ears, a bulbous nose, and a top hat.

The plates at nine o'clock, ten o'clock, and eleven o'clock showed a hooded priestess wearing the mask of a human skull, a manticore, and a humanoid with biceps bulging above each of their four arms.

Although the plates seemed harmless enough, the etchings gave me the creeps. Simply looking at them was enough to turn my stomach and raise goosebumps on my arms.

These creatures are evil. My host arranged the last of the plates. Again, it was more of a feeling than anything else, but I knew it was true. *I hope I never have to meet them.*

Still, I committed the location of each plate to memory. When all of them were in place, my host tapped the gem at the door's center. Again, I got the feeling that if any of the plates had been misaligned, something terrible would've happened. But the door rolled soundlessly to one side.

My host stepped forward.

Behind the circular door was a cave the size of the Stadia. Although it should've been pitch black within, the cave was lit by a hundred thousand stars, which clung to the ceiling overhead. There was a shallow lake in the center of the room, as well as the room's centerpiece: two pillars that stood adjacent to a throne, which rose some hundred feet into the air. Sitting on the throne was a creature that must've been sixty feet tall. Despite its size, it looked human—or like it had been at one point. Now, its skin was a lifeless gray, and the hem of its faded orange skirt was ripped and torn. It sat with its hands in its lap, its feet hanging over an arched doorway leading into a room beneath the throne, and the sightless sockets that had once held eyes staring past me.

Deceased Jewel Guardian (Petrona)

Loot? Yes or No.

The option to loot the jewel guardian was grayed out. That made sense, since I wasn't the one doing the looting. But several other thoughts popped into my mind.

One: *the Heart of the World is supposed to be a jewel, and I bet it's inside that room beneath the throne.*

And two: *that thing is* definitely *going to come alive and fight me.*

I was definitely incorrect on the second point. It wasn't the *deceased* jewel guardian that stood to take my head from my shoulders, but one that was very much alive. This one looked like some type of dragon; it crawled around the side of the throne, its pale pink scales covered in lichen. It resembled a reptilian, though it must've been forty feet long from the top of its head to its feet. It moved with a sound like rustling paper.

Jewel Guardian (Zorlan)

The form of the jewel guardians varies greatly, but Zorlan looks like a giant crocodilian. Brought to Toroth-Gol from a swamp deep in the Nightlands, Zorlan was instilled with magic that grew him to massive proportions and gave him the desire to protect the Heart of the World with his life. Within his mouth are teeth made from diamonds, rubies, and emeralds, though few are foolish enough to try to take them.

On the far side of the room, the jewel guardian slid into the shallow lake with barely a ripple. It moved toward me with sinuous grace, and only its snout, eyes, and the ridge of its back were visible above the surface of the water.

I snapped out of my meditation so suddenly that I yelped and fell backward. My head struck the bed behind me with an audible *thud*.

"Ow!" I leaned forward and rubbed a hand along the back of my skull. No blood, but I'd probably have a bruise. I winced as my fingers brushed against a tender spot.

"What is it?" Spud said from the ground in front of me. His eyes were wide and the concern in his voice was obvious. "Was it a tomato-less future ruled by enemies of our species who use the extreme spiritual power of poor potatoes to fuel their nefarious rituals?" He gasped, his eyes widening farther. "Say it ain't so, Crow!"

"No, Spud, I..."

I trailed off, unsure how to describe what I'd seen. Upon reflection, the answer was obvious, and now I knew why Gatekeeper Valentine had encouraged me to take that course with Mother Baganza.

"I should've been more specific," I said. "I asked the universe what I needed to reach the Heart of the World, though I should've asked what I needed to know that could help me right *now*. But assuming we survive to the tenth level of the dungeon, I know how to run the obstacle course that will lead us to the Heart of the World."

Spud brightened, all traces of concern slipping from his face. "That's cool, I guess," he said. "Though I was hoping for what I said. It would've made a great movie."

Across the room, Xena sat in the pickle jar. Tears glistened on her cheeks. I still didn't know whether there was any truth to Justice's book, but if I was committed to reaching that final room, I'd need to have as much ammunition as possible. Besides, where was I going? I still didn't want to talk to Jocko, and my room was dark.

It's night. I checked my timer. *I was in that trance for a full hour. Guess I missed dinner.*

That was fine, because I wasn't hungry.

I walked over to the jar and unscrewed the lid. "Hey," I said as I turned the jar over. Xena plopped out and I removed the makeshift gag. "I'm sorry about that. I couldn't think while you were yelling. Are you okay?"

I thought Xena might start yelling again. In fact, I was ready to put her back in the jar. But to my surprise, she simply shook her head.

"You don't know what it's like," she sniffled. "I used to be powerful. And now I'm this!"

The exclamation caused a wave of tears to erupt from her. The thing was, I *did* understand. For a decade, I'd fought to make something of myself, only to have everything I'd gained torn away from me.

I understand better than you think. Which you'd know if you'd bothered to communicate. I didn't say anything. It wouldn't have been helpful, and I knew Xena wasn't done.

"I didn't want all those titles," she said. "Empress of Pain, Master of the Necromantic Arts, and Maestra of the Seven Exquisite Tortures. When the War of Fangs broke out, I was a middling historian at a school for second-born children about two hundred miles south of here. Kratha, it was called. The Kratha Institute for Historical Research. I was pursuing an independent study in the history of necromancy. It wasn't even a course in practical applications! Just an academic exercise. One day, I was returning a book to the library in town and the predators razed the school. Burned it to the ground. Most people died, but I hid in the woods and they didn't find me. I survived."

She hiccuped.

If this is an act, it's a really good one. But still, I didn't say anything.

"I only wanted to help my friends!" she wailed. "I used the knowledge I'd gained from my research to bring them back. Turns out, I had a knack for it. I hid with the prey, but when they found out what I could do, they wouldn't let me within a hundred yards of their settlements. And I couldn't leave my friends. So I returned to the ashes of the school and lived my life. The war was all around me, and I didn't want it getting any closer, so I started the rumor of 'Xenandor of Kratha.' It kept both the prey *and* the predators off my back. Can you blame me for actually wanting to defend myself?"

It was a rhetorical question, but Spud didn't seem to get that. "No," he said. "If what you're saying is true, I would've made the same decision."

Xena looked at him like she was going to bite his head off, then laughed and hiccuped at the same time. A bubble of snot blew out of her nose.

"Oh my gosh," she said. "That's so embarrassing. I'm sorry."

"It's fine," I said. I pulled a lamprey hide out of my Inventory and held it out for her before remembering she didn't have hands. "Here," I said. "Blow your nose into this."

She blew while I held the hide. *Have we broken through? Just like that?* But maybe that was all it took, really. She'd been scared and afraid, and had needed some time to cool off.

"Where was I?" Xena said. "Oh yeah. After a time, I got deeper into the necromantic arts. Eventually, I *became* the rumor I'd started for myself. That worked in my favor until the prey won the War of Fangs and set about clearing the woods of monsters. I was captured, my friends put back into the ground. Sirax Sirco himself ripped my soul from my body and shoved it into a gem. That's where I stayed until you found me and placed my body into this. I'm not a bad person. Really. Pretending to be evil was just a habit I learned to protect myself."

At that, I couldn't help but offer a grim smile. *How many times have I had the same thought? Maybe we're not so different after all.*

I extended a hand toward Xena. She flinched, but I didn't pull back.

"I believe you," I said softly. "I'm sorry for what you went through."

Xena looked up at me, her cheeks glistening. "And you?" she said. "What's your story?"

I laughed. "Me? You don't want to hear about it."

"I do," Xena said. "Please. It would help me feel less alone."

I was about to argue with her when Spud interrupted. "You know, now that Xena mentions it, you've never told us your story, Crow," he said. "All Perry knows about his past is that he grew up on a farm, and I've talked about Potato Hell, which is about as much as I can recall from mine. But you? I don't even know your real name."

"It's Nathaniel," I said.

"*What?*" Spud said. "*Nathaniel?*"

"I think it would be good for the team if you shared," Perry said quietly.

"If you don't share, I'll start screaming and never stop," Spud said. He burst into flame. "Ohhhh baby!" he shouted. "*Agh!* That burns! *Arghhhhhh!*"

"All right! Stop that! Just give me a second, okay?"

I closed my eyes. *Am I about to do this?* I didn't like talking about my history. When I opened my eyes, all three pieces of sapient produce were staring at me, each patiently waiting to hear my story.

I guess we're doing this. Here goes nothing.

"I can't remember my childhood," I said. "That makes me similar to you, Spud. And to you, Perry. I must've had parents, but I can't recall them. When I think about that time, I just get nothing. In my earliest memories, I'm working in a warehouse in a part of Steel City called the Dregs. I lived in a tenement with a bunch of other orphans, and I was big for my age, so the overseers made me run scrap metal from one side of the warehouse to the other."

I paused as the memories I could recall threatened to overwhelm me. After a moment, when no one interrupted, I said, "In the Dregs, most orphans looked forward to two things: static and Empire Day. Static was a drug handed out by the overseers as a reward for hard work or good behavior. From what I saw, it made people feel good. At least, it did for a little while. If you've never seen a friend going through static withdrawal, it's a horror I wouldn't wish on my worst enemy. On the other hand, Empire Day was something everyone enjoyed. If your warehouse hit your annual quota, the overseers gave you the day off to watch the screens."

I ran a hand over my head. "Empire Day was the day before the Hunt started. There was always a big lightball match. In the evenings, nobles would come down from the highest level of the city and select new workers for their households. It might sound silly, but it was my dream to get chosen. One year, I was. Sal Valentine brought me to his mansion in Gomindor. After that, my entire terrible childhood had meaning, because it was the precursor to meeting Sal. To him, I wasn't a servant, but a son. In the years that followed, he trained me to become a lightball player, and I might've been the greatest ever until I was accused of treason and sentenced to Toroth-Gol. And that's it. That's my sad story. Everyone happy?"

"I'm sorry for what you went through," Xena said. "Nobody should be falsely accused of a crime."

An image of Sal Valentine flashed in my mind. I saw him as he'd looked on the evening he'd found me in the Salvador Valentine Center for Athletics, standing in the doorway that led to the practice field and leaning casually on his duck-head cane. I experienced a pang of sadness as I remembered how he'd manipulated me.

"I was scared of helping you before, so I didn't reveal my power," Xena said. "I can bring one creature back from the dead and control it. If the offer still stands, I'd like to contribute to the Spud Squad."

That power sounded *awesome*. "Yeah," I said. "We'll practice in the morning. But for now, welcome to the team."

23

That night, I had a dream about my father.

Not my real father; I didn't know him. My surrogate. Sal Valentine. The man who'd changed my life.

In the dream, I stood before the desk in his office. He sat on the other side. Behind him stood a skeleton clock made from marble and gold. It ticked steadily. In hindsight, the constantly changing numbers should've alerted me that I was dreaming, though I didn't find them strange at the time.

"I'm sorry I got you mixed up in all this," my father said. "But you're a brave boy. A strong boy. I know you can do this."

"Do *what?*" I asked. "Whatever you think I'm supposed to do, I don't think I can."

"Oh? Then maybe I don't know you as well as I thought." Sal reached up and grabbed a strange black tab beneath his hairline. "Or maybe you don't know *me.*"

All at once, the dream became a nightmare. Sal pulled on the tab, and his face fell apart in two pieces, revealing it as a mask. Jocko was beneath it.

Jocko had been wearing my father's face.

"Hey, *pacho*," he said, grinning at me. "Do you trust me yet? Do you, Crow? Crow? Crow? Crow!"

I awoke to Spud whispering furiously in my ear.

"Come on, Crow! Crow! Get up, buddy. Crow!"

"Huh?" I said, coming fully awake. "What time is it?"

"*Shhh*," Spud hissed. "Xena thinks there are people in the outer room."

"I don't *think* anything," Xena replied. "I know it. Can't you hear them?"

I listened. Jocko's snores were audible even through two closed doors. Then, something else: the unmistakable sound of whispering.

There are *people in the outside room.*

I slipped from the bed and flipped on my battery pack. I pulled Spud into my hand and crouched inside the door.

"Good job, buddy," I whispered, even as my mind went through different plans.

Should I open it slowly? Kick straight through the door and come in with guns blazing? Or is there a reasonable explanation for this? Maybe Jocko is playing host again?

"Crow, watch out!" Xena yelled.

Her warning came too late. Before I could move, the door exploded inward, ripping away my cover. A hand flashed toward my face, and a crimson nail drew a burning line down my cheek.

I recognize those nails. Lyra.

"Sorry about this, Crow," Lyra said. She stood before me, her eyes hooded by the cowl she'd worn the last time I'd seen her. A sad smile was plastered on her face. "It's a dog-eat-dog world out there. Adam and I want more than an Endless Cup of Coffee." She held her hands before her, staring appreciatively at her nails. "Paralytic venom on the nails. That's about to come in handy."

I would've reached for her but I could only move my eyes. Inwardly, I groaned.

Jocko told you they were coming, and they still got the drop on you. Great.

My eyes flicked to Adam. Lyra's partner stood on the far side of the table, the dim light reflecting off his strange helm.

"Come on, Lyra," he whispered. "Stop fooling around. Let's get what we want and go."

Spud, who still hovered above my glove, chose that moment to try and scream. Lyra must've been expecting it. Almost quicker than thought, she drew a fingernail across him as well.

"Make one wrong move, and I'll kill your friends." She wasn't talking to me or Spud but to someone behind us.

Xena. Or Perry.

I wanted to tell them to attack because Lyra would kill us anyway, but no sound came out.

Lyra wiggled her fingers in front of my face. "This is where that venom is going to come in handy. What I'm about to do will hurt. Luckily, you won't be able to scream."

She plunged her hand through my chest. I couldn't feel the pain of punctured flesh, just the cold, invasive sensation of her hand inside my Inventory.

And the worst part? Lyra had been right. I couldn't scream.

As quickly as the pain had appeared, it was gone.

"Look at this!" Lyra whispered. She clutched the Flameheart, the item I'd looted from Sor'kodich.

"Come on," Adam hissed nervously. "Let's go already! You don't want to wake the other one. I've seen him train."

Lyra pocketed the Flameheart, and her hand returned to my chest.

"Now, where were we?"

From behind her, Adam made a strange noise. A blade sprouted from his stomach. He gasped and coughed, black blood leaking down his chin, and then he stumbled backward through a storm of floating leaves.

To Lyra's credit, she reacted more quickly than I would've thought possible. One moment, she had her hand inside my chest; then, her baton was in her hand, extending even as she whirled to parry the blade that came for her neck. She snarled like a wild beast, swiping at

Jocko with the fingernails of her left hand, but the Grass King disappeared in another spray of leaves.

"You broke into the wrong room, *pacho*!" Jocko yelled. "Now we get to kill you and loot your stuff!"

"Over my dead body," Lyra hissed.

"I'm planning on it!"

Jocko lunged forward, the point of his sword leading his outstretched arm. It was a beautiful strike, quick as a viper, and effective. This time, he passed Lyra's defenses before she could bat him aside.

"Gotcha," he said. However, Lyra must've had some skill that allowed her to partially disassociate because his blade met no resistance as it continued through her body. It skittered along the wall behind her and put him off balance, leaving him open to an attack.

The expression on Jocko's face told me he'd realized his mistake. All Lyra needed to do was lift her left hand and her poison fingernails would easily brush his cheek.

But as she lifted her arm, Adam caught it.

Adam? A moment before, Jocko had stabbed him through the stomach. Now, he seemed very much alive—and trying to help Jocko. A purple glow surrounded him.

With his free hand, the glowing Adam reached into one of the pouches at his waist and brought out a handful of sparkling silver dust, which he blew into Lyra's face. She screamed and stumbled backward, her hands clawing at her eyes.

Blinding Powder

Made from a potent mix of crushed minerals, caustic salts, and finely ground peppers, blinding powder was engineered to irritate and inflame the eyes of anyone exposed to it. The effects are instantaneous.

"What are you doing, Adam?" Lyra yelled. "I thought we were on the same team! I thought you were *dead*!"

That's when it clicked.

What had Xena said to me after I pulled her out of the pickle jar? She told me she could bring one creature back from the dead and control it. That's why Adam is glowing. Xena is using her power on him!

The resurrected Adam—guided by Xena's will—dipped his hand into the second pouch at his waist. This time, he emerged with a handful of sparkling red powder. He blew it toward me.

Curing Powder

Curing powder eliminates any ailment from those who inhale it. The effects are instantaneous.

I could move again. So could Spud. His body exploded in flame as he opened his mouth and screamed, *"Arghhh!* In the name of all that's crispy! Kill her, Perry! Kill her!"

Lyra's back hit the wall behind her and she slid to a seat, her hands still grasping at her eyes. Perry rolled through my legs, stopping in front of her shins.

"Those are my friends!" he shouted. "Nobody hurts them on my watch! I want... *blargh!*"

Acid sprayed from his mouth and settled over Lyra's legs. It hissed like oil in a hot pan and Lyra's screams reached a new octave.

I can't imagine that's any worse than having someone pull items out of your Inventory, I thought, shivering at the memory of her fingers reaching into my chest. Still, I was about to tell Xena to make Adam blow his curing powder on Lyra when Jocko surged forward.

His blade took Lyra through the heart.

It was like someone had turned her off. She gave one final spasm and died, her screams cutting off abruptly.

Deceased Human

Loot? Yes or No.

I felt sick. I turned off Spud's flames and released my magnetism, causing his warm body to drop into my hand.

"I love it when a plan comes together, eh *pacho?*" Jocko said. He yanked his sword from Lyra's body and wiped the blade on the dead woman's pant leg. "She's lucky I didn't use Severance and claim her immortal soul. That's got to be good karma. But she did attack us in cold blood, so let's see what she had." He started to read through her loot. "There are a few schematics and a bunch of crafting materials. We'll have to get those to Brynn the next time we see her. She doesn't have any marks, but there's an IOU for over five hundred thousand, which it says we can turn in at any outpost of Bain and Harding. I think that's a bank?"

As Jocko continued reading, I went down on a knee and held my free hand to Perry.

"You okay?" I asked him as he jumped into my hand.

"I think so," he said. "I'm sorry I didn't realize what was happening sooner. I should've done a better job to protect you guys!"

"You did great," I said. "I don't like that you had to do that. But you were really brave."

"You looked awesome out there, Twinkletoes," Spud said. "I hate to admit it, but it's true."

I gestured at the glowing Adam. "Let him go," I said to Xena.

The eggplant stared up at me. "You sure? Another pair of hands could be an asset."

I shook my head. After Jocko had stabbed Lyra, I'd seen something in his eyes I hadn't liked. Something predatory. A piece of Jocko had *enjoyed* the killing. Maybe he'd been born like that, or perhaps it was something he'd learned. I wasn't sure, but I knew that power was intoxicating. If I didn't control myself, I'd wind up with that gleam in my eye, too.

"I'm sure," I said. The glow around Adam disappeared, and he dropped like a marionette whose strings had been cut.

Deceased Human

Loot? Yes or No.

"And onto the next one," Jocko said, moving to stand over Adam's body. "Lyra had good stuff, *pacho*. But if you remember, it was Adam's item that made me set this trap in the first place. You know which item I'm talking about? The one that made his description appear as a question mark? Let's grab that."

He started humming as he sorted through Adam's loot. "Hmm," he said. "It's not here." He smiled sheepishly at me. "You know what? Maybe that skill didn't come from an item after all."

24

Several hours later, I awoke to the sound of someone pounding on my door. Not the inner door that led into my room, but the outer one that opened to the hallway.

What now? I thought as I swung my legs over the side of the bed. Once upright, I flipped on my battery pack and pulled Spud toward me.

"Huh?" he mumbled sleepily as he smacked into my palm. "Wazzup?"

"Look alive," I said. "Someone is banging on the door. I want to make sure they're not trying to kill us."

I stood, blinking the sleep from my eyes, and crept toward the door. Xena's low voice nearly made me pee myself.

"The person at the door isn't trying to kill you," she said from where she sat in the shadows in the corner of the room. "They've come to warn you about the killers."

Outside, the banging grew increasingly frantic.

"Coming!" I yelled. I didn't care if I woke Jocko. If what Xena had said was true, I needed him awake.

I exited my room. Jocko was already up. He stood beside the front door, one hand on the knob, ready to throw it open.

Of course he's ready.

"Xena says it's a friend," I whispered. Jocko shrugged. To him, it didn't matter. Friend or foe, he'd take the same precautions.

With his free hand, Jocko held up three fingers. Two... one...

Jocko threw open the door. I lifted my hand and sighted down my arm at Spud. Then I stopped.

Feng stood in the doorway, his fist raised for another whack on our door. He wore a full set of fatigues and had a rifle strapped to his back. I could see the barrel poking over his muscular right shoulder.

"Don't shoot!" he said when he saw me pointing at him.

I lowered my hand. "What's going on?"

"The predators attacked early," Feng said. "We thought we'd have months before any type of large-scale incursion." He shook his antlered head. "We need to mobilize now. Get to the switching station. If we can—"

Feng was cut off as an explosion rocked the room. I stumbled and caught myself on the table. Feng held onto the doorframe.

Obviously, Jocko didn't flinch.

Feng grabbed his lapel. Inside his collar was a black plastic microphone, like the kind that field guards wore at lightball games.

A world of magic and they still use technology to communicate. Or maybe the mic *did* work on magic. What did I know?

Feng spoke into the mic. "Duo, do you copy?" he said. "What's going on out there?"

The mic must've doubled as a speaker, because it crackled with static. Then I heard a voice, reedy and tinged with horror. "The preds... know all the switching codes," the voice said. "Defense at... Barracks but... they're—*agh!*"

Devora appeared in the hallway behind Feng. "What in the name of all hells is happening out there?" she said.

Feng glanced over at her. "My friends are in trouble," he said. "Get your weapons and follow me."

I ran back into my bedroom and grabbed the bandolier from where it sat on the small table beside my bed. It was the only thing of value I owned that wasn't already in my Inventory. As I slung the leather over my shoulder, Perry mumbled something, but continued to sleep.

"Al dente," he said. "Ratatouille. Muffuletta."

I met up with the rest of our group in the hallway. Jocko was already there. Devora joined us. She took a swig from her flask before hanging it from her belt.

"Is anyone else in the building?" she asked.

Feng shook his head. "Not in this wing," he said. "Not that I could find. Let's go!"

We followed Feng down the steps and toward the front door. There was a low rumble.

I wonder what that is?

Feng threw open the door, and we stumbled outside. Although it was night, the field that spread out before us was as bright as day, illuminated by spotlights that reminded me of the Stadia. The air was smoky and had the unmistakable, biting scent of cordite.

I shielded my eyes and peered across the field. In the distance was a charging *army*. Leading the pack were death hyenas, their bright red eyes visible even at a distance. Beyond them… well, I wouldn't have known what I was seeing, but the text that appeared in my vision took care of that for me.

Wolf-kin (Fiore Fangblood: Enraged)

Wolf-kin are foot soldiers that form the vanguard of the predator army. The shamanic leopard-kin who leads this tribe is capable of enraging magic, which augments the powers of the wolf-kin and makes them highly aggressive.

How did they all get here?

The shamans the description mentioned were women with the heads of leopards and pelts draped over their tattooed shoulders. There were probably twenty of them interspersed with the slavering wolf-kin. Each carried a wooden staff topped with a skull.

Shamanic Leopard-kin (Krata Bina)

Although each shamanic leopard-kin might have several children, only one lives to young adulthood. Fewer still survive the Trial of Kuan'dar, in which the young shamanic leopard-kin must defeat her own mother in single combat for control of her mother's pelt and staff. The staff is the source of the leopard-kin's shamanic magic, which allows her to control a brood of wolf-kin.

The predator forces were animals in the same way Feng was: inspired by the animal kingdom, though different than the true animals from which they took their inspiration. In addition to the death hyenas, wolf-kin, and leopard-kin, there were creatures that took their forms from panthers, crocodiles, and lions. The air was filled with darting, zipping birds of prey and insects that made the winged imago look like kittens.

The predators are actually predators. I don't know why I was surprised. Almost all the natives of Gray Moor had been some form of prey animal, and the battle with their great enemy had been called the War of Fangs. *Of course* the predators would be predators.

As the predator army charged toward us, they set off mines that lay beneath the soft earth. Explosions sent dirt and the occasional body flying into the air. But the school's defenses weren't enough. Not even *close*.

"We have to fight!" Feng shouted. "We can help the other hunters, and the natives. Look! Up there. Maybe we can meet up with them?"

I followed his finger to a small contingent of friendly snipers that stood on one of the observation decks. From where I stood, I could hear the reports of their weapons. Every time there was a *pop*, one of the predators stumbled and fell.

Keep shooting, I thought, though I knew it was like trying to empty an ocean one spoonful at a time.

Clearly, Jocko thought similarly. "There's no way we make it," he said. "They're toast. And we're gone too, unless someone has another way out."

Toward the back of the charging army was a single scorpion the size of a bus. The insect was the color of obsidian and its barbed stinger must've been as large as a wrecking ball. As I watched, the scorpion turned toward the tower where the snipers hid and its tail glowed pink.

That thing could be on our side. But I knew it wasn't. Neither were the charging troops. They were too toothy. Too spiny. Too *evil*. Their killing intent rolled before them, pushed by the momentum of muscled bodies and thundering hooves. It splashed against my jumpsuit like a driving rain.

"We need to go," Jocko said. "Now."

But all of us were frozen as we stared at the oncoming horde. There was a flash, and something shot from the scorpion's tail. It was a pink laser, so bright that it left a searing afterimage in its wake.

Boom.

The laser struck the tower that held the snipers and the tower *exploded*. Instantly, the spotlight that hung from the tower winked out. Thick struts and burning cables rained from the sky.

"Back inside!" I roared, grabbing Devora by the arm and hauling her through the door. I didn't want to be next. Feng and Jocko stumbled in after us.

"What… the heck… was that?" Devora gasped. It was a rhetorical question. No one spoke. It occurred to me that each of us was waiting for one of the others to take charge.

"I think I have a way out, but once we move forward, we're not coming back to Gray Moor," I said finally. "It's onto the next level or we die trying. And it means abandoning everyone here. With that in mind, is everyone coming?"

I checked the group. Devora was already with me. Jocko gave a single sharp nod. Feng's mouth tightened, but he gave in.

"There's a secret passage down the hall that leads to a part of the level called the Valves," I said. "I don't know what's down there, but at least we won't have to face that charging army."

Feng's eyes grew wide. "Crow, this is a bad idea," he said. "I've heard stories about what happens in the Valves. Terrible things!"

"Worse than facing a predator army?" I asked.

"That's a really good point," Feng said. His shoulders sagged. "But we're leaving my friends behind. Everyone I know is in Gray Moor!"

"It's go now, or stay and die with them." I didn't mean it to sound so harsh, though that was the reality. From somewhere outside, we heard another *boom*, and the building shook.

Feng glanced toward the front door. "Okay, let's go." His face tightened. "Predators. I'll have my revenge against them. I swear it."

I led our group down the corridor that ended in the golden door. As we approached, I pointed to the nearly invisible seam on the floor.

"The floor splits there. Make sure you don't cross that line. Pressing the right keyhole on that door will cause the floor to fall open, and then there's a platform we'll need to reach."

"How do we do this?" Spud asked. "Crow, you want me to hit the button again? Send us all tumbling thirty feet down?"

"Obviously not." I pulled the Ring of Teleportation from my Inventory and both the ring and the anchor appeared in my palm. I handed the anchor to Jocko.

"When I open the door, get to the platform and set the anchor. Then we can each take turns teleporting down. Devora, you go first, then Feng, and I'll go last. Jocko, you'll have to bring the ring back between uses."

"What about us?" Spud said. "Your friendly neighborhood grocery cart?"

"You're with me." To the rest of the group, I said, "If you haven't used one of those rings before, get it in your hand and think the word *activate*. It'll pull you to the anchor, and then you'll hand the ring to Jocko, who'll bring it back up to the next person."

"*Or* you could let me grab the rope between my teeth," Spud said. "You'd hold one end, and then I'd activate my flames, and you could shoot me down to the platform. If you can get me between two bars of the railing that wraps around the platform, I can swing around it, get back on the platform, and tie a good knot. Then, you can tie the end up here and slide down the rope."

"Once the door opens, we'll have fifteen seconds until it closes again," I continued, ignoring Spud. "Last time I was here, the door opened and closed twice before the platform started moving automatically. I think it's safe to assume the mechanics still work the same way. So Devora and Feng, you'll go down after the first open, and then we'll wait for it to close. I'll open the floor again and then Jocko and I will join you. Understood? I want verbal assent."

"Yes," Feng said.

"Understood," Devora said.

"Got it, *pacho*," Jocko said.

"You *sure* you don't like my idea?" Spud asked. "It's got panache!"

I whipped Spud off my shoulder and set him to hover above my palm.

"You want to be the one that presses the button or not? Because the guy that opens the door gets to be a *hero*."

Spud's eyes widened until I swore I could see the dreams dancing within them.

"We'll go with your idea," he said. "It's fantastic. It's incredible!"

"On three," I said. "One. Two. Three!"

I fired Spud at the trigger keyhole. For whatever reason, he lit himself on fire mid-flight.

"Oh *yeah!*" he said. "*Shaboom!*"

He hit the trigger perfectly and the floor opened with a *bang*. Then Jocko was off, the only sign that he'd been standing near us the shower of dry leaves that drifted to the ground. One of the leaves fell over the edge of the pit, though I didn't have time to watch it. I was too focused on Jocko. Without looking, I caught Spud, who'd extinguished his flames before hitting my hand, and lifted him to my shoulder.

"I'm a hero!" Spud said. "Perry, did you see me?"

Jocko appeared on the platform below us and set the anchor. Then he was beside Devora.

"See you down there," he said, pressing the ring into her hand. The two of them disappeared. They reappeared on the platform, leaves rained through the air, and then Jocko stood beside Feng.

"Activate!" Feng shouted. It was proof that, even when people agreed to a plan, they didn't always understand it. But shouting the word meant he was thinking it, so it had the same effect. Feng appeared beside Devora and then Jocko was standing beside me. I waited for the trapdoor to close before I shot Spud at the button, scoring another direct hit.

Activate, I thought as soon as Jocko pressed the ring into my palm. I experienced the now-familiar, extremely unpleasant vertigo that came from teleporting through space before I appeared on the platform.

"Ugh," I said. Feng reached out to catch my shoulder. "Jocko, I don't know how you get used to that."

"It's not so bad, *pacho*," the Grass King said as he appeared beside me. He looked down at the platform and kicked at a leaf. The leaf executed a swift loop before settling where it'd been in the first place.

There was a loud *bang* as the floor above us slammed shut. The only noise was the heavy breathing of four people who'd escaped certain death from an encroaching army. Then Perry's voice split the darkness.

"Hey," he said sleepily. "I had the *strangest* dream. Is it time for breakfast yet?"

25

Spud moaned softly as I activated his light.

"Oh baby," he said. "That's *so* good."

But I shouldn't have bothered. There was a *click,* and a light I hadn't noticed before came to life. It wasn't anything fancy, just an incandescent bulb covered by a wire cage that stuck out from the stone ten feet over our heads. There was another *click,* and another, and then a hundred similar lights turned on to form a line that spiraled down along the walls of the pit.

"I'm—*ugh*—still a hero, right?" Spud said. His flames winked out.

"You're definitely still a hero," I said.

The platform started to rumble.

"That's probably the hero's arrival rumble, and not, like, the predator army tearing apart the building over our heads," Spud said. "Yeah. A rumble for heroes is a *much* more pleasant thought."

But as it turned out, it wasn't a hero's rumble, or the predators, but the displaced energy of the ancient machinery moving the platform. It lurched into motion, nearly spilling Devora over one side, but Feng caught her wrist.

"This looks like a much older part of the school," I said. "I wonder why it was built. Or why they built the school on top of it. Did you guys get the message about the Valves?"

The others nodded.

"I guess we won't know more until we reach the bottom," I said, then leaned over the railing and peered into the pit. I couldn't see the bottom. "Whenever that is."

"I'm scared," Perry said from my chest.

I rested a hand on his bristly stem. "We're going to be fine," I said, though I didn't know if it was true or not.

It took an hour for our platform to reach the bottom of the pit. But finally, the platform settled into place with a *click,* and we found ourselves in a small chamber. In the far wall was a steel door with a wheel in its center, like the kind you might encounter on a bank vault. Strangely, the locking mechanisms were on *our* side of the door, as if the point of the heavy door wasn't to keep outsiders from getting in, but to keep whatever was inside from getting out.

Door to the Valves — Locked

A door that prevents anything in the Valves from getting to the surface. Open at your own risk.

"We're going through that door, aren't we?" Spud asked.

Devora stepped forward and grabbed the wheel. It didn't budge. She squared her hips and put her shoulders into the movement, and a second later, I heard a high-pitched *screech* of rusty hinges.

You got this. Keep going!

The wheel turned. Then, with a *clang,* it stopped. I was worried that Devora had broken something, but then she pushed on the door and it swung open. Beyond it was a long street. To my surprise, it was lit. Not well, but it glowed with a dim, yellow light reminiscent of the bulbs in the pit.

Devora edged through the door. Jocko went next, and I followed him with Spud held before me.

I found myself on a long promenade that ran perpendicular to the doorway. The street stretched away from us in either direction, and the ceiling was sixty feet overhead and arched at even intervals. Each curve was traced by iron girders.

There was a loud *bang* behind us, and I whirled around to see that the door had slammed shut behind Feng. There was no wheel on the inside.

"Guess we're not getting back out that way," Devora said.

I turned back to the street. On the far side were dark windows and doorways that looked as if they'd once opened into restaurants and shops. Nearby, a table umbrella lay on the ground. The fabric had long since been torn away, and its spindly arms were dull with age and rust. I also saw an overturned stall, one wheel in the air. It looked like the kind that sold meat sticks and frozen custard at lightball games.

Whatever food it may have once contained was long gone.

As we stood there, Devora sniffed. "Musty," she growled. "Rats, maybe. And rot. Something *definitely* lives down here."

I inhaled and smelled what she'd described.

"Smells like Perry after one too many burritos," Spud whispered. "I'm kidding, Perry. This is way more reptilian. After too many burritos, you smell like farts."

Reptilian. That's it.

I walked to the overturned stall and ran a finger through the dust on its surface. I didn't know what had happened here, but something had destroyed this city. Once upon a happier time, this street must've been on par with any of those found in Gomindor. Now, it was quiet, though I doubted it was abandoned.

I glanced toward Jocko in time to see his head snap toward the far side of the street. I followed his eyes to a store with a yawning door that looked like a dead man's mouth. Above the entrance, written in what could only be blood, was a single word: "ALPHA."

Only one person on our team had better hearing than Jocko. "Xena, is there anything out there?" I whispered.

"Yes," the eggplant said. "I'm not sure what, though. But something."

"Company at two o'clock!" Feng barked. Jocko teleported, leaving behind a cloud of leaves, and a fist-sized globule of mucus hit the ground where he'd been standing. It bubbled and hissed like Perry's acid as it carved a divot into the hard stone.

I ducked behind the overturned stall, then peered out from behind the relative safety to see what was attacking us. By the dim lights, I spotted one of our enemies. It was similar in size to Devora, but bent over like a gorilla. Its skin was a mottled gray-green, and it had a toad-like face set with cruel, bulging eyes.

Mulcher

Born of foul magic in the Valves beneath the towers of Dungeon School, mulchers are aggressive and territorial. While they might not look particularly dangerous, their speed, adhesive setae, and acidic mucus make them formidable threats.

When I shot Spud toward the mulcher, the creature jumped, its powerful back legs propelling it into the air.

"Adhesive setae means they stick to stuff," Perry said as the mulcher grabbed one of the girders. It held fast, hanging from the girder by one arm.

"It's potato time!" Spud screamed as I pulled him back toward my hand. Before I could bring him to bear again, there was the *crack* of a sniper rifle and the mulcher released its grip on the girder. It fell, hitting the ground with a wet *thwack*. Then it lay motionless, its neck twisted at an odd angle.

I flashed Feng a thumbs up. Then mulchers began spilling into the street. They didn't only come from the dark doorway, but from multiple shops that opened to the street. From deep within those shops also came the sound of a pounding bass drum. *Thump, thump, thump.* And then...

"Is that a guitar?" I asked.

"I said, it's potato time!" Spud yelled. In response, I activated his flames. "*Arghhhh!*" he screamed. "That's right, Crow. Don't embarrass me. When I say, 'It's potato time,' you gotta send me into battle. Or else I'm doing all that screaming for nothing." He turned his attention to the mulchers. "Hey, little froggies," he said. "*Argh!* Feel the wrath of —*ugh*—the Spud Squad!"

The pounding bass was now overlaid by the wails of multiple distorted guitars. *Something* in the darkness was playing a fitting soundtrack to a heated battle. It was the type of music I might've played in the locker room before a big game.

"Now, Crow, now!" Spud shouted. "Let me kill some stuuuuuff!"

My companion's voice trailed off as I shot him away from me. But his screams were audible as he punched through the chest of the first mulcher.

"Oh yeah, baby!" he yelled. "*Arghhh!* Tastes like chicken!"

Twenty or thirty mulchers had flooded from the shops to fight our small team. I tried to keep track of my fellow hunters, if only to avoid accidentally putting Spud through the back of one of their skulls, but I lost them in the heat of the battle. I wasn't only juggling one, but *three* sapient bullets, each with their own power.

"I've got hold of one," Xena said from her spot on my bandolier. Her voice was strained. Purple smoke wreathed her body. "I'll make it attack the others." When she next spoke, she wasn't speaking to me, but the mulcher over which she had control.

"Tear your friends limb from limb," she cried. "Make them pay, those doddering brutes!"

It truly was an incredible power, though I didn't have time to think about it. I fired Spud and Perry as fast as I could release them and pull them back.

"Let's go!" Spud screamed. "*Arghhh!* Spud Squad fight! Spud Squad —*ugh*—win!"

Still, the mulchers kept coming. For every one I took down, it seemed like two more took its place. It was a losing battle, and I could feel myself starting to grow tired. Eventually, I was forced to cycle Xena into my shooting rotation. She didn't pack the same punch as Spud or Perry, though her larger body was good for keeping the mulchers at bay.

Keep going. You have to—

My thoughts were interrupted by a blinding flash of light. The mulchers screeched and recoiled in pain, their eyes overwhelmed by the sudden brightness. I also yelled, shocked by the sudden light. For a moment I couldn't see anything, but then I made out the figure of a man in red armor. He stood in the middle of the street and I could see that he was gripping a pitchfork. The pronged weapon, which he held toward the ceiling, was the source of the light.

"Stop," he said. He tapped the flat end of the pitchfork against the ground. As he did, the light faded, as did the pounding music. A translucent bubble appeared around the man; it was clearly some type of protective shield.

For a moment, I thought we were saved. Then the mulchers fell to their knees where they stood, their foreheads pressed to the ground like the man in red armor was their god, and I knew in that moment we were absolutely doomed.

26

The man who commanded the mulchers was made bigger by his burnished red armor. He had white hair that reached below his shoulders and wore a golden mask with two prongs that jutted out from his forehead like curved sabers.

Sewer Lord (Ferrault / Sor'kodich)

A native student at Winter Ridge named Ferrault accidentally stumbled into the Valves. Recently, he found an ancient magical artifact that allowed him to be possessed by a demon named Sor'kodich, who had once inhabited another body in Gray Moor.

Today, the combination of Ferrault / Sor'kodich lives in the Valves, quietly building an army that owes allegiance to neither predator nor prey.

When I finished reading the description, I groaned. I knew Sor'kodich: he was the same demon Devora and I had fought in the chamber near the Advising Rooms. I thought we'd vanquished him, though clearly he hadn't been as defeated as I'd thought.

Sor'kodich recognized us as well. From within his protective bubble, he smiled at me. The skin around his mouth was pale and his lips were blood red. His incisors poked out of his mouth like fangs.

"My old friends!" he said in a strong voice. "King Crow and Devora. No hard feelings over what happened in Gray Moor. And I do apologize if my followers caused you distress. They weren't supposed to harm you. Though there's not much to do in the Valves, and they often become overzealous. Will you parlay? If so, give up your weapons and come closer. Or don't, and learn more about the army I've been building in the Valves."

Jocko stood to my right, surrounded by severed limbs, and Devora was beside him, one hand lodged in a dead mulcher's torso. I couldn't see Feng.

Can we fight our way out of this? Can we defeat the demon a second time?

None of us were close enough to reach Sor'kodich. Even if Jocko used his ability to teleport toward the demon, it was unclear if he'd be able to penetrate Sor'kodich's glowing shield.

Earlier, I'd fired Xena at one of the mulchers, but now she was nowhere to be seen. Perry had been sitting on my shoulder, but I'd needed to use him as ammunition against a mulcher that had threatened to attack Devora from behind, so I didn't know where he was, either.

I had Spud, though. Honestly, he was probably our best shot at attacking Sor'kodich. I glanced at Jocko and he subtly shook his head. The message was obvious: *don't attack. Let's see what he wants.*

I placed Spud on my shoulder. "We'll parlay," I said.

"Good," Sor'kodich said. "In the spirit of kindness, I'll let you see to your friend."

My friend? I followed Sor'kodich's finger to Feng. The armored buck lay on the ground behind me, and my heart dropped. There was an awful wound in his chest.

"Oh no," Spud whispered into my ear. "He's not moving, Crow. I think he's dead. That was my homie. My boy. He led my fan club."

I didn't have any words as I walked over to Feng and knelt beside his body.

"Feng," I whispered. Could he really be dead? I put my hand on his shoulder, ready to deliver some final benediction over his body that would usher him into the unknown. To my surprise, he let out a weak groan. But as I looked down at him, it was clear he wasn't long for this world.

"Crow," he said, his eyes fluttering open. His voice was barely above a whisper, and his eyes were glassy and unfocused. "You're a good man."

"Is there anything I can do to make it easier?" I asked. I didn't tell him he was going to be okay, because we both knew it wasn't true.

Feng coughed. "No. I can't feel pain anymore, and I'm not scared. It was an honor to fight with the Spud Squad. I'll go back to the lab, I guess, and come back as something else."

I blinked away tears. I hadn't known Feng long, but he'd watched out for us. Not only when we'd arrived at Gray Moor, but throughout our time there. Without Feng, we would've been grist for the mill half a dozen times already.

"Goodbye, Feng," I said. "We owe our lives to you."

"I need to tell you, Crow," Feng said, his voice growing faint, "that… that… destroy the dungeon for me, if you can."

And with that, Feng's breathing stopped. His body went limp, and he was gone.

With trembling fingers, I closed his eyes. Then, I undid the Spud Squad pin from his jacket and put it on my jumpsuit. It wasn't much of a memento, but it'd ensure that I'd never forget the funny, kind creature who'd gone out of his way to help us.

Before I stood, Spud whispered, "Hey, Crow? I lied before, when I told you Potato Hell was *that* bad. I mean, it's not great, don't get me wrong. I wouldn't choose to spend my time there. But they *do* have mini-golf. So if you thought it would help you and the team, I wouldn't mind going back, and then reappearing in twenty-four hours to save the day."

I still didn't know what mini-golf was, but I knew what he was trying to say. At one point, I'd promised Spud I'd never willingly sacrifice him again. It was a promise I'd intended to keep. But now, in my hour of need, he was giving me permission to send him beyond Sor'kodich's reach.

Even if it meant his death.

"Are you sure?" I asked. "We still don't know what will happen. Sor'kodich could turn out to be friendly, and then I'll have crushed you for nothing."

Spud nodded. "He's not friendly, Crow. Let's do this."

I sighed. "Thank you, buddy. I'm sorry. I'll see you soon."

Spud closed his eyes as he slipped from my shoulder and dropped to the ground before me. If Sor'kodich or any of the mulchers noticed, they didn't give any indication.

"Spud Squad," Spud whispered. Before I could change my mind, I crushed him beneath the heel of my boot.

Come back soon, Spud. We need you.

I swallowed the lump in my throat as I turned and walked toward Sor'kodich. While I'd been talking to Spud, more mulchers had appeared around our perimeter. We'd taken out twenty or thirty, but there had to be at least a hundred more surrounding us.

Too many to fight. Any aggression would be a death sentence.

"*Now* we can talk," Sor'kodich said. "I'm sure you're wondering how I'm here. Last we saw each other, Devora was spitting spirits in my face. Well played, by the way. I was sent scampering across the final veil, but for things like me, there's *always* a way back. It takes one person hungry for power to make one wrong move. So here I am! In fact, without you, I wouldn't have all this."

He opened his arms and gestured not just to the mulchers, which had stood and gathered in a loose semicircle behind him, but the Valves itself.

"My own underground kingdom! It doesn't look like much from here, but I've gathered an army. Did you know this was where the prey used to live, before the War of Fangs? When they won the war, they pushed out of these tunnels. You can't really blame them. Not much sun down here, I'm afraid. They left so much behind, and now it's mine. Now, I get to follow in their foot-steps. The predators and prey are already fighting their petty battle, so they don't suspect what's right beneath their feet. I'll conquer them and keep going, to the Heart of the World itself! Given your role in this, it's fitting you're here to witness our ascension."

He pointed to the ground in front of him. "Items, please," he said. "Weapons, armor, and gear. Everything. I can see your Inventories, so I'll know if you're telling the truth. You can make a pile here."

Again, I glanced at Jocko. But what could we do? While Sor'kodich had been speaking, more mulchers had filed into the street. Before, we hadn't stood a chance, and now our odds were worse. Our only viable option was to see how this would play out.

I placed the contents of my Inventory on the ground before me. Devora did the same, and so did Jocko. I still didn't know where Xena or Perry had gone, but I prayed for them to stay hidden.

If we can survive this, maybe there's something they can do to help. If something happens to them, Spud will be back in twenty-four hours.

"Are you hiding anything?" Sor'kodich said.

"That's everything in my Inventory," I said.

"But it's not everything!" came a voice from the other side of the street.

Xena, I thought as the eggplant rolled out from behind a dead mulcher and looked up at the demon.

"Mighty Sor'kodich, I humble myself before you," Xena said. "Like you, I have allegiance to neither predator nor prey. I fought to survive the War of Fangs only to suffer the indignity of this body. In good faith, I offer you the knowledge that these imbeciles have another party member, an entity with a similar shape to my own who can spit acid on command. He might not look like much, but he's formidable. He's over there, hiding in the shadows."

I followed her gaze to a doorway, where I could make out Perry's round form. The tomato shrank farther into the shadows, but it was too late. We'd all seen him.

"There was another, as well, but I see he's dead," Xena continued.

"Help me recover my true form and the rest of my knowledge will be yours."

For the moment, at least, Sor'kodich ignored her. "Come out, young one," he called to Perry.

Cautiously, Perry rolled into view. He must've been crying, because I could see a stream of snot dripping from one nostril.

"There's a special place in hell for traitors," the tomato spat.

Sor'kodich laughed. "What spirit! Perhaps there is a place for you in my organization. Come over here and stay quiet, unless you want to see your friends get hurt."

Tears leaked from Perry's eyes, but there clearly wasn't another option. He rolled toward us. When he was about ten feet from Sor'kodich, a translucent bubble of light popped into existence around him, lifting him into the air to float beside the demon. I could see the tomato yelling, yet no sound escaped the bubble.

Poor Perry. There was nothing I could do for him.

With Perry neutralized, Sor'kodich glanced at Xena. "I accept your offer," he said. "We'll get you a proper form. Come here, Xena, and take your place at my side."

Xena's cruel cackle was about the only thing that could've pulled my attention away from my floating friend. As she rolled toward Sor'kodich, I shook my head.

Didn't Justice Maron say she had to serve me? Unless she plans on double-crossing Sor'kodich.

"I want you to know there's nothing personal in this," Sor'kodich said, turning to face me. "But I need your equipment. And obviously, I can't let you go yet. There's too much risk that you'll bring an army down here before I'm ready."

An idea came to me. "Killing us would be a mistake," I said. "We have knowledge that would be lost with our deaths."

Sor'kodich shrugged. "Every death is the loss of something."

"The Heart of the World," I said. "I know how to get through its defenses."

He raised an eyebrow. "You have my attention."

"I've thought about my death a hundred times since I entered the dungeon. I'm not scared of the pain. The pain is fleeting. It's the permanence that gets me. The idea of disappearing, forever, without anyone to remember me. So I'll make you a deal: give me two days to write my thoughts, so that something lives on after I die, at least, and then I'll give you the information you want."

Sor'kodich looked at me like he was trying to find a trick in my words.

"Deal," he said finally. "But you won't need your friends for that."

With one swift motion, he drove the tines of his pitchfork into Devora's chest. Devora opened her mouth in a scream, but no sound came out. Her body glowed with the same light that wreathed Sor'kodich's weapon. Then the light winked out and Devora was gone.

"No!" I yelled. I leapt toward Sor'kodich, but two mulchers grabbed my arms and held me in place.

It's hard to describe how I felt upon seeing Devora's death. I could describe it in familiar terms by saying it was the same sensation as blowing the last shot of a huge lightball game, but that wouldn't do justice to the stakes. Because at the end of the day, lightball was a game. Losing was disappointing, but no one died.

In Toroth-Gol, one wrong move could kill you. That was never more apparent than when I'd watched Sor'kodich run his weapon through Devora's chest.

I won't mince words, or try to use fancy metaphors. I'll simply say I was *angry*. Maddeningly, ragingly angry. I wanted to activate Giant's Roar, grab my club, and smash everything around me to a bloody pulp. Of course, I no longer had the special ability, nor my club. All I could do was grind my teeth and make myself a promise.

I'm going to get out of this and kill Sor'kodich. I'm not sure how, but it's going to happen.

"So help me, if you kill Jocko, you'll never learn a single secret," I said as tears ran down my cheeks. "I'd sooner die than tell you. If you kill him before you kill me, I'll take my knowledge to the grave. You can rot throwing yourself at the Heart of the World's defenses."

Sor'kodich's eyes widened. *Try me*, I thought as the demon stared into my eyes. I met his gaze with as much fire as I could muster.

"Go on," I growled. "Make your move."

Sor'kodich continued staring at me, likely trying to decide whether I was bluffing. Was I? I didn't know. On the one hand, I wanted to keep Jocko alive. However, the human instinct for self-preservation is *powerful*. I didn't want Jocko to die, though I also didn't want to die, either.

Still, I probably was telling the truth. If Sor'kodich murdered Jocko, I'd keep my mouth shut. It didn't matter how much he tortured me. He'd never learn what I'd seen.

Sor'kodich must've sensed that. "You've earned yourself and your friend another forty-eight hours of life," he said. "But I won't ask again: put all your items into the pile, and then you can start writing your last words."

Beside me, Jocko exhaled a shaky sigh of relief. He put his sword on the ground before him.

"I have your word?" I said to Sor'kodich. I didn't know if that was worth anything, but I figured it couldn't hurt to get assurances Jocko wouldn't be killed. Not before me, anyway.

"You have my word. Forty-eight hours to write whatever you want, and then you're done. He can watch you die."

That was good enough for me. At least, it was as good as I thought I'd get at that moment.

Sor'kodich pointed to the Spud Squad pin on my lapel. "What about that?" he asked.

I touched my lapel and felt the pin beneath my fingers. *He's gonna take the pin.* But I wasn't going to argue.

"Ornamental," I said. "Take that too, since you're taking everything else."

I undid the pin and threw it atop the pile. Satisfied, Sor'kodich turned to Jocko. "And you?"

"Empty as a Thuin's pantry," Jocko said. "You'll regret what you did, by the way. That was a mistake."

Sor'kodich shrugged. He raised a hand to his face. Between his thumb and forefinger, he held a glass disc about the size of his palm. He brought the disc to his eye, staring at me as he said, "All of us might regret our actions, in time." Through the disc, his eye was magnified, a glittering shard of obsidian set into an angular face. "Until then, I sleep soundly."

Whatever the purpose of the disc, it seemed to have been accomplished with me, because he turned to face Jocko and peered through the glass at my companion.

"Ah," he said. "I assumed you might be more cooperative, especially after… well, never mind. The plasma cutter, please?"

My heart sank as a foot-long, metallic cylinder appeared in Jocko's hand.

He tried to hold something back, I thought as Jocko tossed the device atop the pile. It hit awkwardly, bouncing once before rolling down the other side and coming to rest against the foot of a nearby mulcher. *Why did he do that? He must've known Sor'kodich wouldn't trust us to empty our Inventories!*

The answer was written in Jocko's crooked grin as he turned to face me.

He didn't think we had another choice. The realization was like a punch to the gut. *If Jocko thinks we're cornered, we probably* are *going to die. That's not good. Unless this is another test?*

But it wasn't. Two from our crew were *dead.* I might not completely trust Jocko, though I knew he wouldn't go that far in training me.

"It was worth a shot, *pacho,*" Jocko said to me. He turned back to Sor'kodich. "You would've tried the same thing, had you been in my position."

Sor'kodich lowered the glass disc, which disappeared into his own Inventory, and nodded sympathetically. "Of course," he said. "But I'm not. You know what comes next, right? Because you'd do the same thing in *my* position."

Jocko sighed. "Do what you have to do."

As soon as he finished speaking, Sor'kodich leaned forward and grabbed Jocko's arm. Then there was a *crack* and Jocko's sword arm flopped forward uselessly. The noise made my stomach turn. White bone stuck out from Jocko's skin at the halfway point of his forearm.

I could tell Jocko was trying to remain stoic, though he couldn't stop himself from grunting in pain. Still, he forced a smile onto his face, which had turned a ghostly white. A sheen of sweat had appeared on his forehead.

"No hard feelings," he said, forcing the words through clenched teeth.

"None at all," Sor'kodich said. Then, to the mulchers that held us, he said, "Take them both. Put them in the cells. Separate ones. I don't want any more funny business."

That was the last thing I heard before something crashed into the back of my head.

27

I woke up on a hard stone floor. My head throbbed with a dull ache. The last thing I remembered was something connecting with the back of my skull, followed by the feeling of my limbs going limp.

Devora. I forced the thought aside. I didn't want to think about that. I'd made a vow to protect those who trusted in me, and now everyone who'd been stupid enough to try was gone.

I struggled to my feet, but the room spun, and I staggered backward, catching myself on the wall behind me. It was made of thick, gray stones. The only light came from a small crack in the ceiling some thirty feet overhead, and it was barely enough to see by.

I looked around. My captors had taken everything, leaving me with only a pen, a few sheets of paper, and a bucket that I assumed was supposed to be my toilet. There was also a single stone slab on the ground, which I figured was my bed.

Perhaps there's a seam or a hidden lever. I staggered around the room and ran my hands over the walls, but I couldn't find anything. No doors and no windows, and certainly no hidden levers. I must've been dropped into the room from the crack in the ceiling, or else there was some type of strange magic that had put me there.

Nice going, I thought, my self-pity flaring. *Feng and Devora dead, and you've bought yourself another forty-something hours to do... what? How are you going to do anything from here? Wait for a potato to come save you?*

If Spud did arrive at some point, I couldn't see how he would help. Once again, I did a lap, trying to find a weak spot in the wall or a hidden door. There was nothing. The stones were solid, and there was no way out.

I sat down on the stone slab and picked up a piece of paper. Did I bother trying to write my last words? Maybe a confession, or a farewell message to my friends or father? Something else entirely?

I put the pen back down. It didn't matter if I wrote anything, really. My captors were going to kill me either way.

I can still fix this. I'm not completely without resources. I closed my eyes. *Focus. Breathe in, breathe out. Here's a truth, universe: no one should put their trust in me.*

But nothing happened, because I'd used the power too recently.

How do I get out of this? What do Jocko and I need to do to survive this mess?

My stomach growled, and I realized I hadn't eaten since I'd been captured. I wondered if Jocko was in a similar situation. Was he still alive? But Sor'kodich had said Jocko could watch me die, and the demon was still waiting for me to reveal the secrets of the Heart of the World. No doubt Jocko would be at my funeral, only steps behind me on the road to death.

I stood, then paced around the room again, desperate for something to do. But there was nothing. No furniture, no windows, no way out. Only me and my thoughts.

So I sat. After another hour or so, footsteps. Heavy boots, echoing from somewhere nearby. I looked toward the crack in the ceiling, but the sound wasn't coming from there. Rather, it emanated from behind the wall near the bucket.

My heart began to race. *Has it been forty-eight hours already?* There was no way. But what was happening, then?

The footsteps grew louder. I stood and tensed my legs. I wasn't ready to die, and I still had one chance at survival. The fact of the matter was, I'd spent the last several weeks training in hand-to-hand combat. I might not be an expert yet, but I could go down in a blaze of glory.

A voice called out from beyond the wall.

"Time's up, Crow," it said. "Are you ready?"

"It hasn't been close to forty-eight hours," I said as I cracked my knuckles.

"Stand away from the wall, Crow," the voice said. "We're coming in."

Before I could reply, a portion of the wall faded away. I was about to leap forward when I saw…

Feng?

The dead sniper grinned at me. He looked as he had when he'd died, right down to the hole in his chest. Maybe his skin was a tad more gray, and his eyes didn't have a hundred percent of their old luster, but other than that, I was staring at Feng reanimated.

"You should see the look on your face right now," Feng said. He looked down at his chest and placed a hand to the wound. "I know, it's gross."

This didn't add up. "How are you here?" I asked. "I watched you die. Closed your eyes with my own hands. Aren't you dead?"

My question was answered as Xena rolled out from behind Feng's legs. "Technically, he's *undead*," she said.

The pieces came together. "You *did* double-cross Sor'kodich," I said. "You got away from him and brought Feng back to life with your power."

Xena rolled her eyes. "Obviously," she said. "Sor'kodich is *evil*. I wasn't gonna let him get the upper hand. Sorry about the dupe, but your plan with Spud was *terrible*. Like, worse than bad. What was he going to do? Spud is an idiot. Loyal, yes, but *come on*, Crow. I couldn't let you put all your, uh, potatoes in his basket. So, Perry and I came up with an alternative plan. A better one."

"Perry?" I said. *Now* my head spun. "Where is he? Is he okay?"

"Last we saw, he was fine," Xena said. "We know where to find him. Thought we'd rescue you first."

I glanced at Feng, who flashed me a thumbs up. "Is he in control of his own body?" I asked Xena. "When he spoke to me, were they his words or yours?"

"I'm telling you, it's me," Feng said. "Just undead. Now come on, man. Let's grab Jocko and get out of here."

I looked past him and into the hallway, which was lit by glowing lamps. Bodies littered the floor: four, five, or six mulchers in various states of evisceration. That was the only way to describe it. There were disembodied hands and feet and a torso split down the middle, with twenty feet of organs in a trail behind it.

"Don't shed any tears over these monsters," Feng said as he followed my gaze. He bent down and lifted Xena to his shoulder. "They killed me, remember?"

Xena flashed a grim smile. "Feng took out the first mulcher, and then I raised it. Used that one to tear one of his friends limb from limb, then dropped the first and raised the second. Rinse and repeat. Then I brought Feng back. Nothing like a little necromancy to sow chaos among your enemies. And he's telling you the truth. I can control someone if I want, but I'm giving Feng agency. He's doing everything for himself."

"We'll have to work out a more permanent solution for me later," Feng said. "But for now, I want to get out of here before we're discovered. Come on."

He turned and walked into the hallway, and I followed. As I did, my nostrils were assailed with the copper tang of blood. Doorways lined the narrow corridor, except instead of doors, the doorframes were blocked by boulders.

"Earth magic," Xena said. "Powerful stuff. We found a key on one of the guards, and you can tell which cells are occupied by the marking over the doorway. See?"

I followed her eyes to a small black "x" above one of the doorways that looked to have been drawn in charcoal. Feng moved to the boulder that blocked that door, nimbly stepping around body parts and smears of brownish blood, then tapped the stone with his knuckles.

Instantly, the stone became translucent, and I found myself staring into a cell similar to the one I'd left, with one difference: Jocko stood beyond the doorway, his teeth bared and his broken arm cradled against his chest.

"One tap lets you see into the cell, and two lets sound get through," Feng said. He tapped the stone a second time.

"Hey, Jocko, your friends are here," Feng said, his words directed at the Thuin who stood behind the door. "I'm going to open the door and, uh, it would be great if you didn't attack us. Because, you know, you're like a one-man army? I'm not trying to die another time."

Jocko didn't relax. He bent his knees another fraction of an inch and his lips pulled back from his teeth.

"Nice try," Jocko said as he flexed the fingers of his good hand. "I'm not buying it. Play whatever games you want, but I'm not going down without a fight. If Crow is dead, I hope he gave you hell."

"Um, that's not what's going on here," Feng said. "Maybe you could trust us?"

"He's telling the truth, Jocko," I said. "It's us." I wracked my brain for something that would convince him, something only the two of us would know. "Remember when we were sitting next to each other on the train to Toroth-Gol? You told me you were in Toroth-Gol for killing a man who insulted your sister."

Jocko's face softened, yet he still didn't relax.

"Come on, *majoré*, we don't have time for this," I said. "We're going to open the door and I'm asking you to wait for one second before you come out swinging."

Jocko didn't respond. Feng looked at me, a question in his eyes.

"Your funeral," he mumbled. He reached past me and tapped the stone a third time, which caused the translucent boulder to disappear.

I thought Jocko would launch himself forward and gouge out my eyes. Then he saw me, and I watched the tension drain from his body.

"Crow?" he said. His eyes darted toward Feng. "Feng? Xena?" Realization dawned on him. "You double-crossed Sor'kodich. Nice work."

"Never doubt the Maestra of the Seven Exquisite Tortures," Xena said.

"See, a name like that is why someone *would* doubt you," I grumbled.

"Whatever," Xena said. "Jocko, anything you need to grab from your cell? I'd say we should throw the bodies in there, in case someone comes by, but I don't think we're getting the blood off the floor any time soon."

"No chance," Feng said.

Jocko looked over his shoulder. Then he cleared his throat and spit on the ground. "That's all I needed to do there," he said. In my opinion, it was a pretty cool way to leave a jail cell. "Where to?"

28

According to Xena, Perry was with the rest of our gear in an armory down the street from where we were being held captive. But before we left the building, Xena and Feng said they had something to show us.

"This way," Feng said, as he led us up a spiral staircase. As we climbed, I noticed a strange noise.

"What is that?" I asked, trying to place the steady *thump, thump, thump*. For some reason, it sounded familiar.

"That's what we want to show you," Feng said. "It's best if you see it for yourself."

We reached the top of the stairs and emerged into an open-floor-plan room that, at one time, might've been a bar or a coffee shop. All the furniture had been removed, but there was still a long counter on one side.

Whatever the noise was, it was coming from the floor-to-ceiling windows behind the counter.

"Out there," Feng said, pointing toward the wall of glass.

Jocko and I stepped to the windows, and I realized the building in which we stood had been built on the high edge of a deep pit. In the distance, the land sloped gently upward, eventually reaching the level at which we stood.

In the ravine between us and the buildings was a stage. Looking down at it, I remembered where I'd heard the noise. It was the same steady rhythm backing the electric guitars that had started right before the mulchers had attacked us.

"Wow," I said as I looked into the ravine. "I'm so confused."

The bass blasted from a collection of speakers that surrounded the stage. Arranged before them were *thousands* of mulchers that danced, wobbled, and gyrated to the beat.

"I'm thankful to be up here and not down there," Jocko said. "That looks like the worst party *ever*."

"Run by the world's ugliest master of ceremonies," Xena said. "See him on the stage? Crow, your jumpsuit smells like sweat, but it's perfume compared to that guy. I don't know what he keeps under that red armor, but I wouldn't be surprised if it's rotting and consistently damp."

Sure enough, a red figure stood beside one of the speakers.

Sor'kodich. This must be the army he mentioned. I wonder if there's anything we can do to stop him?

But staring at the dancing mulchers, it was easy to guess our odds.

Sometimes, strong leadership was about heading a dangerous charge. Other times, it was about calling a tactical retreat. In this situation, where Sor'kodich's forces numbered in the thousands and our own consisted of myself, an undead sniper, a swordsman with a broken arm, and a necromantic eggplant, the choice was unpleasant but easy.

"Come on," I said. "Let's get to the armory while they're distracted."

We left the building and ran through the shadows on one side of the street. The mulchers that Feng and Xena had killed to rescue us were little more than an honor guard; the rest of the strange creatures were at Sor'kodich's ceremony.

"That's the one," Xena said, after a few minutes of running. "That's the one right there."

We froze beneath the awning of an abandoned café, and I followed her gaze to a three-story building on the opposite side of a long piazza. It had archways for windows and a fountain in the square outside the front door.

"That looks like a hotel," I said.

"They had you secured in the basement storerooms of an old coffeehouse," Xena said. "Sor'kodich didn't build this city. He's been working with what he's got."

"That's a really good point," I said.

After a quick glance down the street, we darted from the shadows and made our way to the armory's front door.

The Valves (Sor'kodich's Armory)

Once a hotel that served the wealthiest of the prey who lived in the Valves, this building has been repurposed into an armory.

"Give me a moment," Feng said as he stepped to the front door. "Need to disable the traps."

I alternated between watching him work and glancing nervously down the street. We were exposed here, and I didn't have any weapons yet. But after thirty seconds or so, Feng said, "All good, my friends." He pushed on the door and it swung inward on silent hinges.

"You're a handy man to have around, *pacho*," Jocko said, and Feng positively beamed.

We filed into the armory and Feng closed the door behind us.

"Nice digs," Jocko said as we looked around. "Makes me wish I had a glass of sparkling wine."

Whatever time had passed since the glory days of the hotel hadn't diminished the lobby's grandeur in the slightest. The floors contained a mosaic made from aquamarine and obsidian, and great pillars of white marble supported a domed ceiling high overhead. There were skylights in the roof, though torches also clung to the pillars. They burned with orange light, filling the room with a soft, warm glow.

"Jackpot," I said as my eyes fell on our stuff, which was heaped into an unceremonious pile inside the doorway. From the way it was heaped, I guessed whoever dropped it there had been in a rush. I ran to the pile and dug through it until I found Perry, who was in the glass jar I'd once used to hold Xena. His eyes were wide and filled with tears, and there was a bandana wrapped around his head, covering his mouth.

I unscrewed the lid, then tipped Perry into my palm and untied the bandana from around his head.

"Perry!" I said as I held him up. "You're alive!"

I dropped the tomato and jumped backward a half-second before a stream of acidic vomit exploded from his mouth.

"*Blargh!*" he yelled. "Ohmygod. Ohmygod. You're safe."

Perry's acid bubbled and hissed against the patterned floor.

"Ohmygod," he said again. Tears and snot streamed down his face. He looked up at me, his eyes shining. "Crow," he said. "I thought I'd never see you again."

"You're okay," I said as I moved toward him. I didn't want him to lose control again and shower me with acid. But his vomiting episode was over, and I picked him up without another incident.

"It was *awful*," Perry said. "Now I know how Spud must feel when he goes to Potato Hell. Is it weird to say I miss that guy?"

Even though Spud could be a bully, I found myself missing him, too.

"He'll be back soon enough," I said.

"The mulchers knocked you out and danced around your bodies, jeering and laughing the whole time," Perry continued. "They looked like screaming monkeys! And I thought Xena was on our side, because we'd made our plan, but it all happened so quickly and she looked so *evil*."

"Thank you," Xena said without a hint of irony.

"Then they took you away," Perry said. "I didn't know where you were going, because they took me in another direction. I wouldn't stop yelling at them, so Xena suggested they gag me and put me in the jar."

I raised an eyebrow at her. "You told Sor'kodich to put him in a *jar?*" I said.

Xena looked sheepish. "I was trying to convince him I was trustworthy."

I shook my head. "You're safe now," I said to Perry. "You're with the team again, and we're in the enemy's armory. Let's see if we can't make something of this setback."

As Jocko and I went through what remained in the pile of our stuff, it became clear it wasn't everything Sor'kodich had taken from us; it was only the castoffs, the stuff he couldn't use. Or maybe the stuff he didn't know *how* to use.

I found my gloves and slipped them on, then adjusted the battery pack on my hip. The flexible leather of the gloves felt as familiar as my own skin. I looped Spud's pouch through my belt and slipped my bandolier over one shoulder, then set Perry against his favorite spot.

"I've had a lot of excitement for one day," Perry said sleepily. "I think I'm gonna rest for a bit. Maybe take a nap."

"You do that," I said as I gave his stem a little pat. "We'll need you at full strength for whatever comes next."

Perry was already snoring softly, so I went back to the pile. All of my pickled vegetables were there, though Sor'kodich had taken the ham. I found Brynn's Radio Frequency Interference Device, which I put into my Inventory along with the vegetables, and Feng's Spud Squad pin, which I held out to him.

The sniper took it reverently and proudly attached it back on his lapel.

"All right!" he said. "Still undead, but now I feel a little more like me."

Other than a few broken arrows, that was it. Jocko's sword was gone, as was everything else of value.

"I'm sorry, Jocko," I said. "I was hoping we'd find something to fix you up."

The Thuin only shrugged. "It's not such a big deal, *pacho*," he said. "When I was younger, my father took me into the Wastes. Tied me up and placed a jagged centipede on my arm. I lay there for three days, baking in the sun and wracked with convulsions." He shivered at the memory. "Once you've felt the bite of a jagged centipede, nothing else really compares." He pointed to his broken arm, which he had cradled against his stomach. "This isn't comfortable, but I'll survive."

"Maybe there are other tools in the armory that can help us," Feng said. He pointed down a long row of shelves that ran the length of the room.

"Good idea, *pacho*," Jocko said. "Let's branch out. Crow, you take this row. I'll get the one on the left. Feng and Xena, take the one on the right. Yell out if you see anything interesting."

I made my way along the shelves. A few feet down, I found a potion.

Minor Potion of Invisibility (Spoiled)

This vial once held a potion that would render a drinker completely invisible for thirty seconds.

WARNING: This potion is spoiled. Drinking this potion will afflict you with poison.

I set it back down and moved down the row. As I lifted another potion, more text appeared.

Major Potion of Fire Breathing (Spoiled)

This vial once held a potion that would allow a drinker to breathe flames at their opponents for two minutes.

WARNING: This potion is spoiled. Drinking this potion will afflict you with poison.

It was like that down the entire row. There must've been dozens of potions, yet all of them were completely unusable. The more I checked, the more frustrated I became.

"Anyone find anything?" I called.

Jocko's voice rang out from the other side of the shelves behind me. "Not going so great over here, *pacho*," he said. "Mostly bare shelves."

"Feng and Xena?" I said. "Anything?"

"Nothing yet," Feng called back. "This armory is picked clean!"

I continued down my row. The potions I came across were spoiled, and the rest of the shelves were either empty or filled with more useless bric-a-brac, like chipped blades or broken arrows. By the time I met up with the others at the end of my row, I hadn't found a single thing we could use.

"Well, there's this," Feng said as he held up a club. "But I'm not sure how much use it'll be."

The club was smaller than the Clockwork Guardian's Club, more of a wooden baton than anything.

Cuddle Club

This weapon is the perfect choice for those who want to bring mixed messages to their enemies. With each strike, the Cuddle Club delivers a warm embrace that will leave your foes feeling fuzzy. Whether you're cuddling up to a pack of goblins or taking on a dragon, the Cuddle Club is the perfect weapon for spreading the love... and the pain! So give it a squeeze and watch your enemies fall to pieces. It's time to bring the snuggles into battle!

"I'm confused, *pacho*," Jocko said. "Does it bring the love? Or the pain?"

"I don't know," Feng said. "But here. You can take it."

I gritted my teeth to avoid showing my frustration. *Of course the armory would be empty. Sor'kodich told you he's preparing for battle. Whatever was in here, it's been taken by the mulchers.*

But at least we'd gotten Perry back, and I still held hope that we might find *something* of value.

I pointed to the nearby doorway. "Let's see what's in there."

We let Feng check for traps first. Once we got his thumbs up, we filed through into the next room. It was a small chamber with elevators on each side, though the doors were closed.

At the back of the room was a floor-to-ceiling window that looked out over a precipitous drop. Like the building where we'd been imprisoned, the hotel had been built on the edge of a high cliff, though instead of seeing into a clearing, I found myself staring into a forest. In the distance, beyond the edge of the forest, was a canyon, the rocky ground pocked with dark tunnels that led deeper into the earth.

"It's too far for me to teleport," Jocko murmured as he stared out the window. "Even if I could, I don't know how we'd get you guys down."

In the middle of the room, a blanket covered something thin that reached to my chest. It was like something you might see in an artist's studio to hide their work, only because of where we were, I looked at it with more dread than anticipation.

"Do I want to know what's under there?" I asked.

"Probably not, *pacho*," Jocko said as he pulled the blanket away.

Beneath the blanket was a Kinetoscope. I was about to turn away from the device when there was a familiar sound: *thump, thump, thump.* I cocked my head and was surprised to realize the noise was coming from the front of the hotel.

"Uh, Crow?" Feng said. "I think the mulchers' ceremony might be over."

I turned and ran from the room. I dashed down the long row of shelves and opened the front door in time to see a wall of mulchers come around the corner at the end of the street.

Oh no. My blood turned cold. I thought the mulchers were simply passing by on their way to conquer the towers, but no. All of them faced the armory.

They knew where we were, and they were coming for us.

"Go!" Jocko yelled from behind me. "Maybe you can draw them off."

With the mulchers a few hundred yards away, there was still time to escape. At least, there was for Feng and me. Jocko, with his broken arm, wasn't in any position to run. There was no way he'd escape the building before the mulchers reached us.

I glanced down the street. Slipping out now meant abandoning Jocko to the mulchers. The lobby only exited to that small room with the Kinetoscope, and all the elevator doors had been closed. It was a trap, plain and simple. Our survival meant Jocko's last stand.

"Get out of here, you idiots," Jocko said.

I glanced over my shoulder and met his eyes. Then, I made my choice.

29

As Feng shut and locked the front doors, I ran back through the lobby of the hotel. Jocko cursed me as I passed, but I ignored him. When I reached the small room, I pressed my face against the Kinetoscope and felt the device lock my head in place.

Confirming... Live on *Elvis Madden's Hunter Talk* in 3... 2... 1...

Then, he was there: Elvis Madden, in all his celebrity.

"Crow!" he said, flashing a bright smile. "I was wondering when we'd—"

"Can it, Madden," I said. I didn't have time to waste. From my Inventory, I withdrew Brynn's Radio Frequency Interference Device and felt the small, cold device between my fingers.

Activate.

You've turned on Brynn's Radio Frequency Interference Device. You're shielded from any broadcasts for the next thirty seconds.

Somewhere in his studio, Madden must've gotten the same

message, because he said, "Dennis, can you confirm this? Crow, what did you *do*?"

"We've got thirty seconds to chat without the Empire knowing what we're doing," I said. "Twenty-eight, now. In the Dark City, you were able to send Perry through the Kinetoscope. Can you still send things to me here?"

"Sure," he said. "But why would I do a foolish thing like that?"

"Am I helping your ratings?"

Madden's brow furrowed. "You're the most-watched feed in the most-watched season of this show. I'd say you're doing really well."

I smiled grimly. There was some satisfaction in knowing how popular I was, even *if* people were watching me fight for my life.

"If you care about your show's ratings, you'll send me something useful, because I'm about to die."

For a moment, Madden didn't respond. Then he looked off cam. His mouth moved, though I didn't hear any words. His eyes widened.

"Madden, help me and you keep the most exciting thing to happen to your show since the Sledgehammers played the Serpents in the Lightning Cup six years ago," I said. "That was also me, I should add."

This time when Madden spoke, the words came clearly. "Ratings *were* good," he admitted.

"Help me out now and I'll stop at the next Kinetoscope I see," I said. "You can interview me. I know you want that."

"Stop at the next *three*," Madden replied. "Commit to staying for at least ten minutes. And you have to answer all my questions with actual answers, not just grunts."

"Two," I said.

"Two, but skip one in between. It'll help build suspense."

"Deal."

Madden glanced up and to the right, to where our countdown timer had reached eight seconds. Did he have a timer, too?

"Dennis, the gold package," he said. "Punch it."

There was a pneumatic *hiss*. A moment later, the Kinetoscope's little door smacked me in the shins.

"Feng," I yelled. "There's a package behind the door near my shins.

Grab it and hide it somewhere in the room. Then pretend like you were looking for something and stumbled across it. You've got four seconds. Jocko, close your eyes. Don't let the broadcast see what Feng is doing."

Madden glanced up and to the right again. "In the spirit of this agreement, you should know that after this level I won't be able to send you anything else," he said. I felt Feng near my legs a split-second later. "And that I'm the one who—"

He stopped as the timer hit zero, then fixed me with his saccharine smile.

"Sorry about that, my friends," he said as his broadcast came back online. "Technical difficulties. I suppose that's to be expected when you're interviewing someone several miles below ground. Ha!"

Of all the times to end on a cliffhanger. What were you about to tell me, Madden? That you were the one who what?

I wasn't getting any answers, though it was hard to be too upset. I still didn't know what Madden had sent, but I trusted his self-interest.

Madden's smile grew wider, and for the first time, his perfect, gleaming teeth *didn't* make me want to punch him in the face.

"Hey, Crow?" Feng said from behind me. "I found something. You probably want to take a look at this."

Madden, you beautiful man. I would've shaken my head in disbelief, but the Kinetoscope held it in place. *You crazy, predictable man.*

"I can't talk right this second, Feng," I said. "Hold onto it for me."

"Crow, you were telling us about your present situation," Madden said. "Barricaded inside an armory with Jocko and the undead sniper. Spud lost somewhere in Potato Hell, though you've recovered Perry, and Xena turned out to be on your side all along. So many twists! So much excitement! Way to keep the audience wanting more."

Time to keep up my end of the bargain. It would pay to keep this man happy, so I took a deep breath and channeled my inner Spud.

"That's right, Madden," I said. "We're down here rolling with the punches. Though all in all, we've gotten pretty lucky."

Madden flashed a coy smile. "You *do* seem to have an angel watching over your shoulder," he said. "I wish I could take credit for protecting Steel City's most popular hunter, but I wouldn't so blatantly influence the Hunt. That would be enough to land me down there with you."

As he pointed at the camera, I noticed the watch on his wrist, and my heart skipped a beat.

I know that watch. It was a one-of-a-kind Pearlmatic made by the most talented jeweler on High Street in Gomindor. The watch had a sun made of pure gold and a little moon crafted from platinum that chased each other around the face according to the time. I recognized it because three days before my arrest I'd tried to purchase it, only to learn someone else had beaten me to the punch.

And not just anyone, but my own father.

But if Sal had bought the watch, how did it end up on Madden's wrist? Unless Sal had given it to him. But why would Sal have given Madden such an expensive gift?

Madden started talking again, though I remained focused on the watch. The pieces clicked into place, and I realized the answer to my question.

"We've got someone on the outside," Jocko had told me early in my journey into Dungeon School, when he'd explained how he'd given us an advantage. "It wasn't cheap, but your father stacked a few things in our favor."

Madden *was* that person. If that were the case, I needed to take advantage of the fact that I was talking to someone who was secretly on our side.

What could I say that would destabilize the Empire?

The answer arrived immediately. "I stand with the Thuins," I blurted, interrupting whatever Madden had been saying.

"What?" Madden said. He looked truly shocked.

"I stand with the Thuins," I repeated. "For those of you who think you're better than them, you're not. For the rest of you, I'm with you. I'm innocent. I'm going to escape. And when I do, I'm going to destroy the Empire."

Maybe, just maybe, we'll get a miracle. If Madden is working for us, he'll find a way to let that clip reach everyone watching.

"Madden, you want that edited out, right?" a voice said from off-screen. "I need your confirmation in the next ten seconds. Madden?"

There was something wrong with Elvis Madden. It took me a moment to realize it, because I was still surprised at myself for having tried something so daring, but Madden was no longer smiling. He looked pained. He stared straight into the camera, his face contorted, and then his hands flew to his chest and he fell forward. His head cracked against the wooden desk and he fell sideways, out of his chair and out of sight.

To anyone watching, it looked like I'd given Elvis Madden a heart attack.

But I knew the truth.

Elvis Madden, you genius. Our man on the outside.

My words hadn't just gone out; Madden had *let* them out. He'd faked that heart attack to buy time, and he had plausible deniability. His weak heart was well-documented, and he'd recently gotten a terrible shock: one of the world's greatest athletes supported the Empire's enemies.

Someone disconnected me from the Kinetoscope, and I stumbled backward, trying to suppress a grin. Feng caught me. He pressed a wooden box into my hands, so I ripped off the top, reaching in and wrapping my fingers around the first thing they touched. It was a vial that fit in the palm of my hand, filled to the brim with clear liquid and capped with a cork.

Potion of Complete Healing

Brewed from a blend of rare herbs and extracts found in the deepest levels of Toroth-Gol, this potion will knit bones, heal wounds, and restore lost limbs.

"Jocko, take this!" I said to the Grass King, who stood beside me. "It should fix your arm."

Jocko snatched the vial with his good hand, ripped the cork out with his teeth, and swallowed the contents immediately. A second later, he grunted as his broken arm snapped back into place with a sound like the *crack* of a leather belt.

"*Yes*," he hissed.

"Don't just stand there," Feng growled. "The mulchers are coming, and I don't want to die again."

As soon as he said it, the front door broke, and mulchers spilled into the armory. They shrieked in anger and started charging toward us.

"What are we supposed to do?" Jocko said. "We don't have any weapons except the Cuddle Club."

"Use that, then!" I said. I looked back at the box in my hand. There was something wrapped in tissue paper, and I tore the paper aside to reveal a pair of boots. They looked like my Empire-issued boots, down to the size.

Steel-Toed Combat Boots of Levitation

These boots are crafted from supple leather and reinforced with steel in the toes. Upon activation, the wearer experiences a weightless sensation as if walking on air. Their magical properties grant the wearer unparalleled mobility, enabling them to traverse treacherous terrains, bypass obstacles, and soar above dangerous precipices. To use, put on the boots and think *activate*.

WARNING: Levitation effect only works for a single two-hundred-pound person.

"Hold them off, guys," I said. "I need a few seconds, and then I'm getting us out of here."

Jocko disappeared in a spray of leaves and reappeared before the line of charging mulchers, swinging the Cuddle Club into one of the toad-like creatures with a form that would've made any lightball enforcer jealous. I didn't get to see if the Cuddle Club had any magical effect on the creature, because the mulcher... crumpled. Another mulcher landed where Jocko had been standing, though the Grass

King was already gone, colorful leaves drifting to the ground in his wake.

I didn't stick around to watch anything else. Instead, I ducked to one side of the doorway and sat on the ground with my back to the wall and set my new boots on the ground before me. I got my left boot off without a problem, but the laces of my right boot were hardened by blood and grime, the knot pulled so tightly I couldn't pick it apart.

"By the Dregs," I growled. I yanked at my boot, but I still couldn't get it off.

Am I going to die because I can't undo a shoelace?

I was helpless. I felt like I had in that dream where I was trying to run from something and my legs wouldn't cooperate.

"Hold me over the boot," Perry said from my bandolier. "My acid can eat that knot."

The thought was unpleasant, though so was the idea of getting ripped apart by mulchers. I pulled him from his spot on my bandolier.

Please don't put a hole through my foot, I thought as the tomato burped. Liquid dribbled from between his lips and splashed against my boot. I held my breath as the knot dissolved into gray mush. I yanked my boot off, not caring that some of the liquid scorched my hands, and pulled on my new Steel-Toed Combat Boots of Levitation.

"Perry, I could kiss your bristly head," I said, hanging him from my bandolier once again. I got to my feet. "We're good!" I shouted to Feng and Jocko. "Fall back!"

I peered around the doorway. I shouldn't have done it, but I was curious.

Mulchers raced around the room or swung like monkeys from the ceiling. Their wet-dog scent was like a slap to the face, as was the music that followed them, the deep, thumping bass and whine of electric guitars.

They were no longer trying to reach my little room. Instead, they were focused on the man that flitted through their midst.

Feng backpedaled into the room, Xena on his shoulder. Jocko appeared beside us and I slammed the double doors shut. They wouldn't hold for long, but I hoped it would buy us at least a few seconds.

"What have you got?" Jocko said as he gasped for breath.

In response, I pulled Perry from my bandolier and shot him at the floor-to-ceiling window that made up the full back wall of the chamber. Clearly knowing what I wanted, he vomited on the glass and it burned away. Cool air rushed through the gap.

"We're jumping," I said. "Hang on."

"Wait a minute, *pacho*," Jocko said. "We're *what?*"

But I didn't wait to respond, because then I'd lose my nerve. Instead, I ran at the gap in the window and lowered my shoulder.

"*Faesala*," Jocko hissed, cursing in Thuin. He pounded after me.

My shoulder connected with the glass, which broke before me, and I jumped. Arms wrapped around my waist. My fingers found an arm and I squeezed tightly as I brought my heels together.

Activate.

The boots whirred to life, and it was like the air had turned viscous. We slowed, but not nearly enough to survive if we hit the ground. The boots were meant to hold one person, not three people and two pieces of sapient produce.

We fell like stones, and the ground rushed to meet us.

30

W ithout the benefit of the levitation boots, several mulchers fell past us. They screamed and flailed their long arms as they plummeted toward the ravine floor.

Idiots.

But who was the idiot, really? The mulchers were little better than animals, sentient but not intelligent. A rational person could hardly blame them for throwing themselves off a cliff in pursuit of an enemy.

Me? I was supposed to be *smart*. Still, I'd jumped off the side of a cliff without thinking of the potential consequences.

As we fell, those consequences caught up to me. Something in the boots whirred, then guttered. We dropped thirty feet in a free fall and my stomach rose into my throat. I screamed before the boots kicked in again.

"They can't support us!" I shouted as another mulcher fell past us. The wind stole my words and made my eyes water. I ran some mental math and realized we only had a few seconds until impact.

Then Jocko was gone, and a spray of leaves blew past me. I looked down, though I didn't see where he landed.

Jocko had said that he couldn't teleport to the ravine floor from the hotel, but we're closer to the ground now. I hope we're close enough.

Without Jocko's extra weight, our descent slowed further. Still, I knew it wouldn't be enough.

"Bring me back, if you can," Feng said.

I should've realized what he meant, but for some reason it didn't occur to me until Xena hopped to my shoulder. Then, Feng let go. Without his added weight, the boots worked as intended, and I slowed.

Feng didn't.

"No!" I shouted. Twice now, Feng had sacrificed himself for me. How many more times would I have to watch my friends die before I escaped the dungeon?

And yet, my survival still wasn't guaranteed. Something in the boots was clearly broken, because they whirred and guttered, and I fell fifty feet before they started again. The ground was closer now, but I still wouldn't survive if I went into free fall.

Hold. Please hold for a few more seconds. Then I crashed through the pine trees, cracking branches and dislodging needles in my fall. I bent my legs in preparation for impact and took a branch to the shins. It felt like getting hit with an enforcer's bat. I grunted as I did a full front flip over the branch, which dislodged Xena from my shoulder and sent her flying off into the forest. I made to snag her with the magnetism from my glove, but lost sight of her as another branch smacked me in the face.

Whump. A huge branch hit me in the stomach. I tipped backward and pinwheeled my arms for a few seconds until I landed flat on my back.

If there'd been anything in my lungs after taking that branch to the stomach, it was ripped out of me upon impact with the ground.

"Ugh," I groaned.

I lay on the ground and watched pine needles fall around me. I couldn't breathe. When I inhaled, my lungs spasmed, and I only managed a series of shallow, hiccuping gasps. Something whined.

Mosquitoes? Maybe even death mosquitoes.

Then, I realized the noise was coming from my boots.

Deactivate. There was a soft *clunk* before the whining stopped. I smelled smoke and had a feeling I wouldn't be using the Steel-Toed Combat Boots of Levitation anytime soon.

"Crow?" Perry called to me from his spot on my bandolier. "I hate to rush you, but if the mulchers have any type of communication system, those forces we saw in the ravine will probably be here any minute."

I stood, finally managing to work some air into my lungs. "Xena?" I called hoarsely. "Xena, can you hear me?"

"Over here!" The eggplant called from somewhere to my right.

I stumbled deeper into the forest and found her next to Feng's corpse. It didn't look good. He must've hit branches on the way down, because half of his face was caved in. One arm lay under him at an angle that suggested it was broken.

"Can you bring him back?" I asked.

Xena glanced up at me. "I'm the most talented necromancer of an age," she said. "Watch this."

Like Spud's Hot Potato ability, I didn't need to command Xena's power. It was something she could wield herself. As I watched, purple smoke poured from her mouth, drifted across the forest floor, and hovered around Feng's body like a shield.

What am I going to say when he gets up? I thought as I waited for Feng's eyes to snap open. *I owe him an apology, at least. He was the one who let go, but I would be dead if he hadn't.*

Behind us, the mulchers' strange music started up again. *Thump, thump, thump.* I glanced over my shoulder.

Is that music coming from the hotel, or did the mulchers find a way down here? I didn't know, though I didn't want to stick around and find out.

"Come on," I hissed to Xena. "Get him back."

"There's a problem," Xena said, a note of doubt in her voice.

"Problem?" My heart dropped. "What do you mean?"

"There's something blocking my magic," she said. "Ordinarily, I could bring him back easily, but he's right on the edge. I can see him, though I can't reach him. It's like there's an invisible wall between us."

"Can you get past it?" I asked as the noise behind me grew louder.

Now, it wasn't only the bass of the mulchers' music, but something else.

Footfalls. The ground vibrated beneath us. *Something is coming. Something big.*

"I might be able to, with time, but I don't think we *have* time," Xena said. "I'm sorry, Crow. We need to leave him."

"We're *not* leaving him," I said. The music was loud now, and I heard the grunting of mulchers, along with the sound of cracking branches, and those loud, ground-shaking footfalls. The whole forest shook, and the tops of the trees swayed as if moving from the path of something large and terrible.

"Let's go, Crow," Xena said. "Run!"

"Throw him in your Inventory!" Perry shouted.

I didn't know if it would work, but I tried. Sure enough, Feng's body disappeared into my Inventory. Whatever blocked her magic didn't seem to stop my Inventory access.

The first mulcher broke the treeline.

They're here. I didn't know how they'd managed to reach me so quickly, but I didn't care. I darted into the woods, heedless of the branches that smacked me in the face. *Better a branch to the face than a spitting ball of acid in the back.*

I ran. Some of the mulchers pounded after me along the ground while others swung through the trees. More than one of them threw their mucus at me, but the trees were too thick for that to be effective. The acidic balls sizzled against the trunks.

Bad for the environment, good for me.

I ran until I felt like I'd collapse. At some point, it'd become darker than it had been. I found that strange, because we were underground. Why bother simulating night and day? But my thoughts on the matter didn't change anything.

With the oncoming darkness, I couldn't avoid all of the branches that hit me in the face, or the logs that banged against my shins. I fell. I slipped into a small creek, the water filling my boots and soaking my jumpsuit up to my knees. I got up and continued running, only to fall again. I threw out my hands to stop my chin from slamming into the ground. My gloves kept me from skinning my palms.

Xena could see in the dark and tried to be helpful, but was too distraught to be much use.

"I'm sorry," she moaned between directions. "Left. No, right! Right! I'm useless. Crow, I'm so sorry!"

"Stop shouting," I growled. "Any sign of the mulchers?"

"No," Xena said. "And before you ask, I haven't seen Jocko either. And for whatever reason, I still can't access my power. Something down here is blocking it."

I leaned against a tree. "I'm not sure if it makes sense to keep running like this," I said. "Soon, it's going to be too dark to see, so I'm worried I might run into something worse than what's behind us. Where are we even going? We don't have a destination."

From somewhere distant came the low roar of something that was definitely *not* a mulcher. I thought of the shaking ground and the trees I'd seen swaying like they were matchsticks.

"On second thought, I could probably go a little farther," I said.

I continued. Finally, it really *was* too dark to run. I stopped and put my hands on my knees. I was hot, disoriented, and angry. But at least I could no longer hear the mulchers' music, and I'd escaped whatever creature had been making those heavy footfalls. Now, there was only the sound of crickets and my own heavy breathing.

"Jocko?" I called quietly. I didn't expect a response, and I didn't get one. "Xena, can you bring back Feng yet?"

"No," the eggplant moaned. "I'm still blocked."

"What now, then?" Perry asked.

I ran a hand over my head. "Xena, watch the darkness and alert me if anything moves," I said. "I'm going to look at the Map and see what I can find."

I pulled up my Map. Since the upgraded Map I'd gotten on the last level of the dungeon hadn't been an Inventory item, Sor'kodich hadn't been able to take it. I found our location in the forest.

I saw something else as well: the icon of a door.

That must be the exit to the next level, I thought, my pulse quickening. *Or one of them, at least.*

The icon was in a part of the Map called the Subterranean Dig Site, which wasn't far off, though it would be difficult to reach. There was a cliff at one edge of the forest, and another several-hundred-foot drop between me and the area with the door.

If I could still use those boots, it wouldn't be a problem, I thought, though I had a feeling the boots were out of commission. They worked well enough to protect my feet, but when I activated them, they sparked and whined.

"What's going on, Crow?" Perry asked. "You see anything?"

I turned the Map. There was another way to reach the dig site, though it required me to get back up to the armory. From there, the streets led to a ramp that zigzagged down the canyon walls and headed straight to the icon.

"I think I've found us a way out of here," I said. "We have to get back up to the streets."

"What about Jocko?" Perry asked.

I didn't know how to respond. If our roles were reversed, would the Grass King try to find me? Or would he leave me to fend for myself, and, if I survived, claim it was all part of some test?

My thoughts were interrupted by Xena. "Hey Crow, remember when you told me to watch the darkness and let you know if anything moved?" she asked. "There's something here. Straight ahead."

I turned off the Map and peered into the forest. Two red eyes stared back at me.

I'm so close to escaping. Now I've got to fight something else?

But there was no way of avoiding it. Whatever was in the darkness had clearly seen me. I pulled Perry into my hand and set him to hover above my palm.

"Let's go, whatever you are!" I yelled to whatever owned the red eyes. "You want to fight? Let's dance."

"That doesn't make sense, Crow," Perry said. "Are we fighting or dancing? Also, I'm not sure it's a great idea to yell at scary things in the woods."

"Shut up, Perry," Xena hissed. "Don't you see he's having a moment? Oh god. I sound like Spud, don't I?"

The red eyes blinked, and their owner stepped from the darkness.

It was a man. He wore a brown trench coat over a deep tunic that was unbuttoned to his stomach, exposing a toned chest. His hands were dyed blue. Instead of a weapon, he held a violin, and something flitted around his head.

Is that a fairy? The small creature also had red eyes.

Pirate Piper (Marland Thorne)

Marland Thorne originally hails from the Red Hills, home to a religious cult of silent adherents that cuts out the tongues of their children. As a result, Marland is mute.

After the sack of the Red Hills by the infamous pirate captain Nile "Whitemane" Thorne, Marland was adopted as a cabin boy aboard the *Rancid Pearl*. When Whitemane died, Marland's sister Cara Thorne became captain of the ship, and Marland took on the role of quartermaster. He was captured along with the rest of the *Rancid Pearl's* crew and sentenced to Toroth-Gol for piracy.

I opened my mouth to speak, but a sultry voice cut me off at the same time that the barrel of a pistol pressed against the base of my skull.

"Hello, Crow," Cara Thorne said from behind me. "I was hoping I'd see you again."

31

I wanted to think of something interesting to say, or at least something that wouldn't get me killed. But then the pistol fell away, and Cara lowered the hammer.

"Turn around," she said.

The fierce woman who stood behind me looked as she had in Contessa Georgia's Ballroom in the Castle of 1,000 Doors. Same trench coat and ruffled shirt, same wavy hair and full lips. Same description I'd gotten in the castle.

The only difference was the weapon in her hand, though maybe I hadn't noticed it the last time. It was a flintlock pistol made of dark, polished wood with silver ornamentation on the butt of the stock and along the barrel. Text flashed across my vision.

Duel-Bound Captain's Flintlock

This pistol passes only through single combat, with each new owner claiming it from the fallen.

The weapon cannot misfire, jam, or lose potency due to water, rust, or environmental hazards. When wielded by a recognized

captain (formal or de facto), the pistol's shots gain enhanced penetration and impact force.

"I'd say fate has drawn us back together, but I doubt that has anything to do with it," Cara said. "Are there others with you?"

"There were, but they're gone," I said. "Only me and my weapons now."

Cara watched me curiously, and then her gaze dropped and she focused on Perry and Xena.

Keep your mouths shut. The last time I saw this crew, they murdered my friend's girlfriend to steal her gear. They're absolutely dangerous and I don't trust them.

"Huh," Cara said. "You're amassing a collection of vegetables. How do they work? You shoot them or something?"

I wasn't going to share *that*. "Technically, they're fruits." It was dumb, but the less the pirates knew about my capabilities, the better.

Cara snorted. She twirled the gun around her index finger, caught the stock, and shoved the weapon into her waistband.

"Don't tell me, then." She stepped past me, moving deeper into the forest. "We were making camp when Marland heard you. You're welcome to stay with us if you'd like."

Cara and Marland walked into the woods, Marland's little fairy narrowing her eyes at us in suspicion before turning a neat pirouette and zipping ahead of them.

Do I follow? I didn't have anywhere else to go, and although I still hated Cara and her crew for killing Geeta's partner, we were united in our desire to escape Dungeon School without dying.

"Stay quiet," I whispered to Xena and Perry. "I want to see how this plays out."

I followed them through the woods, Marland's fairy illuminating the path and allowing us to avoid branches and stumps.

"How'd you get down here?" I asked. "Where have you been since we last saw you?"

"We went through a door called the High Seas," Cara said. She snorted. "Hardly much of a challenge for three seasoned pirates. We found ourselves on the deck of a ship, and it was a raid test. Our fleet was attacking a well-fortified fortress."

"You participated in the raid?" I asked.

"We *led* the raid," Cara corrected. "Pirate law lets anyone challenge a captain to single combat. So I did. Obviously. You should've seen it, Crow: the fortress burning, the masts creaking, and cannonballs splashing around us. I took down their man with a blade to the heart. Got control of the fleet, and the captain's pistol, to boot."

She patted the weapon in her waistband.

"I could've stayed on the ocean all day, but we were racing against the clock, trying to get inside the fortress and find the door to Dungeon School," she said. "When we found it, we ended up on that little platform with the four towers. I imagine you arrived at the same one?"

I nodded.

"We chose Winter Ridge, mostly because we wanted to stick together. Ugly place. More booby-trapped rooms than I've ever seen in my life. I was rather thankful when they told us we could leave."

"Leave?" I said. "How's that?"

She squinted at me. "The final test?" I shook my head. "Why are *you* in the Valves, then?"

"Our school was attacked by monsters," I said. "The Valves were our escape route. You're down here for something else?"

"At Winter Ridge, we were told we'd have a final test, which meant going deep into the Valves and retrieving an egg from some type of lizard that lives down here," Cara said. "If we brought it back to the entrance, the instructors would tell us where to find the door that leads to the third level."

"Right," I said. It made sense the towers would have different graduation requirements. It also meant Rayne was down here somewhere, too.

We entered a clearing with a small fire in the center. A man sat before it. Like Cara and Marland, his hands were dyed blue.

Magic Swashbuckler (Skeev Thorne)

Of the four children raised by the infamous pirate Nile "White-mane" Thorne, only Skeev wasn't adopted. Despite this, he let his sister Cara take over the *Rancid Pearl*, and he took on the role of first mate. He was captured along with the rest of the *Rancid Pearl's* crew and sentenced to Toroth-Gol for piracy.

"Well, well, well, look who it is!" Skeev said in a booming voice. He stood and his joints popped. "I thought we might be getting attacked by mulchers, or have to deal with a random stranger, but it's a celebrity. King Crow! Look at that, Cara. You haven't stopped talking about him since we left the castle, and now he's here in the flesh."

"Shut up, Skeev," Cara said. She shoved him as she walked past him, then dropped to a seat near the fire. But there was no heat in her words or actions. Skeev winked and came toward me, his hand extended.

"Skeev Thorne, former first mate of the *Rancid Pearl*. I don't think we've officially met."

I grasped the pirate's hand. His grip was firm, but not crushing. After we'd shaken, he ran a hand through his shaggy mane and swept the hair from his eyepatch.

"You'll forgive me if I don't stay up to trade ghost stories," he said. "I haven't rested in two days. Now that Cara and Marland are back, I might get some sleep. If that's okay with you, Cara?"

"Go ahead," Cara said. "Marland, you can rest, too. I'll take first watch with Crow."

Skeev smirked, and Cara flashed him an unsavory hand signal.

"I didn't say a word, Cara!" Skeev said.

"Go to bed, Skeev," she said.

Skeev gave us an exaggerated bow, and then walked to the edge of the clearing, where several bedrolls lay along the ground. Marland followed his brother.

"I hope you don't mind that I volunteered you to watch," Cara said after they were gone.

I shrugged. Two weeks before, sitting with a beautiful woman beside a fire would've certainly been my idea of a good time, but

Toroth-Gol had put a damper on everything, and I knew too much about Cara to view her as anything more than a monster.

I sat down on one of the logs around the fire where I could keep one eye on Cara and the other on the forms of her two brothers. We sat in silence for a while, and then Cara said, "Well?"

"Well, what?" I said.

"You gonna say something, or are you gonna make a woman sit in silence?"

"I have nothing to say to you," I said.

"You don't want to ask *any* questions?" She smiled at me, and it made me mad that I felt my heart rate spike. "I know you, Crow. I've always been good at reading people, and the power I got from the dungeon gave me an imperfect form of mind reading. I can't do it perfectly, but I get impressions, which is how I know you have questions. Go on. Ask."

I sighed. A part of me didn't want to let her explain herself. *Good people don't murder innocents. Especially not ones they've enslaved.*

"I'll answer anyway, because I know you want to know," Cara said. "Like you, I'm adopted. I don't remember my parents, only the man who raised me as his own: Nile Thorne, king of the pirates and captain of the *Rancid Pearl*. They called him 'Whitemane' on account of his hair."

"I don't really care," I said.

She gave a little laugh, and her eyes twinkled in the firelight. "There were four of us raised aboard the *Rancid Pearl*: Marland, Hildar, Skeev, and me. Skeev was our father's only real child. Nile found me in the aftermath of a raid. We're probably both too young to remember this, but from what my father told me, Atlantis was preparing to break from the Empire and side with the Thuins. The Empire didn't like that, as Atlantis had the biggest standing navy in the world. So, the Empire raised a navy of their own and sent pirates all throughout the Great Basin to interrupt trade and harass anyone sympathetic to the Thuins. Whatever island I come from was wrecked in that war. We picked up Hildar from a camp of nomads smuggling goods on behalf of the Thuins from Atlantis to Ironwood a few years later, and then got Marland when we razed the Red Hills."

She enslaved your friend. Killed her partner. There's no excuse for actions like that.

"In many ways, it was an idyllic childhood," Cara continued. "Plenty of adventures. Whitemane taught the four of us himself, making us excuse ourselves from our duties so we could review letters, numbers, and history in his cabin. From the crew, I learned swordsmanship and how to cook a mean cod soup. Pretty much everything a child needs to be successful."

"And yet, you turned out like this," I said.

Cara raised an eyebrow at me. *"Rude,"* she said. "I don't know how much you know about pirates, but we're not what you see on the screens. There's a code we follow. Rules that govern our behaviors, like you'd find in any other modern society. It works like this: across the world, there are eight great seas, and each one has a pirate lord who enforces the rules set at an annual convocation. The lords are overseen by the pirate king or queen. That's a lifetime position, though anyone can issue a challenge for it by fighting to the death in single combat. In my lifetime, I saw Whitemane face and kill six challengers."

I thought I knew where the story was going. "The seventh got him," I said.

"No." Cara's eyes blazed. "I was there. I saw what happened. Stephanie Xalarmis approached our ship under the guise of a challenge, but it was late, and when the terms were set, she agreed to duel at first light. But in the night, her crew stole aboard the *Rancid Pearl* and killed our men. All the mentors from my childhood were gone like that."

She snapped her fingers.

"Xalarmis was a Thuin sympathizer, and she didn't like the contract my father had taken with the Empire," she continued. "She could've challenged him, as was the way of our people, but she didn't. She killed him in cold blood and stole the title of Pirate Queen for herself."

"But you survived." Against my better judgment, I was fully invested in the story now. "You and your siblings."

"Stephanie said she wouldn't have the blood of children on her hands. Instead of killing us, she tied us up. Set us in a rowboat and left us off the coast of the Crescent. The waters are choppy there, and I think she expected us to die, but we survived. Without a penny to our names, we made our way north, relying on each other and our skills. It took three weeks, but we finally made it to Helios."

"Capital of the Empire."

"Right. Our plan was to find our father's allies and tell them what had happened. But when we got there, those 'allies' laughed at us. They didn't care about their agreement. They wanted my father's ships. Since we no longer had anything to offer them, they turned their backs on us and sent us back into the streets. That's when I made three promises to myself. The first was that I'd avenge my father by killing Stephanie Xalarmis and retaking the *Rancid Pearl*. The second was that I'd make the Empire pay for abandoning us. And the third was that I'd keep my siblings safe, no matter the costs."

"Are you surprised the Empire went back on their word?"

Cara shook her head. "Not now, no. But I was young then. More trusting. Certainly naïve enough to swear myself to those three vows. Once I did, they became the stars by which I navigated. Do you know what it takes to overthrow a pirate captain? You have to convince scores of people to follow you through terrible conditions, often when food, water, and treasure are scarce, all while you hope they never decide to mutiny. It's easier if the crew doesn't have a choice. So that answers the first question you didn't ask, and tells you why I enslaved Geeta. As to your second, I don't have an excuse other than to say that my brothers wanted the reptilian's Inventory, and they're not afraid to use violence to get what they want. I don't like it, but I know who I am, and I know what I vowed to myself; who would I be if I broke my own code? I'm a pirate, Crow, and that means something. I'm not proud of what Skeev did, though I'm going to protect my siblings no matter what. Even when they do terrible things. Does that make sense?"

"No," I said. "I understand your logic, though I don't agree with it. In my world, the end never justifies the means. I'm sure that's how the Empire rationalizes throwing us all into Toroth-Gol. They say, 'Oh, it gets rid of our prisoners, and the rule-abiding citizens get something to watch.' Meanwhile, we're down here fighting for our lives."

Cara shrugged. "To each their own. You have another question. My power tells me that much, though I can't see what you're thinking. So go on. Ask me."

"Why didn't you kill me earlier?" I asked. "You had a pistol to my head. If you really wanted to protect your family, you could've shot me and taken my items. But you let me live. Why is that?"

Cara laughed. "Isn't it obvious? You have information we need. Right before we caught you, we heard you talking, and you said you knew a way out. We could try to complete Winter Ridge's final test, but this seems quicker. It's much easier to seduce you by a fire than to go on a hunt for some stupid lizard egg."

I snorted. *Nothing like honesty to put a man off balance.*

"That's what this is?" I said. "You're seducing me for information?"

She slid across the log so that she sat directly beside me. "Would it work if I said yes?"

I pushed her away. She laughed and returned to her original position.

"What's to stop you from killing me once I tell you?" I asked.

Cara shook her head like it wasn't something she'd considered. "Pirates follow a code. If we give you our word, we mean it. So I'll give my word: if you tell us how to get out of here, you walk. If you don't, well, you've seen my brothers. They're violent, Crow. If it comes to protecting you or them, you know which way I'll lean."

A shiver ran through me. Cara said they'd let me walk, and that pirates had an unfair reputation, yet I still didn't know if I could believe her.

Maybe I could bargain with them. I have what they need, but what do I want? A few things came to mind. I want Feng and Devora back, and I want to find Jocko and murder Sor'kodich. For good, this time. Can these pirates help with any of that?

I needed more time to think about it. One thing was certain: when I revealed the information, I'd give up my leverage. If I did that with a murderer's word as my only reassurance, I knew I had to be sure they meant it.

"I'll think about it," I said. "Give me until tomorrow."

Cara nodded. "I should be able to restrain my brothers until then. But don't waste time, Crow. They're unpredictable."

The rest of the evening passed uneventfully, with Cara and me staring at the fire and thinking our own thoughts. I didn't realize a few hours had passed until Marland walked toward the fire.

I checked my timer. Sure enough, it was time for him to take over the watch.

Cara glanced at me, then jerked a thumb toward the forest where he'd exited. "Do you want to sleep with us?" I could've been mistaken, but I thought there was a twinkle of hope in her eyes. "You can use Marland's bedroll. Or you could share mine if you want."

I shook my head. "That's all right. I'm going to find another place to sleep. I'll find you here in the morning."

Cara raised an eyebrow. "Sleep tight, Crow. Remember what I said."

"I will. Good night."

I turned and walked into the forest. With every step, I waited to hear the click of the hammer on Cara's pistol, or the *snick* of a blade leaving its scabbard.

If she shoots, will you hear the bang before the bullet hits your skull?

After fifty yards, my thoughts changed from, *She's definitely going to kill you,* to, *She might be a woman of her word.* A hundred yards after that, when I found myself still alive, I realized she was letting me get away.

"Xena," I whispered, after a while. "Anyone following us? One of the pirates, or that fairy?"

"Not that I can see," Xena said. "Which is weird. I could've sworn they were going to take you out."

I didn't wait to see whether or not that was still a possibility. When I was certain the pirates weren't following me, I started running.

3 2

Although I was surprised Cara had let me get away, I still didn't trust the pirates, so I wasn't surprised when—only two hours after I'd fallen asleep—Xena yelled, "Get up, Crow! They're coming!"

In hindsight, I suppose the 'they' to whom Xena referred could have been any of the many groups that had recently attempted to kill me, but I'd closed my eyes thinking, *I'll eat my gloves if I get through the night without Cara or Marland or Skeev trying to rob me.* So when Xena called out, I woke from a shallow sleep and got to my feet expecting pirates.

I was right.

"You've got to be kidding me, Marland," Skeev hissed from somewhere in the darkness. As a precaution, I'd left my battery pack on, and my paranoia paid off as I drew Perry into my hand. "You weren't supposed to let the eggplant hear you. Hey, Crow! We don't want to hurt you. Come out and we'll talk this through."

That *obviously* wasn't happening. It didn't seem like they'd discovered my spot yet, but with them so close, it was only a matter of time before they found me.

What's their play? I listened to them creep through the woods. *Are they hoping to kill me? Torture me? Something else?*

"Come out, come out, Crow!" Skeev said.

They're hoping I run for the exit. Well, I can run, all right, but I'm not going there.

I bolted.

"There!" Skeev shouted. "Go, Marland, go!"

They crashed through the woods behind me. Skeev whooped as he ran, and the manic joy he got from chasing another human chilled me to the bone.

I'm really getting tired of all this running.

Spiderwebs brushed against my face. I cracked branches and sent flurries of pine needles raining in my wake.

Still, I was faster than my pursuers. In a footrace through a forest at night, I had several advantages. For one, Xena's sight cut through the darkness, and she called out major obstacles for me. Additionally, my lightball career had been forcibly paused only two weeks prior, which is to say I was a professional athlete in the prime of my fitness. Also, while the pirates stood to gain some treasure, I was running for my life. Athlete or not, stakes like that would perk up any man's step.

But Marland had his red-eyed fairy. Clearly, she could see in the dark as well as Xena, since no matter how fast I ran, the little creature kept pace. She flitted above us, deftly avoiding branches. Her eyes didn't simply glow, but *shone*. In the dark forest, she was a beacon that drew the attention of the pirates.

"He slipped past you, Marland!" Skeev shouted from the woods behind me. "Follow Hazel's light. Starboard side. Go!"

"By the Dregs," I hissed. I didn't know what to do. With the fairy broadcasting our position, I could backtrack through the entire forest, yet the pirates would still be able to follow.

There was only one solution for it: I needed to get rid of the fairy.

"How much do you trust me?" I asked Perry.

"With all my heart," Perry said. "Though I did just wake up."

"Vomit when ready," I said.

"Oh, so we're doing this," Perry said. "Keep me safe, Crow!"

Ordinarily, this was a shot I would make with Spud. He was heavier than Perry, and harder, far better suited for precision shots than his squishier brother. But at the moment, Spud wasn't an option, and he wouldn't be for at least another few hours.

I didn't stop running as I looked up and found the fairy darting overhead. *This is easy*, I told myself as I fought to control my breathing. *You've made harder shots a thousand times before. She's glowing like a practice flyer. That thing is practically begging to be shot.*

I extended my arm and fired. The fairy didn't have time to dodge. The little tomato performed as well as I could've hoped. I didn't see the vomit splash, but from somewhere behind me, Marland screamed in pain, like he'd been stabbed with a hot poker.

No tongue, but he can still scream. I pulled Perry back toward me. *He must've had a mental connection that was severed when she died. Good. I hope it was agony.*

Perry slapped into my hand, and I didn't miss a step.

"Nice job, Perry," I said.

"I couldn't have done it without you," Perry said. "The shot was perfect."

I slapped Perry against my bandolier and pulled up my Map. From what I could see, I was running *away* from the Subterranean Dig Site, back toward the spot where I'd originally landed. That was fine. I still didn't know if I should try to find Jocko or not. I needed to shake the pirates, and then I could make a plan.

I closed my Map. With my superior speed, and without Hazel to give away my position, it wasn't long before the only sounds were my own heavy breathing and the crack of branches under my boots.

You did it. You bloodied their noses, and you escaped.

But I wasn't ready to celebrate. Not yet.

After another few hundred yards, I broke through the tree line. Ahead of me was a hundred yards of clear ground, and beyond that was the Subterranean Dig Site.

The Valves (Subterranean Dig Site)

Just as the prey built their towers above the Valves, the Valves were constructed atop an older civilization. Thus, when the prey left,

they didn't only abandon the Valves, but the ruins on which it was built.

Today, few know about this ancient civilization, and fewer still have seen their artifacts, though one intrepid group of explorers managed to establish this dig site before the scholars in the towers lost contact with them.

"This doesn't make any sense," I said, pulling up my Map. Sure enough, I stood on the edge of the cliff that overlooked the site.

How is this possible? Back in the forest, I'd checked the Map twice, and I'd been heading in the opposite direction of the site. How was it that the site had come to be spread out before me? Had I been turned around?

"Hands where I can see them, Crow," a voice said from behind me.

I didn't need to turn around to know that Cara Thorne had a pistol trained at the back of my skull. I raised my hands.

"What did you do to me?" I asked. "How did we get here?"

"I told you I could read minds, but I also gained the ability to influence them to some degree," Cara said. "You thought you were heading deeper into the forest, but I had you running toward me. For what it's worth, I told you the truth last night: I'll protect my brothers, but I don't want to kill you. I like you, Crow, and I want you to survive."

"You have a funny way of showing it," I said.

Cara continued as if I hadn't said anything. "My first loyalty is to my family," she said. "So how do we get out of here? Like I said, I don't want to kill you, but if you don't tell me how to get out, I'll do it. You can still walk away. I give you my word: tell me how to escape and I won't shoot."

I snorted. Maybe it wasn't the smartest move to antagonize someone who was pointing a gun at me, but I couldn't let that slide.

"So you won't *shoot*," I said. "You'll stab me instead, or you'll blow me up, or poison me, and the whole time you'll tell yourself you were in the right, that you kept your word, because it wasn't your bullet that killed me."

"I won't," she mumbled, but I knew the truth.

"So you'll have Marland do it," I said. "Or Skeev. I'm sorry, Cara, but if I've learned anything in Dungeon School, it's how to tell when I'm being manipulated. You might think you know people, and maybe you do, but when it comes to manipulation, you're not close to the best of them. I see right through you."

I turned around. Cara stood twenty paces away, her pistol held in both hands and the barrel pointed at my chest. There was something poetic about the scene, a lone gunslinger and her opponent at the edge of a cliff. I looked down the pistol's sights at her bright eyes and saw them narrow slightly. She was deadly serious and wouldn't hesitate to kill me.

Something came out of the trees behind her. At first, I thought it was Skeev, or Marland, but the figure was too small for that, too slight. My heart leapt into my throat as I realized it was Jocko. Despite the broken branches and dead leaves underfoot, the Grass King moved silently, slipping from the forest like an adder. His right hand was wrapped around the hilt of the Cuddle Club. With his left, he raised a finger to his lips.

I saw what he would try to do and swallowed. I didn't like Cara, but I had to think she could change. When she'd said that her words from the previous night were true, I believed her. She liked me. She cared about her family. The desire to protect her siblings and avenge her father manifested in evil, destructive ways, but that didn't mean redemption wasn't possible.

"You don't have to do this, Cara," I said. "Neither of us has any love for the Empire. No one down here does. Let me help you. I want nothing more than for as many of us to escape as possible. When we do, we'll bring down the Empire together."

Behind her, Jocko crept closer. I only had seconds to make a difference.

I thought my words had reached her. Then her eyes hardened and she tightened her grip on the pistol.

"Last chance," she said. "Weapons on the ground. Now."

With her thumb, Cara pulled back the hammer of her pistol. There was a *click* as it settled into place.

"I'm sorry, Crow," she whispered.

"So am I," I said.

Jocko moved with astonishing speed, his club connecting with Cara's head a moment after he disappeared in a spray of leaves. Still, he wasn't quicker than the slight pressure of an index finger on a hair trigger. There was a *crack* as the gun discharged, followed by a ripple like thunder as the sound rolled across the ravine.

At its fastest, a lightball travels around two hundred miles per hour. A bullet moves *five times* that speed, a neat little fact I knew from defensive training with my father. I raised my hands and activated the magnetism in my gloves, and the bullet meant for my heart spun wide. It buzzed over the ravine like a pesky gnat, turning end over end as it fell.

A twelve-gram bullet fired from a handgun can achieve nearly six hundred foot-pounds of force. This was another fun fact I'd learned from my father. All of that force needed to go *somewhere*.

In this case, it was dispersed through me.

I stumbled backward. Under any other circumstances, that might not've been a problem, but I was standing on the edge of a cliff. I took one step, then another, knowing what would happen but unable to stop myself.

"*Pacho!*" Jocko yelled. In front of him, Cara fell to the ground. Half her beautiful head had been caved in by the club. Her brown hair was matted to her face by blood and gore, and her mouth was formed into the shape of a shocked O. Her single undamaged eye, still clear and bright, stared lifelessly past me.

That eye was the last thing I saw before I tripped into nothingness.

Then, I was falling, too.

THE END OF BOOK TWO

AFTERWORD

BY THE DREGS!

You finished *another* book! That either means you enjoyed it, or Spud wouldn't stop singing until you reached the end.

For your sake, I hope it's option one.

If I could make one request: please leave a rating and / or review of the book on Amazon and Goodreads. As an independent author, I rely on those reviews to survive. If I don't hit my monthly review quota, I get sent to Potato Hell.

Also! I love hearing from readers. If you want to be the first to hear about new books and more, join my #SpudSquad mailing list at https://kenny-gould.kit.com/newsletter

Stay crispy,

Kenny G

ABOUT THE AUTHOR

Kenny Gould writes science and fantasy fiction. He holds a BA from Duke University, an MFA from Chatham University, and an MBA from NYU Stern. He lives with his wife, two cats, and a very funny dog in sunny Florida.

Connect with him on social at @thekennygould or through his website at kennygould.com.

THE ADVENTURE CONTINUES!

Get *Prey House*, the next book in the Toroth-Gol series, for FREE on Kindle Unlimited. Also available in paperback and eBook through Amazon, and as an audiobook on Audible!